BRING ON THE NIGHT

The Wild Side - Book 3

M.J. SCOTT

Praise for M.J. Scott

The Shattered Court
Nominated for Best Paranormal Romance in the 2016
RITA® Awards.

"Scott (the Half-Light City series) opens her Four Arts fantasy
series with the portrait of a young woman who's thrust into
the center of dangerous political machinations… Romance
fans will enjoy the growing relationship between Cameron and
Sophie, but the story's real strength lies in the web of intrigue
Scott creates around her characters."
—*Publishers Weekly*

"Fans of high fantasy and court politics will enjoy The Shattered Court. Sophie is such a great heroine…"
—*RT Book Reviews*

The Forbidden Heir
"This story was packed with action, political intrigue, schem-
ing, and high stakes."
—*Alyssa - Goodreads reviewer*

"This is a marvelous book. The world building is unique and complex. The characters are well developed and likable and there is intrigue for days. If you've read the first book in the series it only gets better in this one."
—*Lissa - Goodreads reviewer*

"'Forbidden Heir' is a great rarity: a sequel that I liked better than the original book."
—*Margaret - Amazon reviewer*

Fire Kin
"Entertaining…Scott's dramatic story will satisfy both fans and new readers."
—*Publishers Weekly*

"This is one urban fantasy series that I will continue to come back to…Fans of authors Christina Henry of the Madeline Black series and Keri Arthur of the Dark Angels series will love the Half-Light City series."
—*Seeing Night Book Reviews*

Iron Kin
"Strong and complex world building, emotionally layered relationships, and enough action to keep me up long past my bedtime. I want to know what's going to happen next to the DuCaines and their chosen partners, and I want to know now."
—*Vampire Book Club*

"Iron Kin was jam-packed with action, juicy politics, and a lot of loose ends left over for the next book to resolve that it's still a good read for series fans."
—*All Things Urban Fantasy*

"Scott's writing is rather superb."

Shadow Kin

"M. J. Scott's Shadow Kin is a steampunky romantic fantasy with vampires that doesn't miss its mark."
—*#1 New York Times bestselling author Patricia Briggs*

"Shadow Kin is an entertaining novel. Lily and Simon are sympathetic characters who feel the weight of past actions and secrets as they respond to their attraction for each other."
—*New York Times bestselling author Anne Bishop*

"M. J. Scott weaves a fantastic tale of love, betrayal, hope, and sacrifice against a world broken by darkness and light, where the only chance for survival rests within the strength of a woman made of shadow and the faith of a man made of light."
—*National bestselling author Devon Monk*

"Had me hooked from the very first page."
—*New York Times bestselling author Keri Arthur*

"Exciting and rife with political intrigue and magic, Shadow Kin is hard to put down right from the start. Magic, faeries, vampires, werewolves, and Templar knights all come together to create an intriguing story with a unique take on all these fantasy tropes. . . . The lore and history of Scott's world is well fleshed out and the action scenes are exhilarating and fast."
—*Romantic Times*

For everyone who keeps working to find the light, not the darkness

Chapter 1

I thought you might be thirsty.

The words I'd just uttered hung in the air, so sharp I could almost see them. The vivid green eyes of the man—vampire —I'd said them to let little of what he might be thinking show.

Not that inscrutability was unusual for him.

Lord Marco Sebastiani was an Old One. The oldest vampire in Seattle. Ruler of the oldest vampire lineage in the city. For all intents and purposes, he was the city's vampire king, even if some of Seattle's other Old Ones did not rest easy with that fact.

Not a man to give anything away easily.

"I think perhaps you had better sit down, Ms. Keenan," Lord Marco said after a few more seconds' silence. He gestured to one of the chairs before his desk with a very Italian flourish. If he was more than mildly surprised to find me on his doorstep late at night offering to let him drink my blood, then his voice, like the rest of him, gave no hint of it. His heartbeat, to my werewolf ears, was steady. Unlike my own, which was racing. Though he didn't usually call me "Ms. Keenan," so perhaps he was more surprised than he seemed.

"I'd rather stand," I said, but, to be polite, I walked to the chair. Better not to annoy him. Marco was charming by default, but I knew how ruthless the creature hidden behind that handsome facade was when he wanted to be.

I gripped the curving carved back of the chair. It was old like him, and the deep green silk upholstery matched his eyes. I studied him warily. Even with his expression carefully neutral, his face demanded attention. He was undeniably handsome. The kind of face that might have inspired artists back in his native Italy. Maybe one of them had once caught sight of Marco across a piazza late one night all those centuries ago and carved him in marble. Marco's face wouldn't have changed in the time that had passed. Olive skin unlined. No gray in the near-black hair. Vampires don't age after they're turned.

But a statue would have given away more emotion, perhaps.

Marco put down the document he'd been reading when I'd been shown into his office, sliding it into a black leather portfolio. "I take it from your invitation—and that outfit—that you are offering to repay your blood debt tonight?"

Hearing it stated so bluntly made my stomach squirm. I stood straighter, squaring my shoulders, ignoring the fear. I'd tied my dark hair up. Between that and the strapless black top, my throat was on clear display. The blood debt I owed Lord Marco was causing problems between Special Agent Daniel Gibson—otherwise known as my fiancé—and me. It wasn't the only thing causing us problems, but it seemed to be the most easily fixable. I wanted to be rid of it. I lifted my chin. "Yes."

He lifted one dark eyebrow. "And I am supposed to just walk over there and bite you?"

This wasn't going exactly as I had expected. I hesitated. "Yes?"

Marco sighed. "I am sorry to disappoint you, cara, but I'm afraid I must decline."

My mouth fell open. "Excuse me?"

"I said no. Thank you for the offer, but no." One side of his mouth quirked.

"You can't just say no," I sputtered. It had never crossed my mind that Marco might refuse me. Werewolf blood was something of a delicacy to vampires. One they only usually tasted if it was freely given. Vampires and werewolves are closely matched when it comes to strength and speed. Not many vamps would choose to tackle an unwilling werewolf for a taste of their blood. Not if they were sane, at least.

"Actually, I can, Ashley. You owe me, not the other way around. It is my choice as to how and when I choose to collect that debt."

I clamped my teeth shut before I could say anything I might regret. *Big bad vampire. Do not aggravate.*

Marco nodded. "Take a moment."

I tried to count to ten before I said anything else. But I was too frustrated and only reached four before I blurted, "Why won't you do it?"

"Firstly, as I said, it is my choice, not yours." His words sharpened. "Secondly, knowing what I do about how you feel about vampires, I have no wish to inflict any distress on you when I have no need to call on the debt. Also, Smith's case is not settled. When we made this agreement, I told you we would consider the matter after the case was done."

I'd forgotten that part. Damn it. "It distresses me to have the debt," I muttered.

Marco pointed at the chair once more. "That is a different matter. Sit, and we will discuss this."

I sat. Defiance wouldn't do me any good at this point.

"You understand," Marco said, "that what I have said is fact. This is my choice. Your debt is mine to hold. Mine to end. Werewolf blood has value, but I do not take such things lightly. I would not call on you to pay without great need. Does that ease your mind?"

It made me feel a little better. I didn't think it would improve Dan's view of the situation.

"Or am I to interpret your silence as perhaps the problem being more complicated than you simply not liking the idea of having to submit to me one day? That someone else has trouble with what you owe? Daniel Gibson, perhaps?"

I thought I had a pretty good poker face. And Marco knew how I felt about vampires trying to read my mind. "What makes you think that?" I asked, seeking to clarify before I jumped to any conclusions about how he'd gotten to the heart of the problem so fast.

He shrugged an elegantly clad shoulder. "You are bonded werewolves. It is hardly difficult to deduce that he does not like the thought of you being in debt to me, let alone the fact that you owe me blood."

I sighed. "I don't know how to make things right between us."

"The two of you have been through a lot in a short time. But he cares about you, your Daniel. That is plain. Perhaps you just need time. And whatever it is you need, it is not this. This would anger him, I think."

I knew, with a sudden cold shiver of certainty, that he was right. And that Marco had just saved me from doing something very stupid. Crap. Or yay, perhaps. Either way, I had to find a better way.

I nodded slowly. "Yes. I'm sorry. I shouldn't have come."

His head tilted. "You are always welcome in my house, cara. You are still new to this supernatural world. And I can, perhaps, provide a perspective your wolves cannot." He smiled then, and it wasn't an entirely friendly expression. "Of course, such advice may not always be free."

I suppressed another shiver. No getting deeper into debt with the vampire. That wouldn't do me or Dan any good. Which also meant I couldn't ask Marco for the other favor I needed. The one where I needed him to try to find something my father had hidden in my memories before he'd died. I'd told Dan I wanted Marco to be the one to look for it. He'd thralled me once before to help me, and he'd been kind. The thought of being thralled again by any vampire freaked me out, but I'd thought maybe I could bear it with him. But not if he was going to ask for something else from me in return. Time for Plan B. Or C, or whatever the hell I was up to at this point.

I forced a polite smile. "Thank you. That's kind of you."

That earned me a nod and a smile that wasn't quite so intimidating. "How is the investigation proceeding? Into the elusive Doctor Smith?"

"Slowly," I said. I couldn't say more. Dan, who was leading the FBI Supernatural Taskforce's investigation, wouldn't thank me for sharing confidential information with Marco. Old Ones sometimes operated in some gray areas. Dan wasn't big on gray areas. I would let him deal with telling Marco what he was willing to share. The Old Ones were on the hunt for Smith, too, but I doubted either side was sharing everything they found. "Have you had any luck?"

It had only been a little over a week since I'd escaped from Smith and his vampire conspirators, killing the vampire he loved in the process. So far, Smith—which wasn't his real name—had managed to disappear into thin air once more.

The not-so-good Doctor Smith had created a mutated strain of vampirism. One that could infect a human with a single bite instead of requiring an exchange of blood between human and vampire over a period of time. Basically, vampirism as plague.

If the mutation became common knowledge, it would go badly for the supernatural community. Humans don't react well to threats. They tend to kill first and ask questions later. The supernaturals lived among them, mostly in harmony because the supernaturals played by the rules these days. No one wanted to see that balance destroyed. Marco and the vampires were hunting Smith as hard as Dan and me. They were just doing it through different avenues.

Marco's expression went flat. "No. Which does not please me. Now, the night grows old. Which means I have things to do, and you likely should be sleeping. I will call a car, and it will take you home to your wolf."

* * *

I asked the driver to take me home rather than to Dan's house. I wanted to change and shower before facing him. There were no bite marks on my neck, but Dan would be able to smell Marco's scent on me just from me being in his house. Safer to scrub any trace of it away before I told him where I'd been.

In one way, Marco had done me a favor by turning me down. I didn't like owing him, but he'd been right about how Dan might react. Now, I just felt...weird. Guilty for going to Marco. Relieved he'd refused. Unsure how to explain to Dan what I'd done. At this point I had no idea if I'd just made things worse, even if Marco had more sense than me.

As we headed back to Mercer Island, the limo's wheels shushing softly on the dark wet road, I tried to tell myself that everything was going to be fine. Somehow, I didn't find myself very convincing.

And as I stepped out of the car and smelled another very familiar scent on the air, I realized I'd missed my chance to do even minimal damage control. I should have checked where Dan was before choosing my hiding place.

I hesitated as the limo drove off. My nose told me Dan was sitting on my front porch. I could still sneak in the back, but he'd come find me. Supernatural senses made being sneaky way more difficult.

"How did you know where I was?" I asked when I reached

the bottom of the steps. It was misting rain, and my clothing wasn't any protection.

"Esme," Dan said. He didn't move from where he was sitting on the top step, his dark blue shirt and jeans blending him into the shadows. But the silver of his eyes was bright, which meant he wasn't happy.

I sighed. I thought I'd given my protection detail for the night the slip by heading to my office and then sneaking off in a cab. But Esme Watson, one of Dan's best agents—one of the top guns in the whole FBI Supernatural Taskforce, in fact —was sneakier than me on my best day. Maybe it was because she was a jaguar shifter. Built-in feline stealth or something. Or maybe it was because she was damned good at what she did for a living. I hadn't noticed a tail coming home, but then I wouldn't if she was doing her job.

Which she would do regardless of how I felt about it. Esme stayed well clear of the murky waters of Dan-Ashley relationship issues. Dan was her boss, she'd known him a lot longer than she'd known me, and even though she and I were friends—maybe even as close to good friends as the prickly cat got—she was playing Switzerland like a born diplomat. She would no more choose to put herself in the middle of a post-Marco confrontation between Dan and me than she would appear in public looking less than immaculate from head to toe.

"She said you were at Marco's," Dan said after the silence stretched a bit too long.

I nodded. "Yes."

"Any particular reason you were visiting an Old One in the middle of the night?"

Might as well just get it over with. "I went to pay off my debt."

I didn't see him come down the stairs. One second, he was standing looking down at me, and the next, I was staring at his chest, breathing in the smoky electrical scent of angry werewolf.

I froze. Dan wouldn't hit me. I knew that deep in my bones. But a werewolf in a rage was a chancy proposition, even for another werewolf.

"Show me." The words only sounded half human.

I tilted my head back even though baring my throat wasn't necessarily the smartest move. Push an alpha past a certain point and submission might well be met with aggression. But at the moment, I had limited options.

Dan drew in a deep breath, anger rumbling in his throat as his fingers touched my skin, resting on the place where my pulse beat. "He didn't do it."

I slanted a glance up at him, not moving away just yet. "No."

"Why not?"

"He said it was his choice, not mine. And that I was being…rash."

He squeezed his eyes closed, grimacing. "It's rare that I totally agree with Marco, but I have to this time." When his eyes opened, the silver blazed even hotter. "Can I ask what you thought you were doing?"

"Trying to make things easier."

He growled. The back of my neck prickled in response, my own wolf's desires warring between submitting and fighting back. Which was the story of our life at the moment. Dan was a dominant wolf, alpha but not Alpha. So was I. Finding how that worked as a couple was tricky. Particularly when our lives had been full of kidnapping, chaos, and danger since Dan walked back into my life a few months ago.

Situations precisely designed to push all the wrong buttons when it came to our instincts.

"How?" Dan asked, voice rough.

"We fight about my debt to him all the time. I wanted it gone."

His expression didn't change. Damn it, why couldn't he

understand? "I just wanted us not to fight. To focus on what's important."

"And what is that, exactly?"

"Finding Smith. Stopping a plague of vampires." His expression darkened, and I hurried on, stomach churning. "You want me to say 'us,' don't you? Well, I want to say that, too. But can't you see that we're never going to be able to relax—never going to be just us—while Smith's still out there?"

Dan's stance eased fractionally, a change so slight a human wouldn't have noticed. But it was enough to make me hope that maybe I was getting through.

"You going to Marco doesn't get us any closer to finding Smith." He paused. "Unless you asked him to look inside your head?" His tone was too controlled.

"No. I don't think that's an option."

Dan's head tilted. "Why not? You said you trusted him." His brows drew tighter. "Did he do something to scare you?"

I shook my head. "No. But he made it very clear that his advice won't be free all the time. I don't want to owe him another favor."

The idea was to get rid of my debts, not add to them.

"We could always get a court order. It's related to the case."

I flinched. "No, thank you. I barely want to let any vampire in. I definitely don't want one who's annoyed and only doing it because he has to. And you don't need to wreck your relationship with Marco. He's too important." I didn't even know if the Taskforce would let Dan antagonize Marco, given who he was. Though, thanks to Smith, the threat we faced was maybe more important than politics. And we needed Marco to help us with the case. I would find another way, even if the thought made me shiver.

But I didn't want to think about that now. If I thought about it now, on top of everything else, I was going to scream.

I shivered. The rain had saturated my thin top, and I was

getting cold. Werewolf metabolism helps us ignore bad weather, but not forever.

"Can we just go inside?" I laid a hand on Dan's arm. Felt the rock-hard bicep soften. "I'm sorry. It was a dumb idea. I just wanted to make things better. Have one less thing to worry about. I didn't want Marco to be able to call on me in the middle of the investigation." Not that it was likely that Marco would do such a thing while we were all chasing Smith. But the constant feeling that he could didn't help me focus. "I'm just trying to make this easier for us. I'm tired of fighting. And you don't like the fact that I owe Marco."

"No," Dan agreed, still frowning. I'd never quite figured out whether it was just the fact that Marco would get to drink my blood one day that he hated, or whether it was guilt because I'd incurred the debt to save him.

"Wouldn't you feel better if I didn't owe him? I would. I'm working on the other debt. I wanted this one gone, too." I'd incurred two debts to Marco in the last few months. To settle the lesser of the two, he'd asked me to help Lord Esteban, another of the Old Ones, with an embezzlement issue. Given Lord Esteban ran some of the nastier dark clubs in the city— places where people and supernaturals went for pleasures involving blood and pain—it wasn't a pleasant task.

To make things worse, Esteban's case had turned out to be tangled up with Smith's. I had yet to get to the bottom of the mystery of how exactly. I was a damned good forensic accountant, and I was used to dealing with supernatural clients and how complicated their affairs could grow over their long lives, but Esteban's were like a spiderweb spun by a very deranged spider. Every time I tugged at a thread, it snapped, or divided, or landed me deep in a pile of data that made no sense. But I would win in the end.

I stepped closer to Dan, looked up into his face. "I just want it to be over. I know it might have been dumb, but I want our lives to get to some sort of normal." I dropped my forehead onto his chest and breathed for a moment, listening to the thump of his heartbeat, feeling his muscles ease and his scent calm at the contact.

This. This was what I wanted. Dan and me. Time to be just us. Time for me to lean against him and just be with my mate, without worries of imminent disaster. To enjoy the bond we shared rather than fight it. To live in the place where everything felt right because we were together and not have that shattered by death and destruction and sorrow.

"I know," he said, the sensation rumbling through his chest as his voice hit my ears. His arms closed around me. "I know. We'll figure this out. Together."

I didn't know whether he meant us or the case. Or both. Whichever it was, I hoped like hell he was right.

We needed to find Smith before the situation got worse. Dan thought he'd left the state or even the country, but I wasn't so convinced. Smith—whoever he was—had roots here. He'd known my father, maybe even worked with him at Synotech or one of the other pharmaceutical companies where Dad had done his immunology research. Obviously there was something about Seattle or Washington that meant something to him.

Or there was something here he needed. Like whatever it was my dad had buried in my head.

So he wouldn't have gone far, even if he was freakishly good at hiding his trail. We just needed a break. Something to clear the path a little. Until then, we'd keep following the money. Research was expensive. He needed cash. For equipment. For a laboratory. For facilities to house the plague vamps. There hadn't been a rash of people being turned with one bite, so Smith had to be containing them somehow.

All that required serious dollars. I had to find the money. Follow the money. That was a very basic tenet of tracking down fraudsters.

Someone helping Smith had been siphoning cash from Lord Esteban, so we could keep digging there.

If that didn't work, then we'd look at other options. Maybe Smith had targeted other Old Ones. That was an unpleasant thought. In order to find that out, we'd have to speak to more Old Ones. Which would possibly mean enlisting Marco's help yet again.

I didn't want to do it. But I would if things got bad enough. The FBI wanted to catch Smith, wanted to stop his plague vamps. But I wanted to stop him because he was, perhaps, behind the events that had warped my life. He'd supported McCallister Tate, the vampire who'd killed my parents, my best friend, Julie Anders, and a whole raft of people in my hometown thirteen years ago. McCallister Tate, whose resurfacing had brought Dan back into my life a few months ago.

Tate was the reason Dan had needed to bite me, turning me into a werewolf. A change I'd never wanted, though it had saved my life, saved me from being turned into a vampire sired by Tate.

Not to mention it was something in my father's research that Smith had apparently used—twisted—to create his plague vamps.

And most recently, Smith had been responsible for the death of yet another person I loved. Rhianna Anders. Julie's little sister. Mine, too, in all but blood.

Though that was where my own guilt came into play. Smith was the reason Rhi had died, but the truth was she'd sacrificed herself to kill a vampire threatening me. And she'd used me to cause their deaths, thralling me and giving me an order I hadn't been able to refuse. I hadn't told Dan that part yet. I couldn't face it.

My gut twisted just thinking about it, the rage I tried to keep banked flaring to vicious life that burned away the sadness.

Dan wanted to bring Smith to justice.
I wanted revenge.

Chapter 2

DAN LEFT the house before I woke. I operated my forensic accounting practice from late afternoon to midnight to cater to my vampire clientele. Dan technically worked similar hours, but the FBI definition of office hours tended to be kind of bendy.

Right now it was bendy and stretched. Dan was working days and nights. I was working on the case and trying to keep my business running, so my hours had expanded, too. But clearly he'd thought I still needed to rest. I'd recovered from being shot while escaping Smith, but physical wounds were the least of my problems.

The emotional roller coaster of grief and anger and frustration was exhausting. I was actually looking forward to the full moon later in the month, because with the moon came an energy boost I desperately needed.

I was pouring myself a second cup of coffee and wondering whether my desire for steak for breakfast was due to me being extra tired or just being a werewolf when the doorbell rang.

Ratty sweats were not my favorite things to be wearing when unexpected visitors arrive, but there was nothing to be done about that. I checked the security screen by the door and was startled to see my aunt standing on the doorstep, a small wheeled suitcase by her feet.

I fumbled with the lock, opening the door as fast as I could. "Aunt Bug? What are you doing here?"

"Did you really think I wouldn't be coming to see you after you were in the hospital again?" She cocked her head, smiling. The expression was a little too wide. Too stretched. Her gray hair was back in its usual neat bun, and her outfit was far more pulled together, but something felt…off.

Dan had told her she didn't need to come when I was in the hospital after the doctors had said I'd only be in overnight, and I'd spoken to her on the phone most days since I'd been released, but the last week or so had been hectic. Maybe she'd been hinting she wanted to come see me and I'd missed it?

Guilt twinged. "I'm really fine," I said, stepping back to let her in.

"Well, if that's true, then I'm worried about you," she said with another odd smile that tugged at my instincts. She moved at her usual brisk pace, wheeling her bag into the house, and I followed, trying to work out what about her had me so worried.

Maybe I was just overreacting.

Bug was always the one who coped. The one who'd picked me up when my world had shattered. Who'd helped me build a foundation again after my parents died and then did it again when I'd become a werewolf. I wasn't sure what to do with a world where she wasn't standing firm and certain to anchor us all.

But I couldn't let her see that. If something was bothering her, I needed to be there for her like she always was for me.

Bug paused when she reached the kitchen, her eyes scanning the room. No doubt noting the plate and silverware I'd pulled out, intending to make myself breakfast, still lying unused on the counter.

"Have you had breakfast?" I asked as she lowered herself into one of the chairs at the kitchen table.

"Hours ago," Aunt Bug replied. "Have you?"

"I've had coffee. I just woke up. My hours are weirder than usual at the moment."

Bug put her bags down and walked across to the fridge. "I'll make you something."

"You're the guest," I protested.

"You got shot," she said pointedly. "Let me fuss a little." She studied the contents of the fridge. "Bacon and an omelet?"

I knew better than to argue with Bug in mother hen mode. And when it came to her cooking for me, I didn't want to. "That sounds perfect."

I poured myself more coffee, refilled the French press to make a fresh batch, and found some cookies. Even if she'd had breakfast, she might be hungry, too. Bug worked her magic with my frying pan, and before I knew it, we were sitting at the table. I tried not to eat too fast, starving now that food was actually in front of me. Bug poured sugar and cream into her coffee and stirred it slowly, gazing out the windows into my backyard.

My instincts prickled harder, accompanied by a growing knot in my stomach. "You should have let me know you were coming. I would have cleared my calendar."

Her eyes met mine and then moved away again. Bug wasn't the prevaricating kind. She was a firm believer in the "rip the Band-Aid off fast" school of dealing with trouble. "I know you're still busy, but I wanted to make sure you're taking care of yourself."

I took her hand. "I'm never too busy for you. And I'd have told you if I wasn't okay." That was something of a lie. I wasn't telling anybody about what happened with Rhianna, and Bug didn't know about the plague vamps. She, like everyone in Caldwell, had been told that Rhianna died of her injuries following a vampire attack. "So why don't you tell me what's going on?"

She sighed, the clink of the teaspoon in the coffee mug getting louder as she stirred harder. "I wasn't going to tell you straight away. But Ani said she thought you might need some company, and I'm not going to lie to you."

Crap. My instincts were right. Something was wrong.

And wait, what? Aunt Bug was talking to Ani? Ani and Sam were the Alphas of the Seattle pack. Aunt Bug had met Ani at the hospital after Dan bit me and turned me into a werewolf, but I wasn't aware that they'd stayed in touch.

But I'd deal with that part after I found out what Bug was hiding from me.

I made myself smile, trying for reassuring. If she needed me to be fine so she could be not-fine, I would be. "Tell me what you need to tell me."

Her mouth flattened. "Rhianna's funeral was yesterday."

It took a moment to sink in. Then it hit me like a baseball bat to the stomach. They'd buried Rhianna, and no one had told me. No one had *invited* me. To go to the funeral of my de facto little sister.

Tears stung my eyes, and I fought them back. I wasn't going to lose it in front of Bug. "They didn't want me there." My voice cracked despite my efforts to not react.

Bug's face twisted. "No. I'm sorry. The mood in Caldwell is…difficult right now. What happened at the memorial service, well, the attack has brought back a lot of old hurt. They asked me not to tell you or Dan. I don't agree with it, but they're grieving parents, and I wasn't going to argue with them."

I hadn't thought about checking the papers or social media for funeral notices. I'd assumed Bug would let me know. The Taskforce might have been monitoring things to make sure the story of how Rhi died stuck to the lie they planted, but apparently if they'd seen anything about the funeral, it hadn't occurred to anyone to tell me. Or maybe I'd been one of the things they'd been trying to control, too. After all, I was one of the few people who would have known the coffin was empty. Rhianna had burned to ash, so there wasn't a body. Hell. How had they managed the funeral? Clearly it had seemed normal to Bug, or she'd be asking me questions.

"Define difficult," I said. If there was trouble brewing in Caldwell, I needed to know. And focusing on that let me push away the harder task of dealing with the fact that the people I'd once considered a second set of parents hadn't wanted me at their daughter's funeral. Didn't want me in their town, it sounded like.

Caldwell, where all the trouble in my life had started just over thirteen years ago when a vampire killed my family and nearly twenty other people in the town. Where only a few weeks ago, the memorial of that event had been ambushed by more vampires. Plague vamps. Leading to Rhianna's death.

People are meant to feel nostalgic about the places where they grow up, but if it wasn't for the facts that Aunt Bug still lived there and my family was buried in the cemetery, I could have lived happily without going back to Caldwell for the rest of my life.

Sounded like the feeling was mutual now.

Aunt Bug sipped coffee. Took a cookie but then just put it down on her plate untouched. "There's been some talk. Rumors and gossip." Her brows drew down.

"Talk about what?"

"About why the vampires came at the memorial. And what happened to Rhianna afterward."

"Rhianna was too badly hurt. She died," I said automatically. And just as automatically shoved away the flare of grief and guilt. I didn't like lying to Bug, but she was in no way cleared to know the real story. Rhianna was dead, and that was all that mattered. Bug knew we were hunting for the people responsible. Knew the people responsible were connected to Tate, but that was all the detail she had.

"I know that," Aunt Bug said, and I had to school my face not to react. Not to wince from the pinch of guilt that she had such faith in me. Or that maybe she knew I was lying to her and didn't want me to know she knew and was pretending to believe me to keep me happy.

Either way, her blue eyes were serious. "But some people in town want to believe otherwise. Those who like to stir up trouble. Talking nonsense."

Was that a faint hitch in her voice? One I might have missed without wolf hearing? Not much unnerved my aunt, but something was bothering her. "Aunt B, has someone *threatened* you?"

She humphed. "Not threatened. But there were some boys speaking rubbish about werewolves the other day at the grocery store—"

"About me, you mean?"

Her answering nod was reluctant. "I gave them a piece of my mind, told them exactly what you'd done for Caldwell. Reminded them you saved people that night at the memorial. That you were the one who dealt with Tate in the end. They slunk out of there. But there were others who paid attention. And then not wanting you at the funeral. I hope it's just grief, but…."

"You can stay here with me," I said. Screw Caldwell. Bug could live with me as long as she wanted if she didn't want to deal with their bullshit.

She sipped coffee. "I'd like that. For a few days. Just to make sure you're okay. But then I need to go home. They need to hear some common sense to counter whatever nonsense is being bandied about."

"I don't want anything to happen to you."

She shook her head. "I'll be fine. No one in Caldwell is

going to bother me. And I think that sentence is backward. You're the one who keeps getting herself into trouble."

"Believe me, I don't want to. But this case isn't closed yet."

She sighed. "Are you getting anywhere?"

"Slowly. The Taskforce is throwing a lot of resources at the problem. We'll catch him, don't worry."

Much like what had happened to Rhianna, Aunt B only knew the basics about what had happened to me. She knew Smith had worked with Tate and that he was behind the vamp attack at the memorial. I was sure she'd filled in a few more pieces for herself—she was smart enough to read between the lines, and obviously she'd been talking to Ani—but she hadn't ever pressed me for more information.

Aunt Bug frowned, and I noticed the shadows beneath her eyes. She wore makeup but not enough to hide the fact that she looked tired. And older than the last time I'd seen her. I squeezed her hand. "We'll get him. I promise."

She nodded and squeezed back. Then sat back, straightening her shoulders. She tilted her head. "While I'm here, I'd like to meet some more of your pack."

I blinked. That was a definite change of subject. And not one I'd expected. "You would?"

"Of course. These people are part of your life now. I'd like to get to know them. Talking on the phone with Ani isn't the same thing as spending time with her."

"I'll see what we can arrange." I wondered if this was Bug's way of reinforcing the idea that she was taking my side. Socializing with werewolves carried some risk for a human. Lycanthropy was more infectious than the Stoker Variation, and even with vaccination, accidental transmission could happen. But maybe Bug had decided she was okay with that risk when she'd stuck by me after I'd become a wolf. And if she was willing to take the risk, I couldn't argue with her. After all, surrounding Bug with werewolves would ensure her safety from Smith and anyone else who might try anything. It might not improve her popularity in Caldwell—I was smart enough to read between the lines, too, and there was definitely more going on in Caldwell than she was letting on—but that was her choice to make. I would have to put some feelers out and see how bad the mood in the town was.

Aunt Bug sipped her coffee, looked thoughtful. "All right, then, I'll stay. But only for a day or two. Like I said, I'm not letting them chase me away. I have things to do back home."

I picked up my cup again, sipped to hide the anger making me want to grind my teeth. This was Smith's fault. It was one thing to disrupt my life and come after me, but it was another thing entirely to stir up the wounds of my hometown and drive my aunt from the place she'd lived her entire life. Not to mention turn Rhianna's family against me.

If we didn't stop Smith, we might not be the only ones to suffer. Caldwell wasn't the most supernatural-friendly town in Washington, and I couldn't blame them for that after what Tate had done, but even places that were more inclusive might find their tolerance stretched if they learned about plague vampires. It wouldn't take long for anti-vampire sentiment to stretch to all other supernaturals as well.

And I was one of them now.

War between the races would be bloody, and I suspected the humans' weight of numbers would lead them to a victory. And what exactly would such a victory mean? Vamps and shifters interned? Confined to reservations? Or simply wiped from the face of the earth?

I couldn't let that happen.

I *wouldn't* let that happen.

We'd been following the money trail for weeks now, and the Taskforce had been over the building where Cilla and Smith had held Rhianna and me with a fine-tooth comb more than once and we'd come up blank. The leads that had come from the estate of the vampire who'd sired Tate had dried up, too. Tate had spent her money, and the properties she'd left behind provided no more clues as to where Smith might be now.

There was one other way to go. Circle back to the beginning.

To my father. And whatever the hell it was he had hidden in my head.

* * *

"We need a Plan B." I hip-bumped Dan's office door shut behind me with a decisive click, pleased that I had managed not to spill the drinks I carried. The coffee machine in the Taskforce's kitchen was temperamental and it had filled the take-out cups near to the brim. But it was after 9:00 p.m., and I figured Dan could use a caffeine fix if he was feeling like me. I'd spent the day with Bug, had an early dinner with her; then she'd insisted I go to work, claiming she was perfectly happy to watch a movie and have an early night.

Dan looked up, but he didn't put down the tablet he was holding. "For what?"

I put one cup in front of him. The quality of the coffee the machine produced was as random as the foam level. But Dan's years as a cop had killed any hint of coffee snob, and now he mostly cared about hot and sweet when it came to caffeine. And, after a restless night and what was going to be a very long day before I got to bed tonight, I'd take my chances as well. "For me trying to let someone find whatever it is Smith thinks is in my head. If Marco isn't an option, I need someone else."

He dropped the tablet, narrowly avoiding the takeout cup. "You think you're ready to try?"

"I have no idea, but I need to." My stomach twisted at the

thought. My experiences with letting vampires into my head wasn't good. First Tate had thralled me multiple times, then Marco to make sure Tate hadn't planted anything that would let him back in. I learned to shield—a werewolf form of a psychic barrier—after that. A little too well. When I hadn't been able to let Cilla, the next crazy vamp who came my way, thrall me thanks to my instinctive shielding, she'd forced Rhianna to do it. I'd trusted Rhi enough to let her in, but it had given her the chance she needed to order me to open a blind and kill both her and Cilla with sunlight.

"Didn't everyone say you needed to give yourself some time?"

If by everyone he meant him, the doctors at the hospital, Ani, and the counselor the hospital had referred me to, then yes.

I waggled my coffee at him, trying to act nonchalant. The heat of the liquid was starting to make my hands uncomfortably warm. A contrast to the cold gnarl of fear in my gut. "I know, but we don't have time to wait, do we?"

"It could make things worse," Dan said. He was watching me, concern clear in his eyes. "Your counselor said—"

"I know what she said, but I want to try again." My counselor, Ella, wanted me to take things slowly in dealing with everything I'd been through. I didn't disagree with the principle, but we were still in the middle of a major investigation and risking a plague of vampires. I couldn't afford to coddle myself.

"Why the rush?"

"I want this case to be over."

"You've wanted that all along. Did Bug say something to you?" He moved the tablet a safe distance back from the coffee, then picked up the cup, swigged, grimaced, and swigged again.

I'd messaged him to say Bug had arrived, and I'd be late

into the Taskforce. I hadn't yet told him anything she'd said. But now it was confession time. I sighed as I perched on the edge of his desk. I sipped coffee again, trying to gather control. I didn't want him to see how upset I was. Didn't want to upset him more.

"Rhianna's funeral was yesterday. We weren't invited." My voice cracked again.

Dan flowed out of his seat and had his arms around me in an instant. "Oh, Ash. I'm sorry."

I tried not to give in to the urge to just cry. That would hardly convince him that I was ready to let a vampire read my mind. "They didn't want me there," I said, leaning into him. "They hate me."

"They don't hate you. They're grieving parents. Not thinking straight."

I knew that feeling. I wasn't sure I was thinking straight now. But I knew I had to do something. Had to act. To try to catch Smith. "I know, but…."

"It sucks," he said. "I'm sorry, love. But you still don't have to do this if you're not ready."

I flinched.

He sighed, pressed a kiss into my hair. "There's something else, isn't there?"

"Bug said there's been a lot of talk. About Rhianna and the vamps who attacked. The kind of talk that isn't good for supernaturals."

"That's somewhat understandable in a place like Caldwell."

Dan had visited Caldwell with me. He'd been popular because people knew he'd been involved in the situation that led to me killing Tate. But that was before the latest vampire attack, and no one had known he was a werewolf. I doubted he'd get such a warm welcome now.

"The powers that be in Caldwell have done a lot of work

to help people heal," I said. "This sort of stuff isn't normal for them."

"Is it anything more than talk yet? I can talk to Sheriff Thompson, find out what he's hearing."

Kenny Thompson was a small-town sheriff, and he'd grown up in Caldwell like me. He was a decent guy who believed in doing the right thing and the rule of law. He wouldn't be happy about this kind of thing happening on his watch.

"If it's moved beyond just talk, we need to know," Dan said. "A minor act of aggression like that can be a slippery slope, Ashley. Something that seems small can start a nasty snowball into something a lot worse. Let me talk to the sheriff."

"Okay. But don't mention it to Bug unless there's something you think she needs to know about."

"Maybe she should stay with us for a while," Dan said. He eased back on his embrace, stepping back so he could see my face.

I smiled at him, my heart lightening for the first time all day. This was why I loved him, even when we butted heads. Because I knew he would do anything for me and mine. If Bug wanted a break from Caldwell, he wouldn't blink at her staying with us or doing whatever was necessary to make her comfortable and make sure she was okay.

"Well, she said she's here for a few days. She said she'd come to check on me, but I'm not sure it's only that."

"That's a start. Gives me time to feel things out with Kenny."

"She said she wants to meet some more of the pack. Is that something we can arrange?"

I didn't know what the protocol was for human relatives of pack members hanging out. The pack guarded its privacy carefully. Supernaturals were accepted for the most part in Seattle, but, like Caldwell, everywhere had humans who'd be happier if the only people who were around were the ones who were just like them.

Dan shrugged, not fazed by the request. "I'll call Sam, see what we can set up."

"Is that normal?"

"We get new wolves with human families from time to time. Most people don't want to give their families up."

He hadn't. I hadn't. But I was still new to werewolf life, and I hadn't been to any pack gatherings where humans—other than kids not yet old enough to turn—were present yet. "I guess I hadn't thought about it."

"Well, we haven't had any mixers lately." He smiled at me. "But don't worry, we know what we're doing. We'll take things slow. Ani and Sam can set something up for Bug. Probably at their place. We keep things away from the Retreat as much as possible. Some humans get to come there eventually—not at full moon, of course—but usually we stick to the city. Ani has met Bug already, so I can't see that it would be a problem."

"She said she's been talking to Ani on the phone."

Dan grinned. "That sounds like Ani. And your aunt. Don't worry, it won't be a problem."

He leaned across the desk, drained his coffee, crushed the cup, and tossed it to the recycle bin. "So, Bug is why you want to try this so soon? The vampire thing?" The smile faded from his face.

I nodded. "Bug is all I have left, apart from you and Jase. I want her to be able to live her life. I want her to be happy. Safe. Which she'll never be if any more of those plague vamps get loose. We need to stop Smith. Now. Whatever it is he thinks I know is part of that."

Silver eyes were steady as they searched my face. "You're sure?"

"Yes. Ella said she had a colleague, a vampire who helps clients with vampire-related…issues." Trauma was the word she'd used. But I wanted to keep that term out of my head and out of Dan's. And a vampire counselor would have to respect my privacy. If they got a sneak peek of anything in my other memories, then they wouldn't be able to tell Dan.

"That sounds like a good idea," Dan said carefully. "Are you going to give her a call?"

"Yes." Before I lost my nerve again. "I want to try."

Chapter 3

"YOU NEED TO RELAX."

Sylvia's voice was gentle as she settled into the chair opposite mine about an hour later. Hair the color of cherries swung around her face, falling neatly back into a sharp-cut bob. The frames of her glasses matched the hair, as did her lipstick.

Too much red. Red had bad associations.

My tongue darted out to wet my lips. "This is about as relaxed as I get when it comes to vampires digging around in my head." The room we were in felt too small. It wasn't. It was large as offices go, decorated in soothing earth tones, cozy and warm. I told myself to stop being dumb. After all, this was my idea. And Sylvia had kindly agreed to see me on short notice.

Her smile was sympathetic. "Your heart is racing. Are you sure you want to try this tonight? We could take a few sessions, work up to it?"

"I'm sure."

Beside me, Dan shifted in his seat. I wondered if he was going to try to talk me out of this, but he stayed quiet. He was with me for moral support but had agreed to not interfere with whatever Sylvia was going to do.

"Take some deep breaths. There's no rush. We'll take our time." Sylvia leaned back, folded her hands in her lap. The glasses, hair, and lips were the only colorful things about her. Her eyes were a very dark brown, near enough to black. Her skin was vamp pale, a fact only highlighted by her white shirt and black suit.

I forced my hands to relax, rubbing them along the arms of the chair. The leather squeaked under my palms.

Sylvia lifted an eyebrow.

"I want to do this," I said. I didn't know if I was trying to convince her or me.

"Just relax. Think of something pleasant." Her voice was low, pitched to be soothing. The trouble with that was that I'd had enough vampires thrall me now to know that low and soothing sometimes equaled "a vampire wants in your head."

Which was not soothing at all.

"I'm trying," I repeated. *Think of something pleasant.* Right. That sounded easy but there hadn't been many happy place moments in my life lately. I closed my eyes, tried to summon a memory of safety. The moon shining down on the forests surrounding the Retreat, silvery light flooding over my skin.

"Maybe try something else," Sylvia said.

My eyes snapped open. "Why?"

"Whatever you're thinking of, I can feel your shields going up."

Damn. I'd forgotten the shields. Werewolf mojo. Ani had taught me to erect mental barriers to protect against vamp mind powers. For some reason picturing myself in a glass box, moonlight streaming over me and around me, was the image that worked for me. Shields had their place, but I needed to let the nice vampire in, not keep her out.

"Okay." I closed my eyes again, tried to think of something else. Then opened them. "Wait, you can feel me shielding?" Not all vampires could.

"It's one of my skills," Sylvia said. "Not all of us can. But think of something else."

Sunshine. Daylight. Flowers. Aunt Bug's roses. But the thought of Bug brought a mental image of confronting idiots back in Caldwell. My shoulders tensed.

I forced them down again, releasing a slow breath before drawing in another to try again.

This time I kept it simple and pictured Dan's face. Focused on breathing in his scent, letting it drown out the sharper smell of vampire. Another breath. Another.

"That's better," Sylvia said, her voice barely above a whisper. "Whatever that one is, stay on that. Now, when you're ready, open your eyes."

My stomach tightened, but I kept breathing, sinking into it to chase the fear away. Thinking of Dan.

After about a minute, I made myself open my eyes.

Sylvia had crept forward to the edge of her chair, leaning toward me. She stayed still for another few of my breaths, then slowly—so slowly that I knew she was taking a lot of care to be unthreatening—extended a hand. Not far enough to touch me but close. Palm up, extended in invitation.

Just a hand. No big deal.

Still, the muscles in my arm locked in protest as I thought about laying my hand over hers.

Another breath. Another lungful of Dan's scent.

"Take my hand, Ashley," Sylvia said in the same quiet soothing tone she'd been using all along. Like a rider trying to gentle a horse.

Or a vampire seducing a victim.

No.

I banished that thought from my head. Another breath. But I was losing my ability to focus only on Dan, my werewolf nose sorting out the other smells in the room.

A hint of dust and whatever chemicals the cleaners used. The bland smell of office furniture and air conditioning.

Sylvia's perfume, something lightly spiced with a base note of warm flowers. Not strong. Vampires and werewolves are sensitive to smells and careful with the scents they wear. Still, Sylvia's was enough to minimize the smell of vampire, so maybe she'd put it on to make me feel at ease.

There was no need for my heart to race. She was no threat.

Regardless, my right hand shook as I reached out and laid it in hers. Her skin was cool, as I had known it would be. Vampire cool.

I shivered.

No different to touching Jase. If I'd been going to let Marco feed from me, I could do this.

"Good," Sylvia said, still in that same gentle tone. "Now, when you're ready, I want you to look at me."

It was an effort to raise my eyes and meet her gaze. All my instincts screamed at me not to. Every primitive part of me, including the wolf, knew this was a predator. One that could maybe take me down.

I gritted my teeth, locking my arm muscles so I wouldn't snatch my hand back.

My instincts were wrong. Sylvia wouldn't hurt me. She was trying to help me. Help me find the information we needed so we could catch Smith and make sure nobody else got hurt.

She didn't say anything, just smiled encouragingly as I clenched my jaw and curled my left hand over the arm of the chair. Luckily she'd bought furniture designed to withstand an accidental supernatural show of strength. The chair creaked, but I didn't break it or tear the upholstery.

I willed each muscle to relax, flexing my fingers back to straight one by one, while I ignored the part of me that wanted to throw a shield between me and the vampire. That was what had happened when Cilla tried to thrall me. I hadn't been able to let down the shields.

Ultimately, Rhi had paid the price for that failure. I'd let her in, and she'd chosen to die to protect me, taking Cilla down in the process. But she had confirmed there was something in my head. Something left there by my dad. I had no memory of him ever doing it, but apparently he had. And whatever it was, Smith wanted it.

Which meant I had to get to it first.

I didn't want to lose anyone else to get hurt. Beside me, Dan was very still, but I could tell he was tensed, ready to act if I needed help. I was safe. And I had to do this.

"Go ahead," I said to Sylvia.

She nodded. "All right. You know how this works. Just keep looking in my eyes. Relax."

I nodded again, trying to obey. I stared at her eyes, trying to only see Sylvia, a person, not a vampire.

But then she said, "Ashley, let me in," in a soothing tone, and I flung up a hand, jolting back with enough force to send my chair skidding back a few feet on the wooden floor, heart pounding.

"Ash!" Dan said, and he was out of his chair and on his knees in front of me, his hands clasping mine.

"Sorry," I said. "That was stupid." I knew he could hear how fast my heart was beating. Sylvia could, too. That was the problem with working with other supernaturals. Harder to pretend you weren't freaked out.

"Let's take a break," Sylvia said smoothly. She flowed out of her chair in that effortless vamp way, which did nothing to make my instincts back the hell off, and walked out of the room, closing the door behind her.

I hung my head, biting my lip with frustration, tears prickling my eyes.

"Sorry," I muttered again. "I can do this. I know I can."

"I'm sure you can," Dan said. "But maybe today isn't the day. Let's try again tomorrow or the next day. You can work up to it."

"We might not have a few days," I said. "Smith could

make a move any time he wants." And I wasn't sure practicing with Sylvia was going to help.

"That's true," Dan said. "But for now, he hasn't. And I'm not going to let you hurt yourself trying to do this. That doesn't help anyone either. I know you want to protect Bug. I'll do everything I can to help you do that, but you're not expendable, Ash. I need you, okay?" He leaned forward, brushed his lips against mine. "We'll figure this out together."

I rested my forehead against his. Touching him soothed the panic. That was how it was supposed to be between bonded wolves. A team, not a pair butting heads every other minute. I needed to lean into the moment, remember how it felt. Work to have more of them.

"Okay," I agreed. "Tomorrow. If that's okay with Sylvia."

"Good," he said. He climbed back to his feet, not letting go of my hand. "Now, how about you go home and hang out with your aunt? Andy is still double-checking data, so there's not much for you to do back at the Taskforce. You can have a night off."

Andy Ramirez was the agent helping me with the financial side of the investigation. He was good.

"Bug will want to see you, too," I said. Dan had been working the same long hours as me. Longer, maybe. I took some time away from the investigation to handle my regular clients. He was all Taskforce all the time.

He nodded. "I won't be too late tonight, and we can all have breakfast tomorrow. And I'll talk to Ani and see if we can set something up tomorrow night for Bug to meet some more of the pack."

Tomorrow was Friday. It wasn't that unusual for pack members to get together over the weekend. Hopefully Ani and Sam didn't already have plans that we'd be disrupting. As the Alphas, they were the most in demand to keep our pack together and connected. That included all the social stuff.

Wolves were social creatures. I was still getting used to that part. I'd always been more of a loner since my parents died. It had been just Bug and me, and though I'd had friends at high school and college, it had always been a small select group. Which had only grown more select as my hours became increasingly nocturnal. When I became a wolf, I'd gained a family of about sixty overnight.

Hopefully they'd welcome Bug as well.

* * *

"It's very kind of you to invite me," Aunt Bug said to Ani, handing over the bottle of wine she'd brought as a hostess gift.

Ani smiled, shaking her head as she took the bottle. The gesture made her red curls bounce around her face. "Thank you for this. But we're always happy to include the people important to our members." She looked over her shoulder as a shriek came from the backyard. "Sorry, it's a bit crazy with all the kids." She tucked the bottle of wine under one white linen-clad arm as she turned back. In her white shirt and faded blue jeans, jade green Birks on her feet, she didn't look old enough to be worrying about kids. Or running a werewolf pack. But looks were deceiving. Ani was tough and smart and ruled us with a velvet-clad paw. Well, she and Sam together.

Bug smiled. "I like kids. I was a teacher before I retired."

Ani looked at me, a question in her green eyes. "I don't think you told me that, Ashley. I'm guessing you had to behave in school, then."

I nodded. "Even before Bug took me in, she was the principal at my high school. Hard to get away with much when that happens. Especially in a small town."

"Ashley was a good kid, mostly," Bug said, smiling at me. "You have a lovely house here, Ani."

Ani and Sam's big family room backed onto their yard. Light and airy like the rest of the house, it was decorated with comfortably squishy furniture, family photos, and flowers.

Toys spilled out from a basket tucked under the coffee table, suggesting a hasty cleanup. The french doors were open. The yard was huge. Which made sense. The pack had the Retreat outside Seattle where we gathered at the full moon, but Ani and Sam needed enough space to host a bunch of werewolves at a moment's notice here as well.

"Thanks," Ani said. "We like it. Even with all the craziness. But let's get you both a drink. What's your poison? Shall we open this wine, or do you like something stronger? I make a mean martini, or Sam made a batch of sangria earlier."

"A martini sounds perfect," Bug said. It was her favorite cocktail. I didn't think I'd mentioned that to Ani.

"Great. I'll make some. Ash, you, too?" She waved us toward the big granite counter that separated her kitchen from the family room.

"Sure," I said. Dan was designated driver. And really, the sangria was likely to be as strong as a martini, anyway. Werewolves burn off alcohol fast, so they tend to like their drinks to pack a punch.

Ani made drinks and started introducing Bug to the others. I stuck by Bug's side for a while, but she seemed perfectly at ease, so I excused myself and went to join Dan, who had wandered out with Sam and the other guys doing manly things near the grill and keeping an eye on the kids. Natalie and Kara, two of the other female wolves I was getting to know, were sitting on low-slung deck chairs on the edge of the deck, wine in hand, laughing and chatting.

"Are girls allowed near the sacred flame of beef?"

Sam grinned at me. "Sure. As long as you walk around it three times widdershins and stand on one leg to remove the curse of girl cooties."

"I'll take my chances." The steaks smelled delicious. We were not yet near full moon, but the case and Bug had me on edge, and the wolf prowled not too far beneath my skin.

"How does your aunt like her steak?" Sam asked.

"Rare," I said. "She'll fit right in."

He laughed, nodded, and flipped a couple of the steaks over. "Not long now."

Dan glanced back at Bug. "She seems fine with all of this."

"Bug loves me," I said. "She's going to make the best of whatever comes along with me, I guess." Bug had never had children of her own. I was it. "And she's always tried to be fair with how she treats people. Even with what happened in Caldwell. She was the one who always pushed me to keep an open mind about supernaturals." I'd gone through a phase of hating vampires after the massacre. But it had been Bug who insisted I have therapy and deal with it as best I could, knowing it would be hard to function in the world if I didn't. Not everyone in Caldwell had thought it was the right thing to do, but she didn't care about that.

She'd been right though. I hadn't had a close vampire friend until Jase, but I'd built a very lucrative business specializing in supernatural clients who others weren't always willing to take on.

Bug hadn't wanted me to break up with Dan when he'd been bitten by a werewolf as a cop, but that had been a bridge too far for me back then. I could be civil to supernaturals, but I hadn't wanted to become a werewolf myself. Which was a high risk if I dated one.

Of course, it seemed fate hadn't cared much about what I thought about that, because here I was, a werewolf now anyway. And it was Dan who had bitten me. It was still an adjustment, but the best part about it—after the fact that it had brought Dan and me back together—was the pack. A whole new group of people who felt more and more like family each day. Maybe they could be that for Bug as well.

"Have your folks been here?" I asked Dan. His mom and dad lived in Hawaii now. They'd moved a couple of years after Dan was bitten. Not because of that—or so Dan said—

but because his dad had developed arthritis that Seattle's damp cool weather didn't help.

We hadn't seen them in person since Dan and I had gotten back together, though we video-chatted and talked via email and text and phone. It was taking a little while for them to adjust to the idea of me being back in Dan's life.

I couldn't blame them for being cautious. From their point of view, I'd abandoned their son at a difficult time. But things were easing between us, and I was looking forward to seeing them again once the case was settled. Until then, neither of us wanted them to come back to Seattle. We didn't need to provide any more tempting targets for Smith. He'd used Bug to get to me in the past. I wasn't going to let him turn the people we cared about into leverage again.

Dan finished his beer and tossed the can into the recycling crate near the grill. "A few times. They were okay with it, I think." He glanced over at Bug, who was laughing at something Ani had said. "Maybe not quite as relaxed as Bug."

"She's always been good with people." Even idiots in Caldwell.

"Guess it's that teacher thing," Dan said. He smiled ruefully. "Maybe if my folks still lived here, they might have gotten used to it by now, too."

"They still love you," I said. That much was clear on our calls. The Gibsons were a little wary with me, but their love for Dan shone through every word.

"Loving me and loving the pack aren't quite the same thing."

"Well, they weren't used to sharing you. That's the problem with being an only kid."

We had that in common. Growing up with no brothers and sisters. At least Dan still had parents.

I sighed and leaned into him, suddenly exhausted. I wanted our lives to be simple.

Safe.

To have family around to grill steaks or go on vacation to Hawaii and lie on a beach. Or run on one under the moon.

"You look like you need a steak," Sam said. He handed me two plates and put a steak half the size of my head on each one. "Take one of those to your aunt."

I sniffed appreciatively, thanked him, and did just that. Bug and I filled our plates with salads and sides and found a seat at one of the tables set around the garden. I left a spot for Dan to join us but was too hungry to wait to eat. Wolf metabolism meant I ate more than I used to, especially as the moon waxed. Something I took advantage of. My steak was two-thirds gone before Bug had made much of a dent in hers. I remembered my manners and slowed down.

"Is the steak okay?" I asked her.

She nodded. "It's delicious. Sam knows what he's doing with that grill."

I nodded, reaching for my drink to make sure I didn't start eating again. "He does."

"It helps that he grew up on a beef ranch," Dan said, sliding into the chair next to mine.

I blinked. "He did?" I didn't think I'd ever heard Sam mention his family. He worked at one of Seattle's biggest ad firms, and I had a hard time picturing him on a ranch. But hell, I'd grown up in a tiny town and left, too, so it shouldn't have been a surprise.

"His dad and his older brother still run it," Dan said. "This steak is probably one of theirs."

"Don't say any more." As a werewolf, I was never going to be a vegetarian, and having up close and personal encounters with prey in wolf form made it hard not to be realistic about where my food came from, but I still didn't need visions of cute calves dancing in my head as I ate steak.

Dan snorted at me but changed the topic to baseball. Bug and Pen, one of the older wolves in the pack seated on Bug's other side, joined in. They'd been talking earlier and seemed to have gotten along like a house on fire. Which made sense. Pen was tiny but fierce and no-nonsense like Bug. Her short-cropped black hair showed no signs of silver, but she was around Bug's age. Wolves aged more slowly than humans, but we weren't like vampires. We still got old and died eventually.

I let the chatter wash over me, making vague encouraging noises as I focused on eating. I finished my steak and decided that yes, I wanted a burger as well. I was halfway back to the grill when Ani stepped into my path.

"Bug seems to be enjoying herself," she said.

"Yes. Sorry, I know this is a lot to pull together last minute. She just wants to make sure I'm okay," I said, chancing a smile. Despite the smile on Ani's face, something in her posture told me she hadn't just bumped into me accidentally.

Ani glanced back at the table where Bug, Pen, and Dan were laughing. "And the two of you seem…better?"

I hitched a shoulder. Had Dan told her about Marco? I leaned toward a no on that. I figured I'd be getting a scolding it he had. Something had felt easier between Dan and me since our post-Marco convo, like we'd taken another step closer. I didn't think he would have told Ani. "I think so. We're figuring things out. It will be easier when the case wraps up."

She smiled. "That's good. Lean into that. The bond will help both of you once it really snaps into place."

I nodded, a little wary. Easy for her to say. She hadn't turned and formed a bond with Sam in the middle of the level of craziness Dan and I were dealing with. But I knew she was right. The closer I let Dan in, the easier things were to bear. It was just hard fighting myself and letting down my walls sometimes.

"Dan said you tried to let a counselor into your head?" Ani continued.

Okay, so he *had* told her about that. Ani knew a bit more about the case than Bug did. Smith and his cronies had killed one of our wolves and injured another. Plus, Ani was the one who'd had to deal with me being a reluctant new wolf while I was dealing with the reappearance of the bogeyman from my past. She needed to know what was happening so she could do her job. Our pack was the largest in Seattle, so she and Sam were the highest-ranking wolves here. Wolves don't live for centuries like vampires, so they don't tend to build power bases and empires like the Old Ones, but Ani and Sam had clout. Political power, even if they were subtle about it. I should have expected that Dan would tell her things more directly related to the case. Like me trying to find the information in my head. "Yes. But I panicked."

She smiled sympathetically. "You need to go easy on yourself."

"Easier said than done when I know whatever's in there must be important."

"I understand that. But that doesn't change the fact that no one wants you to hurt yourself trying to find it out."

Least of all me. I tilted my head, struck by another option I hadn't thought of. An Alpha werewolf had power over her pack members. "Could you order me to remember? Would that work?"

Her eyes widened. "That's a question with a less than simple answer." She glanced around the yard. "And not something to discuss here and now. Can you and Dan and your aunt hang around when everyone leaves?"

Pack parties tended to linger. But the kids would be getting tired, and lots of them had sports or other activities on the weekends. I'd noticed that, other than Pen, Ani had invited married wolves, and most of them had kids. So maybe she'd wanted to make sure there was a natural earlier ending to the gathering so Bug wouldn't get overwhelmed.

"Sure," I said. "Bug won't mind. Though she'll insist on helping you clean up."

Ani grinned. "Well, I'm never going to say no to that. All right. We'll talk later. Now, go get your food."

Chapter 4

A COUPLE HOURS LATER, Ani led Dan and me back to her study. Sam and Bug were, as I'd predicted, cleaning up after the last few stragglers had left. Bug just smiled and waved us off when I explained that Ani wanted to discuss some pack business for a few minutes.

Dan and I settled onto the sofa, and Ani swung her desk chair around to face us, sipping the mug of green tea she'd carried with her.

"So, is there anything you can do?" I asked. Might as well get the conversation started.

"Can I find what's hidden in your head? At best, that's a maybe," Ani replied, and my heart sank. She had seemed like the perfect option. If she could make me remember, then no need to let anyone into my head, and no need for my secrets to come out.

"Why only 'maybe'?" I asked.

She shrugged, swinging one of her feet back forth. "Alpha powers don't work the same way as a thrall. I can give you a command that you'll be hard-pressed to disobey, but I can't take over your mind the way a vampire can."

"Doesn't that mean you could order me to remember?"

She put her mug on the desk. "I can try, but I suspect that, in your case, it's unlikely to work."

"Why not?"

"You have no memory of your dad doing this to you, do you?"

I shook my head. If Rhianna hadn't told me she thought my dad had put something in my memories, I wouldn't have believed it. I still wasn't entirely sure I did. She'd been half crazed from being turned and desperate for a way out. Cilla and Smith were convinced my dad had been working on something that could help them, but that didn't mean he'd buried clues in my brain. Why would he? He hadn't expected to die.

"So," Ani said. "Your dad buried—or had someone bury—something deep in your subconscious, so deeply you don't have any memory of it being done. I can tell you to remember what you were wearing last Wednesday for lunch, but without something to link the information you're trying to find to, your mind has nothing to zero in on. You don't know when or where this happened. I can't say 'Ashley, remember what your dad left for you on your fourteenth birthday' or whenever it was, so you have nothing to search for. "

That was true. The best we could narrow it down to, if it had happened at all, was somewhere in the couple of years before he died, when my dad worked for Synotech. He must have crossed paths with Smith back then. Smith knew him, but we hadn't figured out how. "Can't you try anyway?"

"I can try. But don't get your hopes up. Unless there's more detail you can give me to work with?" She looked across at Dan, who shook his head

"Do it," I said, tucking my legs up under me.

"Would it really be so bad to let another vampire try?" Ani asked. "It might be easier for them. Minds are strange, and vampires are the experts at this kind of thing."

"I tried with Sylvia. I couldn't stop my shields going up. It wasn't fun." My hands flexed, remembering the panic that had flooded me.

Ani nodded. "It's understandable though, given what you've been through. Most people in your position would avoid vampires altogether." She was a web designer by trade, but she was great at counseling people, too. Alphas needed to be.

I blew out a breath. "I can be around them. It's just the thought of letting one of them rummage through my head that freaks me out."

"Who was the last vamp to thrall you?"

I looked down. The answer to that was Rhianna. But if I confessed that, I'd have to explain the rest. I wasn't ready.

"Cilla," I lied. "At the Retreat that night." When I'd first met the crazy bitch and she'd managed to partially control me. Not a full thrall, but she'd still had power over me. It was after that I'd gotten Ani to teach me to shield. A lesson I'd learned a little too well, it seemed.

"Anyone before that who wasn't a psycho? Someone you trusted?"

The sofa creaked as Dan shifted besides me. Ani looked from me to him, then back to me. There was no hiding the tension between us from our Alpha. But she stuck to the subject at hand.

"Marco," I said quietly. "I was able to let him in after… after Tate." I bit my lip as I heard the rumble in Dan's throat.

"Is Marco an option now?" Ani asked.

"No," Dan said bluntly before I could answer.

Ani cocked her head. "Why not? Besides the fact that you seem to be jealous of him?"

My mouth dropped open. Guess Ani wasn't avoiding the subject of Dan and me after all.

"Because I'd rather not have any more of us in his debt," Dan said.

"Wouldn't he do it if the Taskforce requested?"

"Lord Marco rarely does anything out of the goodness of his heart." The words nearly snapped out. "We'd probably have to get a court order. And I'd prefer not to stir things up between the Old Ones and the bureau right now."

"You could still ask," Ani said. "Maybe he'd take the debt from you if you're concerned about Ashley."

Dan stared at her, his silver eyes darkening. "Having a senior FBI agent in the debt of an Old One of the city isn't a good idea."

"Usually I'd agree with you." Ani looked at him sternly. "But whatever this information is, you seem to need it pretty badly."

"Not that badly," Dan said, jaw setting in a stubborn line.

"Yes we do," I said. "But I agree, Marco isn't the best option. Not if we can find another way."

He looked at me, expression softening before he nodded and turned back to his Alpha. "If this doesn't work, can you teach her to relax her shields? Make it easier on her?"

"That might take more than an Alpha suggestion, too," Ani said. "Ashley's been through a lot, Dan. If her shields are going up unconsciously, she might need therapy for this to work."

I sighed. "That doesn't sound like a quick fix." And we didn't have months to waste. Smith had vanished temporarily, but I doubted he would let things stand as they were. He'd be back. "Ani, let's try this. It's worth a shot."

Ani rose. For a moment, she considered me with a half frown, and then something in her stance changed. She was short and slender, and her red hair was escaping its messy bun, but there was no mistaking who had the most power in the room when she used her Alpha abilities.

"Ashley Keenan," she said in a tone that no one in the pack could have ignored. "I want you to remember what is hidden. I want you to remember the thing you have forgotten, remember the information you need." Her eyes blazed a moment, the green wild and powerful.

The urge to obey was overwhelming. I braced myself against the cushions, half expecting a flood of memories to burst into my head and sweep me away. But none came.

The silence lingered, stretched, and then the atmosphere eased back to normal as Ani blew out a breath.

"Anything?" she asked.

I shook my head. "Not yet." Which meant it wasn't going to work. When an Alpha gave a werewolf an order, the werewolf obeyed. As soon as humanly, or maybe wolfishly, possible. If nothing had risen from the depths of my subconscious in response to Ani's command, then it was unlikely anything was going to.

"What if Sam tried?" Dan asked.

Ani tilted her chin up, green eyes fierce. "Are you suggesting Sam has stronger Alpha mojo than me?"

The look of consternation on Dan's face would have been funny in any other situation. "No, ma'am," he said meekly. "I am not."

"Good." Then she laughed. "You should see the look on your face."

I bit my lip, trying not to laugh, too. I didn't think Dan was in the mood to share the joke.

"But to answer your question," Ani continued, "if it hasn't worked with one Alpha, it's not going to work with two."

I reached out and touched Dan's arm. "We'll think of something else."

"Like what?" he asked. "You want Jase to try?"

"Jason?" Ani sounded startled. "Is he strong enough to do that?"

"Marco says he's strong. He's been teaching Jase for a while now," Dan said, looking at me rather than Ani.

I didn't reply, just as startled as Ani. I hadn't thought about Jase as an option. He was my friend, but I had to admit that his blossoming psychic abilities made me nervous. Most vamps took longer to start to develop significant powers. Jase was apparently an early bloomer. Hence Ani's surprise.

The fact that Jase had drawn Marco's attention was an indication of his potential. He could end up very powerful indeed.

The sort of powerful that meant, if he decided to play vamp political games—and survived them—that maybe one day he could end up an Old One himself.

A fact I had been trying to ignore. Vampires had taken a lot from me. Jase was the first one I'd ever let close. We'd been friends before he turned, and I hadn't wanted to lose him when he'd made his choice based on a terminal diagnosis. I still didn't want to lose him.

I wouldn't allow it. My issues with his powers were just that. My issues. I had to deal. Accept that vamp powers were part of the package, and that most vamps—including Jase— weren't going to abuse them. Just as most werewolves didn't go around biting people willy-nilly to infect them intentionally. And by the time Jase reached Old One status, I might be dead anyway. Marco was at least four hundred years old. Were- wolves lived to something more like one fifty. Jase's eventual vampire status was likely not my problem. I just had to accept him for who he was now.

Which might mean I had to do some apologizing if I wanted him to try this.

* * *

They say revenge is a dish best served cold. In the case of Smith, it was starting to feel like it was going to be frozen solid.

Bug stayed another day after the cookout at Ani's, but then she headed home, insisting she didn't want to be underfoot.

It had been almost a week since she left. Dan and I had

slipped back into working too hard on the case, though we were trying to spend some of our virtually nonexistent free time together. Between Smith, Dan's other cases, my clients, and my continued work trying to figure out where Smith had been siphoning money from Lord Esteban's accounts to, the days and nights blurred together.

And even with werewolf energy, we were both running close to empty.

I hadn't even found time yet to raise the subject of trying to find what was in my head with Jase. Dan had asked me to wait a few more days, insisting—like Ani—that I needed to give myself a break from the stress of trying to overcome my instinct to resist.

To be honest, I hadn't fought him. I knew I had to ask, knew sooner was better than later, but the thought still scared me. Losing myself in work seemed easier, and I hadn't even been in the same room as Jase yet. I'd been working from home or the Taskforce, and he'd been holding down the fort at my office. It wasn't a conversation I wanted to have on the phone. But despite how hard we were working, the week brought no new breakthroughs on the Smith front.

I was running out of time. But being exhausted when I tried again hardly seemed likely to help me control my fear.

Tonight—well, it was early morning, really—I wanted sleep.

I barely summoned the will to scarf down the last of Bug's freezer lasagna that she'd left us. Revenge would have to wait a bit longer. Right now, I longed for soft cotton sheets and the familiar scents of our bed and more than five hours of sleep.

Dan ate as silently and steadily as me. He looked up as he swallowed his last bite. "Wanna watch some TV?"

Thank God for streaming services that made the life of those with weird working schedules easier. But I needed sleep more than a fix of the latest small-town comedy we'd been bingeing.

"I'm wrecked. Can we—"

I broke off as my cell phone shrilled to life. *Please, God, let it not be Jase with some work emergency.* I rose to grab it off the counter, hitting the Answer button just before my voice mail kicked in.

"Ashley Keenan," I said, trying to sound professional just in case it was a client.

"Ashley, it's Sheriff Thompson," a gravelly voice said in my ear.

The edges of the phone dug into my fingers as they clenched, fear sliding down my spine. "Kenny? Is something wrong with Bug?" My voice sounded too high.

"She's okay, but you need to come home," he said, his usual professionally calm voice edged with something that sounded like fury.

I resisted the urge to clutch the phone even tighter. I'd killed a couple of phones in my first few weeks of werewolf life. It was an expensive mistake. "What's happened?" My mouth was dry.

"Her house is on fire."

"I'll be there as soon as I can."

* * *

Dan broke just about every speed limit on the way to Caldwell, but the drive still felt endless. I tried to call Bug every five minutes as we sped through the night, but her phone kept going to voice mail. She was all right, I told myself over and over. Kenny had said she was all right. Maybe the fire had fried her phone. Or maybe it was switched off because she was dealing with the fact that her freaking house was burning down.

In between trying to dial Bug, we got hold of Esme and asked her to find out more about what had happened. She couldn't tell me much more than Kenny had. Police, paramedics, and the fire department had been called to a fire at Bug's address. It was too early for a damage report.

I wound down the window as we reached the outskirts of Caldwell. The stink of smoke was faint at first, growing stronger as we neared Bug's house. A parked patrol car blocked the end of her street. I left Dan to deal with the deputy, clambered out of the car, and hit the ground running, heading for Bug's house. Even in human form, I moved fast. But it still felt like slow motion as I searched the small crowd of people gathered in the street, looking for Bug.

Smoke hung in the air, stinging my eyes and nose. The firemen were still hosing down the house, and the noise from the pump and the water seemed horribly loud.

Where the hell was Bug? I pushed through the neighbors standing around, struggling not to shove them with werewolf force. The smoke blotted out any trace of her scent.

Sheriff Kenny found me first. His hand on my shoulder made me jump and whirl.

"Where is she?" I demanded when I recovered enough to realize who he was. "Where's Bug?"

"She's okay," Kenny said. He jerked his chin toward the far end of the street. The fire trucks blocked the view. "The paramedics are monitoring her. So far she's resisted going to the hospital."

"If she's all right, why does she need to be monitored?" I started walking in the direction he'd indicated. Fast.

Kenny kept pace with me. "She's almost seventy, and she just escaped from a house fire. It's a precaution." He was using one of those deliberately calm tones I'd learned law enforcement people use when they're dealing with people who they think are being too emotional. Well, screw him. I had a right to be emotional. Like he said, Bug had just escaped from a fire. And "precaution" was a weasel word I didn't trust.

I sped up. As we passed the house, the choking ash scent was almost overwhelming. After one quick glance, I didn't want to look any closer. Bug first; then I'd worry about the house. Houses could be rebuilt. People couldn't.

I ducked between the trucks, Kenny's presence smoothing my way when a female firefighter stepped into my path asking who I was. I ignored her and kept walking. Two ambulances were parked at the end of the street.

Two?

"Was someone else hurt?" I asked.

Kenny shook his head. "Not so far. But both units were free, so they both came down to help out. They'll take care of the firefighters if they get any minor injuries."

"How did it start?" Bug was always careful. She wasn't the kind to leave a stove unattended or a candle burning.

"We don't know yet," Kenny said. His voice was grim. Never the most effusive man in town, the degree of serious in his smoke-roughened rasp was high, even for him.

I stopped, staring at him. "Do you think this was arson?" Blood rushed in my ears. Had someone just tried to kill Bug? Or, at best, scare her out of Caldwell?

He shook his head. "It's too early to tell."

"Tell what?" Dan appeared through the smoke haze, coming to stand with me.

"Whether the fire was set deliberately," I said, voice going way too high. Who would do that to Bug? She was popular in town. She'd lived here all her life. Hell, she'd taught half the current adult population.

Dan's gaze snapped to Kenny. "Is that likely?"

"The house is old, but Bug had it rewired just a year ago. She's careful." Kenny didn't look happy.

I tasted bile and swallowed hard against the nausea. Kenny was trying to sound professional, but I could hear the worry in his voice. No way he thought this was an accident.

I turned to Dan. "We're taking Bug back to Seattle with us. I want her somewhere safe."

He nodded, still frowning. "Fine with me. The question is whether she'll agree to that."

"I'll convince her. I'm not going through this again." The fact that someone might be trying to scare Bug or chase her out of town made me sick, but that might not be the only danger. Smith and his various vampire conspirators liked leverage. They'd used Bug and Dan to force confrontations with me before now.

Not this time. This time no one would be left vulnerable. Or taken from me.

I scowled, then focused on Kenny. "You need to figure out who did this. If it was someone from the town, then that's your issue. If it wasn't, then there might be a bigger problem."

His expression turned grim. "A problem like what happened at the memorial service?"

I didn't deny it. Kenny wasn't in the need-to-know group when it came to what had really happened to Rhianna, but he wasn't a stupid small-town cop. He knew there was something bigger going on. In the last few months, I'd become a were-wolf, I'd killed Tate, and then there'd been another vampire attack here. These days, vampires usually played by the rules. Even in the cities, random attacks by individual vamps were rare, and when they happened, it was usually a young vamp out of control. I couldn't remember the last time there'd been a group attack like the one at the memorial service.

It was plain that things weren't exactly situation normal.

Maybe the fire was simply the result of the attack stirring up old wounds and anti-supernatural sentiment in Caldwell. Or maybe not. "I don't know. But I'll take Bug home with me. If this is related to me, then hopefully nothing else will happen here."

If it hadn't already. My chats with Bug over the last week had been brief, both of us trying to be lighthearted. She hadn't mentioned any other incidents, but maybe she hadn't told me everything.

"Has anything else happened? Bug mentioned some problems. Is she the only one who's been targeted?" I asked. Dan had spoken to Kenny when Bug visited us, but Kenny said nothing had been reported to him. But that was a week ago. Things might have shifted with Bug returning, or it might be that it wasn't only me the town had a problem with. Bigger cracks could be forming between those who wanted nothing more to do with supernaturals and those who were reasonable.

My hands clenched. Perhaps Caldwell wasn't a perfect reflection of how humans would react if they found out about a vampire plague. The town's history with Tate meant the residents were predisposed to be suspicious toward vamps and shifters. But the town leaders had worked hard not to let that hatred blossom into ugliness over the years. To try to make sure Caldwell was a modern town and didn't cut itself off from the supernatural world.

If what happened at the memorial service was undoing all of that, inflaming the fear to the point where it would win and raise the level of hostility against *all* supernaturals, then that was scary. Exactly the sort of thing we'd feared might happen if people learned about the plague vamps.

This was why we needed to catch Smith. To stop the world going to hell.

"There have been a few things," Kenny said. "A bit more vandalism than usual. People complaining about prank calls. Nothing I would have called serious until now. But I'll have a word with the mayor. People can be angry about what happened, yes, but I'm not having this sort of shit tear up my town. We're better than that."

I hoped he was right. But until I had more reason to believe he was, I was taking Bug out of there.

I nodded at Kenny, then pointed at Dan. "Tell him all the details. The FBI is still investigating what happened at the memorial. There might be a link they can find that you can't. I'm going to go find Bug."

I didn't wait for Dan to protest about me offering the Taskforce's services. I was right. They needed to look into this. Bug was too close to me not to be a target for Smith. Again.

The thought quickened my pace.

I made my way past another small group of neighbors, braced for any signs of resentment, but I saw only concern on the faces that turned toward me as I headed for the nearest ambulance.

Bug sat on the edge of the truck, an oxygen mask over her face. A female paramedic who looked familiar stood next to her, typing something into a tablet. I took that to be a good sign that Bug was doing okay.

"Aunt B," I said, leaning in to give her a careful hug. She smelled like smoke, the harshness of it almost hiding her normal lavender and soap scent. My eyes prickled. I wanted to grab her tight and spirit her away someplace safe. "Are you okay?"

She rolled her eyes and tugged down the mask. "I'm fine. Aisha here is being overly cautious."

"I'm just doing my job," Aisha said, rolling dark eyes at me. "Smoke inhalation is no joke." She stowed the tablet in a rack in the back of the ambulance. "Ashley, it's nice to see you. Your aunt is doing well. She got out fast. No burns. It would be good if she stuck to the oxygen a little longer." She reached out and gently put Bug's mask back in place. "Then she should come to hospital and let the doctors confirm all of that."

"Thank you, Aisha. Is there any reason why I couldn't take her back to Seattle and get her checked out there?" I asked.

Bug yanked her mask down again. Her eyes were reddened from the smoke but fierce. "I'm not going anywhere."

I held up my hands, palms out. "Don't shoot the messenger, but you need to stay somewhere. They're not going to let you back in the house for a few days, I'd say." That was probably optimistic. The fire was still burning. I couldn't even begin to work out how much damage the water and smoke and flames might have done. "And I want you to come back with me."

"I just got home," Bug said, expression mulish. "I have things to do."

She always did. Bug had always been big on volunteering and diving into all the little community rituals that made up life in a small town. Since she'd retired, she'd only increased her involvement. Sometimes I wondered why she hadn't just kept working if she was going to spend so many hours a day on all her various projects and causes.

Not that I'd say that to her. That would only earn me a lecture about responsible citizenship and civilized communities. I'd heard it before. Even before Dan came back into my life, the weird hours I worked to service my supernatural clients ruled out many opportunities to give back the way Bug did. Now the pack and the case took up any fraction of spare time I had. I wrote nice big checks to charities, including some Caldwell organizations, and left it at that.

"I'm sure Caldwell can continue to function for a few more days without you. If they can't, you're not training them right." I smiled, giving her my best version of puppy-dog eyes, trying not to let her see how much I wanted to get her the hell out of there. "Come back with me. I'll take you shopping." It was our usual way to hang out when she came to town. I'd take some time out, and we'd wander through our favorite shops and finish the day with martinis at one of our favorite swanky downtown hotels. We hadn't been able to do it when she'd been in Seattle last week. She'd been too tired for a late night and I'd been too busy.

This time she really would need to go shopping. The thought made my stomach turn again, and I fought to keep the smile on my face. Who knew what state her clothes might be in after a fire? Bug had lived in her house a long time. All those memories. All her things. How much had she just lost?

Because of *me*. Because I was a werewolf now, and I had brought the worst of the supernatural world back to town.

I glanced back toward the house, but the firetrucks blocked my view. How much damage had I done?

As though she knew what I was thinking, Bug reached for my hand, squeezing it. "Stop fretting," she said. "I'll come with you."

Chapter 5

A FEW HOURS LATER, I was tucking Aunt B into bed in my guest room. The fire chief hadn't wanted to let her into her house yet, so it was just her, her purse, her phone, and the few things she'd grabbed on her way out. In typical organized Bug fashion, she had a small file box in the front hall closet with her passport and insurance docs and such. I'd sent Dan to the nearest drugstore to buy some basic toiletries and a toothbrush, and to fill her prescriptions.

Bug had been quiet on the drive back from Caldwell, and she was pale now, her face drawn and, for once, looking her age. We'd stopped at the hospital the Taskforce worked with most often, and Dan's badge got us through the waiting area in record time. The doctor on call had cleared Bug, prescribed some medications to help her lungs, told us what to watch for, and sent us home. Bug had been half asleep when we'd finally reached Mercer Island. As much as she needed clothes, shopping was going to have to wait until morning.

She'd showered as soon as we'd arrived, trying to get rid of the smoke smell. I washed her clothes and cobbled together an outfit of one of Dan's tees and a pair of his sweatpants I'd shrunk in the wash that were now too small for him but too big for me. Bug was taller than me, so they fit her. I had a huge old robe I wore in winter, and I wrapped her in that, then plied her with scrambled eggs and herbal tea before convincing her to go to bed.

The fact that she let me do all of it without a single squeak of protest told me she was far more shaken than she was letting on. But sleep was a good start. We could deal with any other fallout in the morning.

I stayed outside the guest room door until I heard her breathing shift into the rhythms of someone sleeping deeply. Then I retreated to the kitchen and poured myself a drink while I waited for Dan. My hands trembled as I tipped the tequila bottle toward the glass, and I had to pause, biting my bottom lip for a moment, determined not to have a meltdown.

I'd been putting on a brave face in front of Bug, but it was hard to keep it together now that she was asleep. Someone had set fire to her goddamn house. She could have *died*.

And once again, the blame had to be laid at the feet of Tate and Smith. Tate had been psychotic, a man who should never have been made into a vamp. I could understand him, in a way. He lusted after fear and power. Hardly a new story. But we'd been hunting Smith for months now, and I still didn't know what his motivation for teaming up with Tate and Cilla was.

He'd told me he'd killed Cilla's daughter, and, if it were true, then yes, that was horrifying and tragic, but even that didn't justify choosing to create vampires who could potentially wipe out the human race. That didn't make sense for humans or vampires.

But whatever the hell his goal was, I wasn't going to let him win.

My grip tightened around the bottle and I poured a shot, threw it down, and let the alcohol chase away the fear and focus me on what I needed to do.

I heard the front door opening as I poured a second shot.

Dan lifted his eyebrows at me as he walked into the kitchen, a bag of supplies swinging from his left hand. "Any left for me?"

"Maybe," I said. I reached for another glass and filled it for him.

He put the bag on the counter and came around to stand beside me. But instead of picking up the glass, his hands reached for me, pulling me close. He was big and warm and strong, and smelled like safety.

"Bad day, huh?" he said.

"Not the best." I wrapped my arms around him, fighting back tears. I couldn't lose it. If Bug woke up and found me crying, she'd try to take care of me. I was the one who should be taking care of her. "She could have *died*, Dan."

"I know," he said, holding me closer. His right hand stroked my back. "But she didn't. Concentrate on that."

He'd never been one for dwelling on the past. Maybe it was part of his FBI training or even the lessons he learned as a cop, how to compartmentalize and move forward after something went horribly wrong. But they didn't teach you that when you became an accountant.

Well, not how to deal with the really bad stuff. I could manage a difficult conversation with a client when I needed to, and I'd dealt with fraud and divorces and other tricky legal situations, but accountants weren't supposed to have to deal with murderous vampires.

But I was no longer just Ash the stable, normal, human accountant. I was a werewolf caught up in an FBI investigation and trying to stop the world from potentially being overrun by vampires. I had to deal.

"If we don't stop Smith, if news gets out about the plague vamps, stuff like this will just be the beginning." I said, the words shaky. "People are going to get hurt." And we could be those people. I didn't think humans would make neat divides between shifters and vampires in their mind when it came to a threat to their lives. Lycanthropy was a virus, too. I knew how human logic worked. If one virus got classed as a bigger threat, both would. Lycanthropy was already more infectious than the vamp virus. It was only the fact that werewolves appeared more normal and didn't drink blood that made us seem the less scary kind of supernatural.

As good at appearing calm as he was, Dan was worried, too. The subtle tensions in his muscles told me that much. And his scent was developing that smoky edge. He wasn't outright furious, but he was angry about what had happened to Bug.

"I know," he said. "But that's not going to happen, Ash. We'll stop him."

I wanted to believe. But in my gut, I knew something needed to change if we were going to succeed. We needed a new lead, new threads to follow. And I was the one who maybe had the answer to all of it buried in my mind. Fear or no fear, freak-out or no freak-out, I had to find out what it was.

"I'm going to talk to Jase. Tomorrow. As long as Bug's okay," I said, voice muffled against his chest. "We need what's in my head if we're going to find Smith."

"I doubt your dad left a map of his whereabouts," Dan said.

"We have no idea what he left," I said. "If he was still alive, I'd be having very stern words with him. Of course, if he was still alive, I wouldn't need to." I banged my head gently against Dan's chest. "Why the hell he thought using my head as a backup drive was a good idea, I'll never know." Normal people would have just hidden stuff in a safe-deposit box somewhere. Which told me my dad had been beyond a normal level of concern when he'd done whatever he'd done to me. I was sure he'd never thought it would turn me into a target.

"I think that comes under the same general category of

things not to focus on," Dan said. "As far as I know, seances aren't real. Short of that, we might never find out why your dad made his decisions. You'll tie yourself up in knots wondering. Better to focus on finding out what he left. And why the vamps want it."

That was the scary part. It was weird enough finding out my father had messed with my memories. But Rhi had discovered what he'd done before she'd died, taking Cilla with her in a blaze of sunshine and fire. She'd told me there was a secret in my head. She just hadn't had time to find out what that secret was before she'd sacrificed herself so I could escape.

No wonder I had trouble letting people poke around in my head. Every time I did, bad stuff followed. Not to mention that every time I did, it stirred up all the memories of losing my family.

"You're right," I said. "So, Jase is the answer. I hope. We don't have time for me to get comfortable with Sylvia. Not if things are escalating." I stepped back, looking up at Dan, seeking reassurance. If I couldn't trust Jase enough to let him in, then I would have to go back to Marco. He'd thralled me before. I had no doubt he'd be able to do it again. The question was what price I'd have to pay. And what that would do to Dan and me.

The thought made my head hurt. It had to be Jase. He was the only vampire I could think of who I might be able to trust enough to let in.

Ironic when, not that long ago, I'd made him promise never to use his burgeoning psychic powers on me ever again.

"We'll figure this out. Something will work," Dan said. He nodded at me, steady as a rock. "In the morning, we'll see how Bug is. If she's okay, you can talk to Jase. If not, well, we wait a few more days until she's feeling stronger."

I sighed. "Okay." He was right, Bug was the first priority, but I suspected she'd put on a brave face regardless of how she actually felt. I didn't want to leave her alone, but she couldn't be with me while Jase did whatever he was going to do. Not only because she had her own bad memories of vampires but because it was all related to the case. Bug didn't yet know there was something hidden in my head. She didn't know Rhianna had found it.

"I wonder if Ani would ask Pen if she might come spend some time with Bug?" I said. "They seemed like they were hitting it off at the party." If Bug was going to pretend everything was okay, company would be good for her. A distraction.

Dan smiled. "That's a good idea. Penelope is no one to mess with. Bug will be safe with her."

"I'd ask Stanley to come up here, too, but I think Bug might murder me." I stepped back and shook my head. "Why she won't admit he's her…gentleman caller is beyond me."

Stanley and Bug had started as bridge partners. Bug, who'd claimed to be perfectly happy with single life, spent a lot of time with him these days. They had plenty of interests in common beyond bridge. Stanley was a mad keen gardener like Bug, and they both swam and threw themselves into just about every volunteer organization in town.

But she steadfastly refused to call Stanley her boyfriend, insisting they were just friends. Given I'd heard Stanley in the background a few times when I'd called Bug either early in the morning or late at night, I was certain they were more like friends with benefits, at the very least. Which was perfectly fine by me. Bug deserved whatever made her happy. And that was a train of thought I wasn't going to follow too much further. I was on board with Aunt Bug having a satisfying love life. I just didn't need to think about it too hard.

"She likes her privacy, I guess," Dan said. "Small towns are hard."

Small towns had tried to burn her out of her house. I wasn't going to let that happen to anybody else.

* * *

"You're here early," Jase said, brows lifting, as he walked into the office the next evening.

His moss green eyes swept over my desk. I'd made a start on the emails he'd been sending me about things that needed my attention, and now my desk looked like I'd camped there for a week, littered with my notebook, tablet, pens, an empty coffee cup, my half-eaten candy bar, and a pile of sticky notes.

The truth was I'd been more focused on the case than my business for weeks now and not giving my clients my full attention. Jase had been holding down the fort, putting off clients and rearranging my schedule and doing his usual stellar job on the admin side of things. I'd taught him to use a lot of the analytical tools we had at our fingertips, but he wasn't an accountant. That part was my job. I was going to have to figure out a better solution soon or I wouldn't have a business to come back to when this was all over.

Jase was probably shocked to see me. We'd been communicating by text and video and phone over the last few weeks.

I'd wanted to beat him to the office so I could figure out how best to broach the subject of him trying to find what was hidden in my memories.

Vampires didn't really eat or drink, so I couldn't bring him coffee and pastries to butter him up like a human employee. But then again, Jase was my best friend. I shouldn't need to butter him up.

But I did. We'd hardly had any serious fights in the years we'd known each other, but we'd had one not long ago.

When Jase had tried to use his psychic powers on me without asking.

I'd lost it, and the fight had been nasty.

Our friendship was strong enough to get through it, to find a new footing, but we were still at that delicate stage where we were navigating to that place. Tiptoeing around each other, being overly cautious. Part of the reason I'd been working from the FBI building instead of the office was that it was just easier, in a way, if we gave each other some space.

But now I had to poke at the wound that was only just scabbing over. And hope asking him to do this wasn't going to ruin things between us if I had the same reaction I'd been having so far to other vampires trying to do what I was asking him, too.

Jase knew exactly why I had issues with vampire mind powers, and he'd know exactly how it could go wrong between us.

Besides which, Marco had only been working with him for a few months. He might not even be able to do what I wanted.

"I thought I should try and catch up on some things," I said. "Or make a start, at least." I waved my hand at the monitor. "You'll see the updates in the database."

"Okay. How's Dan?" He sat in the chair opposite me. He looked more awake than I felt, his charcoal suit sharp, the pale gray shirt and violet tie immaculate as always, making his eyes look greener and his hair somehow a deeper shade of red.

But put together or not put together, I knew he'd be as worried about Bug as I was. I hadn't actually told him about the fire yet. I'd been so focused on Bug last night, I hadn't thought of it until this morning, and I hadn't wanted to wake him. His need for sleep was decreasing with each year, but he wasn't like an Old One who could stay awake all day and all night. He still liked to sleep the day away when he could.

"Dan's good," I said, trying to think how to break the news. He'd be hurt that I hadn't told him straight away. Not a great start when I needed us to be okay.

Jase frowned. "Ash, is everything okay? Did something happen?"

Damn it. He'd always been too quick to read my mood. But maybe it was better to just get it over with.

"Yeah," I said. "It did."

"Was anybody hurt?"

Reasonable question. There'd been too much death since Tate had reemerged. I'd ended up in the hospital twice. Dan had, too. Rhi had died. And Ben, one of the werewolves.

"No. But Bug's house caught fire."

Jase swore under his breath, a string of curses hissing past his lips. His eyes turned very green. I was right, he was pissed. But not at me.

I held up a hand. "She's okay. Well, physically anyway. She's doing the stiff upper lip thing at the moment, but I think she's pretty freaked out."

"*I'm* pretty freaked out," Jase said, easing back a little. He adored Bug. He tilted his head at me. "And you're pretty freaked out, too, I'm guessing. Is she staying with you?"

I nodded. "Yes. We won't even know if her house is safe to go back to for a few more days. Then it will have to be repaired. Cleaned." I only had the vaguest idea about what cleaning up after a fire might entail, but I knew it was going to be a lot of work. And if there was structural damage to repair, it could take months. "But she's okay. Or pretending to be okay. I don't want to push her too hard. Penelope is staying with her for today."

"Penelope from the pack?"

Jase knew a lot of the pack. He'd known some of them before Dan and I had gotten back together. And he'd attempted to learn more about the pack since I'd joined it. "Yes. They hit it off at Ani's dinner last week."

"That's good that she has company. Are you going to the Taskforce tonight?"

I shook my head. "I've already been in. And I have that appointment with Esteban later on." I resisted the urge to pick up my favorite pen and start clicking it. Jase knew my nervous tells. And a looming meeting with the lord of the dark clubs along with the conversation we were about to have had me plenty nervous. Of course, he could hear my sped-up heartbeat and draw his own conclusions. "Actually, I could use a break. Why don't I grab a coffee and we can go up to the roof?"

He stiffened. "You're not about to give me the 'I'm joining the FBI and closing the business' speech, are you?"

I blinked. "What? No. *Nooooo*." Crap. Was he worried about his job? Had I been that bad a friend-slash-boss lately? "The last thing I want is to work for the Taskforce full-time. What we do is more fun."

He shook his head at me. "Most people don't consider forensic accounting to be more exciting than fighting crime."

"Most people are wrong. And they've never come near the kinds of crime the Taskforce does. That's why they exist, so the rest of us don't have to deal with that stuff." Because it was freaking terrifying. "Besides, you and I fight crime in a way. A way that involves fewer bullets and less blood. So, I'm in favor. Besides," I said, smiling, "if the FBI wanted me, I'd tell them we're a package deal."

His expression lightened a little. "Good. But the FBI can't afford us, you know."

"You're probably right."

I grinned and then busied myself at the coffee machine. Five minutes later, we stood on the roof, looking out over the lights of the city, still bustling despite the darkness. Sometimes, when we were working true supernatural hours, we'd come up here and it would be nearly peaceful, the city's traffic gone as most of the humans slept.

I sipped coffee and watched while Jase stood next to me, hands shoved into his pockets, standing very still in that way vamps sometimes did.

"What was it you wanted to talk about?" he asked after a minute or so.

"Can't we just be hanging out?"

"You're so busy, you barely have time to sleep. And honestly, I don't think I've been high on your list of people to hang out with lately."

My guilt pinged. "Jase—"

He held up a hand, grimacing. "I know we had a fight. We'll get past it. Things have just been…weird."

"I can't argue with that," I stepped closer to him. Bumped my shoulder into his upper arm gently. "But even if we're fighting, you're always one of the people I want to hang out with."

"I know," he said, bumping me back. "And I know you've been through a lot. Hell, it took me years to get used to being a vampire, and I didn't do it in the middle of an FBI investigation with bonus psychopaths interfering." He flicked a smile at me before his expression turned serious again. "But all that aside, I don't think your pulse would be quite so fast if you just wanted to hang out. Is there something more about Bug? About what happened?"

I winced. "It's connected. Maybe. Or, at least, we can't rule out it being connected."

His brows flew up. "Someone set the fire deliberately?"

"Kenny says he doesn't know, but I think that's just sheriff talk for 'he doesn't want to say anything without proof.' But I'm going to be very surprised if it was accidental. Bug said there'd been some talk." I bit my lip. "Rhi's parents didn't invite me to her funeral. It was last week."

"What?" Jase looked horrified. "God, Ash, I'm so sorry. That's…."

"They're upset," I said. "It's understandable." My brain agreed. My heart still didn't. It hurt. Which was why I hadn't mentioned it to Jase before now.

I drained the rest of my coffee and put the mug down on the stack of milk crates we'd hauled up here to act as an impromptu table at one point not long after I opened the business. I could afford proper outdoor furniture now, but we were used to our makeshift version.

"So, people in Caldwell aren't happy about vampires." He frowned. "And werewolves, too. Shit, Ash. That sucks."

"Yeah, it does." I shoved my hands deeper into my pockets. Jase was my friend, but I'd hired him because there was a very clever brain inside his handsome head. He was on the need-to-know list when it came to the case because I'd needed his help to do the work I was doing for Esteban. And now I needed it again.

"Trouble is, it's not going to stop sucking until we stop Smith," I said. "As long as those plague vamps are out there, there's a risk the humans are going to find out and freak out. None of us will be safe if that all boils over."

"No," Jase agreed. He stared down at the city, chewing his lip. "And we're still stuck on the case."

"That's what I wanted to talk to you about."

His gaze turned back to me, face suddenly wary. "If this is about Niko—"

"No. Not this time." Niko worked for Esteban. He was as beautiful as sin but, as far as I could tell, had few morals. At least, not enough to stop him for working for one of the scarier Old Ones in the city.

Not the kind of guy I would have picked for Jase, but he had other ideas. I'd made up my mind not to interfere anymore. It would only make him more stubborn. But there was a part of me that hoped the attraction was going to burn out once Jase lost his lust goggles. I couldn't really blame him for being attracted to Niko. The guy was the kind of gorgeous usually only seen on movie screens. He had women and men sighing in his wake wherever he went.

Which was part of the reason I was fairly certain Niko was going to break Jase's heart. People that beautiful were no good for ordinary people. The other part of the reason was that I wasn't entirely convinced that Esteban hadn't sent him to seduce Jase to keep an eye on me somehow—or gain some sort of leverage.

Maybe that was just me being paranoid, but after the past few months, my paranoia felt justified.

But there was nothing I could do to stop Jase from getting hurt. I trusted that he was loyal to me and wouldn't tell Niko anything he shouldn't. I wasn't so sure Niko wouldn't do his best to snoop if he got a chance, but the FBI had layered my office network over with some genius level security systems since I'd started working for them, and I didn't think Niko had hacker skills that could crack that level of encryption.

I just had to hope Jase's good sense would reassert itself over time.

"Then what is it?" Jase asked, bring me out of my thoughts.

I braced myself, feeling my heartbeat speed up again. It was just a short sentence. It shouldn't be this hard. "I need you to thrall me," I said. "You have to see if you can find what my dad left in my head. Find what Rhianna saw."

Instead of flinching, he went very still. And very quiet. The pause grew very long.

"Have I stunned you into silence?" I bumped his shoulder again. He didn't bump back, just stared out over the city.

"Why me?" he asked when he finally looked back at me.

"Because so far, I freak out when anyone else tries it. I trust you."

"You told me never to use mind powers on you again."

"And now I'm asking you to ignore that," I said. "I'm asking for your help."

His mouth set in a stubborn line. "And if something goes wrong, what then? Are you going to hate me? Or be scared of me, if this freaks you out? You're my friend, Ash, not just my boss. I don't want that to get messed up."

"I won't let it mess up us, Jase," I said. "I know what I said. At the time, I meant it. But I need you to do this for me. You're one of the few people I really trust. If you can't do this, if I can't let you thrall me voluntarily, then I'm going to have to ask Marco to try do it against my will."

Jase's eyes narrowed. "That sounds like a bad idea. You'd owe him another debt, for a start."

"I know," I said. "Which is why I'd like you to do it. Will you? I promise that, whatever happens, it won't come between us."

"That's not something you can guarantee."

"Please, Jase."

He looked away. For long enough that I thought maybe he was going to turn me down. But then he sighed and turned back. "Okay. I'll do it."

"Thank you!" I hugged him then, hard and fierce. We didn't often hug, and at first, he was stiff in my arms, but then he hugged me back. When we finally released each other, he was smiling ruefully.

"Let me guess, you want to try now?"

"No time like the present." Before I had time to think about it. "Let's go back inside."

Chapter 6

"Here?" Jase asked as I took a seat on the reception sofa. I'd washed my coffee cup and put it away after we came back inside, but that was as much procrastination time as I'd given myself.

"It's as good as place as any," I said, sliding nearer to the sofa arm, trying to find the softest spot. The sofa was office sturdy, not squishy. It looked good, but it wasn't designed to be relaxing to sit on. "I'm comfortable here. But lock the door and put the 'office closed' notification on the elevator. I don't want anybody interrupting us."

Jase still looked uncertain, but he went to his desk and hit a few buttons on his keyboard to activate our do-not-disturb settings. Then he crossed to the door and locked it, pulling the blinds down for good measure. No one was going to get past the elevator, but the blinds made it feel more private.

I leaned over and flicked on the lamp that sat on the side table with a stack of magazines. We rarely used it. Bug picked it out when I'd been decorating the office. A quirky take on an old-fashioned banker's lamp, it had a heavy brass base engraved with constellations and the glass shade was purple, shading to deep blue rather than the standard green. Bug said it was like the night sky and claimed it would make my clients feel comfortable.

Given a lot of my clients were supernaturals, I didn't think many of them had confidence issues, but I'd liked the lamp. The light it gave off beneath the shade was warm and golden, cutting through the clear white from the LEDs set in the ceiling.

"Turn off the main lights," I said. "It might be easier." The last two times I'd tried this had been in brightly lit rooms. I had no idea if that had contributed to my inability to give in to the thrall, but it was worth trying something different.

Jase did that and then dragged one of the reception chairs closer to the sofa. "How do you want to do this? Do you want to lie down?"

I settled back into the sofa, running my hands over the navy fabric. Safe. I was safe. "I think sitting is better."

"Okay." He settled into the chair, looking oversized in its depths.

Note to self: bigger office chairs required.

"Are you sure you know how to do this?" I said, sounding breathless.

"I know how to thrall someone," Jase said, one corner of his mouth lifting. "We all do."

"Yes, but there's more to it, right? If you're going to make me remember."

"Well, as for that part, we'll just have to see, won't we? It's not like I've ever had to do anything like this before." He made a little "settle back" gesture at me. "But I wouldn't have agreed if I didn't know what I was doing. I wouldn't put you at risk."

"Okay, good." My voice squeaked that time. Then I remembered Rhianna. "Can I ask you a weird question?"

"You can ask me anything."

I squeezed my hands together, not meeting his eyes. "Can you see my memories if you go into my head?"

"Not unless I'm trying."

I looked up. "Wouldn't this count as trying?"

"I'd be trying to get you to remember your dad and whatever he planted. If he did. I don't need to see anything else."

My shoulders relaxed a fraction. "Okay. That's good." I believed him. So that would mean he shouldn't stumble over my memories of Rhi's death.

"Does this have something to do with what happened with Rhianna?" Jase asked.

"No." But the word had come too fast. "Why would you ask that?"

"Because what went down was clearly not good. And if you're worried about me seeing some of that in your memories, maybe it was way beyond not good. Worse than you're letting on. Your aunt isn't the only one who's good at pretending everything is okay, Ash." His smile was lopsided. "It's okay if you're not ready to talk about it but you're going to have to at some point."

I looked away again, shoulders hunching. "Maybe."

"Definitely. But that's your decision. And I'm not going to do anything but help you find what your dad left for you. But if you don't trust me, then you should get Marco to do this."

I shook my head, swallowed hard before I look up at him again. "I trust you. I want it to be you."

"Okay."

"Okay," I agreed. I did trust him. My head knew I was going to be okay. I just had to convince the rest of me that was true. My palm rubbed restlessly over the arm of the sofa.

"Ash, if this is going to work, you have to relax," Jase said gently.

"Easy for you to say."

"Maybe. But it's true. I'm not going to force you. If you won't go under for me voluntarily, then we'll have to go back to Marco. He's stronger than me." He put his hands on his knees, watching me.

I nodded, fighting my instincts. The wolf inside me

wanted to run. She didn't like feeling like prey. But she wasn't in charge, I was. And I didn't want to wind up back at Marco's asking him to force his way into my head. He could probably make it enjoyable, but only for as long I was under his thrall. I knew from experience that after that, I'd be in all sorts of trouble. "I'm trying."

"I could sing to you," he said with a smile.

"That isn't relaxing," I said, smiling back. Jase loved old musical theater with a passion. But his voice was the kind only a mother could love. I tried to get him to keep to a hum in the office, but we'd had some alcohol-fueled nights in karaoke bars that were best forgotten.

"I know some soothing numbers."

"Soothing for banshees, maybe," I retorted, then laughed.

He grinned. "That's better. Okay, no singing. How about bad jokes?"

"Thanks, but let's just do this." I was feeling more relaxed.

His smile disappeared. "Okay. So, you know how this goes. I'll sit here, and you look at me when you're ready. And try to avoid that wolf shielding thing. Think of beaches and piña coladas and Dan in a bathing suit, not moonlight, okay?"

"Right," I said, then, "Why are *you* thinking about Dan in a bathing suit?"

"I'm not. He's your happy place though. Lean into that. As long as you keep it in daylight." He leaned forward, closing the space between us a little. "I'm right here. Whenever you're ready."

I closed my eyes and summoned Dan again, smiling as I put him in a Hawaiian shirt, holding a piña colada. He looked happy. I needed to lock on to that. Dan happy and relaxed. Bug safe. Everybody safe. That was why I was doing this. I tried to sink into the sensation. What would it feel like if all the trouble Tate and Smith had brought to me all went away? To find out, I needed to trust Jase.

I couldn't put it off any longer. Holding an image of Dan

and a glorious tropical beach in my mind, I looked up and met Jase's gaze. His mossy green eyes caught mine, the way they'd done a million times.

My best friend.

I steadied my breathing. Jase breathed with me, not saying anything yet.

"I'm ready."

Jase slowly eased one hand up toward my face, and when I didn't flinch away, he laid it on my cheek. Marco had touched me to do this, too. "Hey," he said. "It's me. Let me in."

I stiffened, but before the recoil came, I found another breath. And another, staring into his eyes. And suddenly, the familiar sensation of a breeze wafting over me took hold. I'd half expected Jase to feel green like Marco. Marco felt like a forest, old and deep. Rhianna had felt like cool blue water. But Jase, well, he felt warm. Cozy. There was a golden glow around us, a sense of comfort, like fall leaves crunching under-foot or sitting by an open fire.

I smiled. Maybe it was the thrall rather than our friend-ship giving me this sense of security, but I'd take it over panic.

"Good," he said. "Now, let's take a walk."

My awareness shifted, the room around me fading away as the gold and the warmth and the safety wrapped me tighter. Then I was standing with Jase on a leafy trail, both of us dressed in jackets and boots and scarves. The path we were on wound through a wood that reminded me of the forest around the Retreat. Dense and close, the light tinted green.

Though the woods there had few clear trails. Wolves made their own way.

The path beneath our feet wasn't well worn either. Leaves scattered over the dirt and tufts of grass grew here and there, breaking the patches of bare earth up. It felt abandoned. But also faintly familiar. An odd sensation. I looked ahead, but I couldn't see around the bend in the trail. "Where are we?" I asked.

Jase shrugged. "This is your brain. You tell me."

I frowned. "I'm not sure." This was different to the other times I'd been thralled. They hadn't felt so real. Marco had been a voice in my head telling me I was safe. And Rhianna and I had stood in something more like a void, talking.

"Then I guess we just keep walking," Jase said. "But think about your dad for me. Try to remember him."

In the warmth of the thrall, I didn't resist the suggestion as I might usually. It still hurt to think of my parents. Not always the terrible fresh grief of my teens but a well-worn ache that sometimes still stung too sharply. Wallowing in my memories of them wasn't a luxury I allowed myself very often.

But I closed my eyes and summoned my dad's face. Laughing brown eyes and the dark brown hair just starting to show the odd silver strand when he'd died. The scruff of stubble across his jaw from the days when he was too caught up in his work or some project around the house to remember to shave.

I smiled at the thought, and Jase said, "That's good."

I opened my eyes. The path, which had been shaded by trees, was now dappled with patches of sunlight, and the sense of warmth was stronger.

"Think of another memory," Jase said, and I obliged.

Dad teaching me to drive, pretending not to be desperately resisting the urge to grab onto the steering wheel at some of my wilder moments.

Dad mowing the lawn and laughing when Mom brought him lemonade, not beer.

Dad asking me about my hated chemistry homework.

Dad laughing again as he held up the last Tootsie Roll in the bag and offered to flip me for it. We both loved them. Mom just shook her head at us when we made ourselves half sick gobbling our way through a pile and threatened to never buy them again. Which only ever resulted in Dad buying the biggest pack he could find the next time he went for groceries or did a Costco run. In my mind's eye, he held out a Tootsie Roll in one hand and a quarter in the other.

"Heads," I yelled. And watched as he sent the coin spinning through the air, sunlight sparking off the edges.

"There!" Jase said. "Hold on to that one."

I froze, the memory stilling as well, then opened my eyes. "Why?"

He pointed ahead of us. "Because something just appeared on the path up there that wasn't there before."

I looked where he was pointing. I might not have spotted it without the assistance of werewolf-sharp eyes. There, ahead, right at the edge of another bend, lying in a clear patch of dirt, was a Tootsie Roll, the tiny bands of red on the wrapper all that made it stand out from the path. And suddenly, I was bending to pick it up without having walked the distance between.

"Tootsie Roll?" Jase asked, looking amused.

"His favorite." I walked around the bend, trying to think of another memory of Dad and his obsession with the candies. His last birthday when Mom had made him a Tootsie Roll-shaped cake and he'd been so delighted, he'd just stared at it for five minutes with a silly grin on his face before kissing her soundly.

"Another one," Jase said. Sure enough, on the path ahead, another roll had appeared. I walked to it this time, bent to pick it up. It felt real enough in my fingers, the right weight and shape. I resisted the urge to unwrap it and eat it in case I broke the illusion.

"This is all feeling very Hansel and Gretel," Jase said.

"Dad liked fairy tales. And myths and legends."

"He was a scientist though, wasn't he?"

"Yes. But he always said stories were how we tried to make sense of the world. Back then, before they had the science to explain things. Even now when we're trying to express things that we can't yet explain." I rolled the candy between my fingers, trying to remember exactly what he'd told me about science and stories and the way the world worked.

"Well, maybe whatever he left hidden is something we can't explain," Jase said. "Let's follow the Tootsie Roll road." He waved me on. When I didn't move immediately, he shot me a "get on with it" look, and the warmth glowed around me again.

I started walking, still thinking about my dad. Tootsie Rolls continued to appear. I gathered them all until there were too many to hold in my hand and I had to shove them into the pockets of my…

I realized suddenly I was wearing one of my old favorite hoodies under the jacket. A UWA hoodie that had been my dad's. I'd stolen it from his wardrobe early in my teens, even though it had been way too big for me. I'd lost it in a house move years ago.

"The woods are getting thinner," Jase said, and I came back to the present again. He was right. The path was growing lighter, and in the distance, I could see where the trees ended. And another glowing Tootsie Roll ahead on the path.

When we reached the tree line, I hesitated. Around me, leaves rustled, and the light dimmed a little.

"Something wrong?" Jase asked.

"I just…what if it's something bad?"

The glow of the thrall flared brighter, and another wave of safe-warm-relax rolled over me. "It's your dad. He loved you, Ash. He'd never do anything to hurt you."

"He hid something in my head."

"Because he trusted you. Not to hurt you. If he was here, you'd do this to help him, right? So now you can do it to help everyone else you care about. Bug. Me. Dan. The pack."

He was right. I straightened my shoulders. "Okay."

We stepped past the edge of the woods and onto the lush

grass of a large field. The kind Sam's dad probably raised his cattle in. The kind that surrounded Caldwell.

Not all that different to any other field. Lots of healthy green grass bordered by post and wire fences and edging onto other fields. A couple of green squares over stood a white clapboard house with a cheerful red roof. But no signs of life. No cattle or sheep in the field itself. The only living thing besides us and the grass was a giant oak tree, its branches reaching out and up, creating a circle of shade on the ground beneath them.

I thought I caught a glimpse of something dangling from one of those branches, but it was still too far away to be sure.

I racked my brain for any memory of this place, but nothing came. Whatever it had meant to my dad, I didn't think I'd been here before. But maybe it was my dad just playing with symbols again. There were plenty of myths that featured big-ass trees, after all. I just hoped he wasn't expecting me to climb it and get transported somewhere else.

As I walked toward the tree, the grass sighing around my feet as a soft breeze ruffled it, I didn't think that was likely. Somehow this felt like the end of the road.

Jase walked beside me, his presence strong and steady, a golden glow in the back of my head, telling me I was safe. When we reached the tree and stepped into the shadow of the canopy, he began to laugh.

"What?" I asked.

He pointed ahead of me. A Tootsie Roll bag dangled from one of the gnarled lower branches. It was a stretch to reach it, but it came away easily to my touch. And it felt weighty in my hand.

OPEN ME was scrawled across the plastic in black Sharpie. When I looked more closely at the bag, I realized the top of the package was taped together. I peeled back the tape and peered into the opening. It was full of candies, but peeking out from beneath them was the corner of an envelope. I withdrew it with two fingers, handing the pack to Jase.

"All this for a note?" It felt kind of anticlimactic. Rhianna had said she could see numbers and letters in my head. But she'd been less than coherent, and I had no way to know now what she'd meant. Or even what powers the virus had granted her. It should have been too soon for her to have any meaningful psychic powers. But maybe what Smith had done to the virus to make it more contagious had altered that, too.

Jase shrugged, then tipped his chin at the envelope. "Maybe he explains it all in that."

I ran my finger across the heavy paper. ASHLEY was written across it in my Dad's spiky black scrawl. Along with GOOD JOB, KIDDO in smaller letters underneath. I smiled even as my heart twisted, fighting back the emotion. Time enough to get sentimental after I had my dad's message.

I studied the envelope. It seemed harmless, and my wolf was quiet, not sensing any danger.

"Here goes nothing," I muttered as I ran my fingernail under the flap and lifted it. Instead of a piece of paper, there was a flash of light, and then suddenly my father stood before me.

"Dad?" I said, bewildered.

The image turned toward my voice. "Hi, honey," it said. It was his voice. His tone. A voice I hadn't heard for so long. And had never expected to hear again. I groped for Jase, felt his hand close around mine.

"I guess you're wondering what this is about?" Dad continued. "If you're seeing this someday, then either I asked you to get this for me or maybe I'm gone." He hesitated a moment. "I hope it's not that. But if it is, and you need this, then I'm sorry, honey. Didn't mean to leave a mess for you. I hope you never see this. But as you are, then I'll just say, 'I love you. I'm proud of you.' And if I'm not there, then wherever I am, I miss you like hell."

He blurred in front of me, and it took me a few seconds to realize it was because I was crying, not because of anything wrong with the memory or whatever the hell this was. I swiped at my eyes, not wanting to lose a second of him. For a moment he was studying my face, that easy smile—oh, that smile I missed—breaking my heart all over again with the knowledge it wasn't real. That he was gone, and this was all that was left.

Then he seemed to look past me, over my shoulder. Almost as though someone was behind me. But I couldn't feel anyone there, and Jase hadn't reacted, so I didn't look. He nodded once, and then his gaze came back to mine.

"Now, listen to me, darling girl. Remember this." He reeled off a string of numbers, then repeated them. Then, before I could do anything more, he was gone.

"No!" I stepped forward, the hand not in Jase's reaching for him.

Jase pulled me back. "Ash."

"*No!*" I struggled. "Bring it back."

"He's gone," Jase said, and very deliberately stepped in front of me so our eyes met. "He's gone, and you need to wake up right *now*."

Gold light flared around me, and my eyes flew open. Pain crashed over me. The ache of loss. Of grief. I curled my hands into the sofa, heard something snap.

"Ash," Jace said. "Ash, tell me those numbers." His voice was demanding and strangely compelling, as though he hadn't yet set me free of his influence.

He had his phone out, recording. "Ash, remember them. Now."

I reeled off the numbers, surprised they were still in my head, as I battled the overwhelming sense of grief and loss. Like I'd just lost my Dad all over again.

"Good," Jase said. "That's good. That's what I heard, too. You did it, Ash. You remembered."

I burst into tears.

* * *

Jase let me cry, making soothing noises and passing me Kleenex. Eventually I wrestled myself back under control, and he rose and drifted off into the back of the office. I didn't pay much attention until he reappeared with water, a cookie, makeup wipes, and eyedrops.

"Do I look that bad?" I managed, only half hiccupping the words.

"That depends," he said.

"On what?"

"On whether you're still going to meet with Esteban tonight."

Crap. I'd forgotten all about that. I finished blowing my nose and straightened. It was just a memory. I hadn't just lost my dad. I was okay. Or I would be. I pushed the sadness away as best I could. "Yes, of course I am."

He frowned. "Are you sure? That was a lot."

That was an understatement. Having my dad right *there*. It had felt so real even though I knew it had all been in my mind.

Brains were weird. And sometimes they could screw you over.

"It wasn't real," I said. Maybe if I repeated that a few more times, I'd start to believe it was true. "And Esteban won't want to reschedule."

"Are you going to tell Dan what just happened?" He put everything he was carrying down on the chair he'd been sitting in, then dug into his suit pocket and extracted a piece of paper. "Here. I wrote down the numbers from the recording. Looks like location coordinates to me."

I took the paper and unfolded it. He was right. I hadn't made the connection, but it was definitely latitude and longitude. I'd never been a Girl Scout, but one of my high school gym teachers had been into orienteering and made us learn all about compasses and maps and hiking with coordinates for a semester. "Did you look this up?"

He shook his head. "I figured it's up to you what you want to do with it."

I glanced at my watch. It was closing in on 2:00 a.m. I kept weird hours, but most of the world still slept through the night, and it didn't seem smart to go flying off to wherever this was straight away.

If it was a business of any kind, it would probably be closed, anyway. And I'd been telling the truth when I said Lord Esteban wouldn't wait. He'd cooperated with our investigation and let us freeze his bank accounts and various other assets while we tried to root out how someone had siphoned money out of his businesses, but he was growing impatient for that to come to an end. Tonight I was supposed to be telling him what progress we'd made—which boiled down to "not enough"—and giving him clearance on which accounts we were handing back to him.

Both things that could have been done via a phone call, but when an Old One asked for an in-person meeting, you didn't say no. Not when you were working for him because of a favor you owed to another Old One. Technically Esteban could demand all his assets be handed back and the Task-force would have to do it. They could get court orders to force him not to, but that would all take time we didn't have. Even Dan—who didn't like Lord Esteban one bit—hadn't argued about tonight's meeting when I'd mentioned it. He was supposed to be picking me up in about thirty minutes to take me there.

"I'll call Dan, give him these coordinates. Someone in the Taskforce can look into it, and I guess tomorrow we'll take it from there," I said.

"You'd think your dad might have offered up a bit more of

an explanation," Jase said. He was frowning, frustration underscoring his words.

I knew how he felt. In fact, as the worst of the shock of seeing my father again receded, irritation was building in its place. Whatever the coordinates led to, I hoped there was some sort of better explanation at the end of it. Maybe Dad had thought he was protecting me when he'd put this stuff in my head, and maybe he'd never expected that I'd need it one day—or at least need it without him there, despite his little speech.

No one really ever believes that they're going to die, do they?

But I couldn't help feeling as though he'd indulged his love of puzzles and pranks a little too much. What was wrong with a good old-fashioned safe-deposit box and a key and some sort of secure message in his will?

"I guess he had his reasons," I said, trying to sound calmer than I actually felt. Heading to deal with Esteban in a temper wasn't a good idea.

I took the makeup wipes and headed for the bathroom. Cleaning my face and reapplying my makeup made me feel a little calmer. When I returned, Jase was seated at his computer working.

"Thank you," I said, leaning in to kiss his cheek. "I should have said that first."

He went red, looking pleased. "You were upset. I would have been, too, in your place."

"Maybe. But I mean it. Thank you. You're the only one who could have done that for me. It means a lot." I hugged him, even though the angle was awkward, trying to express what I felt. He'd given me a few more moments with my dad. And even though that hurt, it was also a gift I'd never be able to repay.

"I love you, too, Ash," he said. "Now, call that wolf of yours so we can find out what the hell this is all about."

I laughed, let go of him, and went to grab my phone off the side table.

Dan sounded surprised when he answered. "Is everything okay? We're heading your way in a few minutes."

"I have some new information," I said. I'd told him I was going to ask Jase before I'd left for the office, but there'd been no way to know if it was going to work.

"Oh?" There was a lot of hope in that one syllable.

"Jase and I tried again," I said, keeping my tone casual.

"Okay." Fabric rustled, as though he was moving around. "I take it, it worked?"

"Yeah."

"Are you okay?"

"Mostly," I said, smiling. I loved that he asked about how I was first rather than what I'd found. "It was weird. We can talk about that part later. But turns out that what Dad left me was a set of location coordinates. At least, that's what I think they are." I rattled off the string of numbers.

"Yep, that's what they are," Dan said. "Okay, I'll get someone to work out where this is. Unless you did that already?"

"No. I'm leaving that part to the experts. Plus, it's the middle of the night. If it's a bank or something, it's not like I can go bang on the front door. But the Taskforce can."

"Let's see what turns up," Dan said. "Do you want me to wait and find out before I come to you?"

"No. I don't want to keep Esteban waiting."

Chapter 7

"THIS PLACE still makes you nervous, doesn't it?" Esme asked as we walked up to Infradark's black mirrored doors.

"It's a dark club. It should make everybody nervous."

I slanted a look up at her. She was her usual all-under-control self. Showing no sign of nerves. That unflappable air was a Taskforce thing. All the agents had it. Maybe it was a class they took. And, in Esme's case, it was also a personality thing. She was reserved and somewhat enigmatic most of the time. Tonight she'd worn black jeans and a leather jacket instead of one of her usual suits—a nod to blending into the club crowd—but she still managed to look cool and kind of regal. Maybe it was a cat thing, too.

Cats were good at saving face. Esme, being a jaguar shifter, was wired differently to a werewolf. And she'd been an FBI agent a long time. So maybe she truly wasn't nervous about dark clubs.

I still didn't like them despite the fact that they were no longer unfamiliar. I'd been in quite a few of Esteban's other clubs investigating this case, and I'd been back to Infradark a few times as well. So far none of the visits had been as eventful as the first one.

That had been my first encounter with Esteban, who'd felt the need to flex his powers, which hadn't been fun. It had also been my first encounter with Cilla, though I hadn't known it at the time. My more recent visits had been more straightforward. The staff who ran Infradark for Esteban knew me now and knew my FBI connections. They didn't necessarily like them, but they mostly just ushered me up to Esteban's office rather than toying with me.

That made the time I spent in the clubs more bearable but didn't change the fact that they smelled like fear and blood and sex and sweat and other bodily fluids to my werewolf nose. The people who enjoyed the clubs liked that mix. I did not.

I especially didn't like it when I had just had an encounter with my dead father and a meltdown. Being with Dan had helped calm me down, but I still felt like the ground beneath my feet had shifted and I hadn't yet found my balance.

But I didn't have a choice in the matter, so I had to ignore my nasal passages and grit my teeth and just get on with it. I yanked the closest of the enormous doors open, and we went inside. I didn't know where Esteban found the music that always pounded through the air, but it was a weird mix of electronica and what sounded to me like death metal. And every so often something more disturbing, like a scream, seemed to float under the music at the very edge of hearing.

Dance music with a side of creepy. It didn't seem to stop the clubbers from enjoying themselves though.

The vamp manning the entry station nodded at me, recognition lighting his eyes. The club staff didn't wear name badges, and Esteban wasn't exactly the kind of boss to take me around and introduce everybody. I knew a few of the employees' names, but not all of them, so I just nodded back. He waved us through, touching his earpiece to announce our arrival. By the time we reached the main stairs that led up to the levels that held the private playrooms and Esteban's office, Leah, Esteban's second-in-command, was waiting for us.

"Ms. Keenan," she said with a nod. "Agent Watson." She wore a suit as sharp as mine rather than one of the long slinky dresses she favored. It made her look more real somehow. Less like she'd stepped out of someone's fantasy painting of a vampire. She eyed Esme with an unfriendly expression, and I thought for a second that she was going to announce that Esteban had changed his mind about the FBI yet again.

The first time I came here, he'd insisted that Dan wait outside for me, and for several of my encounters with him after that, the FBI had been barred from the clubs altogether, and Jase and Marco—or one of the other vampires of Marco's lineage—had done escort duty. But after my last round with Smith and the FBI's ramping up of the investigations, Dan had insisted that an agent accompany me. Esteban had relented and agreed. Not Dan, which was a pure power play on his part, but we'd gone along, wanting to try to maintain Esteban's cooperation.

Esme's presence was the compromise. I liked her, Dan trusted her, and Esteban, for whatever arcane vampiric reason, accepted her, too. Given she was tall, blonde, and gorgeous in that Valkyrie/Amazon/"I will seriously hurt you if you mess with me" way, I guessed that had something to do with it. Dan was waiting in his Jeep, parked a few blocks away, so as not to give Esteban any cause to claim he was breaking the ban.

"Hi, Leah," I said, trying for overly chirpy.

Esme hadn't said anything about my slightly red eyes, but I had no doubt that Dan had told her I'd finally unearthed what my dad had hidden in my head. But if she was professionally curious or wanted to offer a friendly shoulder for me to decompress on—it was hard to tell with cat shifters sometimes —she wasn't letting on. Nor did she react to my forced bubbly tone now.

Leah merely raised one dark eyebrow, nodded, then turned on her high black heels and led the way up the staircase.

I followed her, watching my step rather than the swish of her long ponytail. The stairs were steep and the bannisters coated with silver-laced paint. I'd learned that the hard way on that first visit. I wouldn't give Leah the satisfaction of seeing me stumble and burn myself now. We'd pretty much had dislike at first sight. The fact that Jase and her brother were dating hadn't eased our relationship any. I didn't know whether she had her doubts about the relationship like I had, or whether she was offended that I disapproved of her brother. I didn't care much either way.

I had the pack, I had Dan, I had Jase, I had Esme. I didn't need a vampire gal pal. And, even if I'd wanted one, Leah would hardly have been my choice, given who she worked for.

We reached Esteban's office quickly. Leah didn't try to shock either of us by stopping to activate any of the two-way mirrors that gave a view into the private playrooms lining the hallways, which sped up the process. She ushered us into Esteban's office, but he waved her away when she asked whether he wanted her to stay.

I tensed when he dismissed her but kept unpacking my tablet from my bag. I preferred not to deal with Esteban on my own. Though, if I was honest about it, it was unlikely that Leah would stop Esteban if he tried anything. Esme, at least, I could count on.

Esteban merely watched me, his disconcerting summer sky eyes alert. Like many vampires, he was beautiful. If you didn't think about what he actually was. Most vamps made an effort to tame the creature within. To suppress their appetites and keep them within the laws the world had established for supernaturals. Esteban kept to the law, but he didn't always hide his inner monster. Because he liked people to be afraid of him. And his strongest power was a particularly troubling one. He could evoke desire in anyone he chose.

Without a full thrall.

He'd shown me that power once. I'd fought, but it had been nearly impossible to resist him. He'd stopped before I'd really reached breaking point. Maybe I would be more resistant now that I could shield, but I had no wish to provoke him to another display of power. I'd rather just do what I had come to do and then get out again before what lay beneath his all-American rugged blond handsome face had any reason to surface.

But before I could start talking, the office door opened, and Leah came back in. "My lord, we have a situation."

My spine stiffened. A situation that Leah couldn't handle on her own couldn't be good.

Esteban rose. "My apologies, Ms. Keenan."

"My lord, I think this may be something Ms. Keenan needs to see as well. And Agent Watson."

That couldn't be good. The tension in my spine turned into a shiver that landed in my stomach like a lump of lead. Beside me, Esme had gone very still, her eyes fixed on Leah.

Esteban raised an eyebrow at Leah. "Are you certain of that?"

"Yes, my lord." She nodded, dark eyes serious. But she didn't offer any more details.

Esteban turned back to us. "Very well. Please follow me."

Esme and I exchanged a look as we followed Esteban out, but she shook her head fractionally. I took that to mean "don't ask any questions yet" and stayed quiet as we walked. I knew where we were. Each of the large darkened glass panels in the walls hid one of the club's playrooms behind it. The places where things could get really nasty even if it was consensual. I was hoping they'd stay dark. But as we reached the very end of the hallway and Leah waved her hand at the wall in a familiar gesture, I knew that wasn't going to happen.

Do not react, I chanted to myself. Then, as the glass cleared and I saw what was inside the room, surprise chased my determination away, and I stepped closer without thinking.

The room behind the mirror was empty apart from one man lying on the bed. The covers had been stripped and dumped in a messy pile on the floorboards, leaving him spotlighted against the white sheet. He looked like he was peacefully asleep. Almost normal apart from the wound in his neck. Blood stained the sheet beside it, not an alarming amount but enough to tell me the wound hadn't yet healed over.

"Did one of your…clientele get overly enthusiastic?" I asked cautiously when Esteban just stared at the man, not speaking.

"He was found outside the club. Out back," Leah said softly.

I glanced at Esme. She frowned. In a city the size of Seattle, there was a certain level of supernatural crime, but random vamp attacks on humans were unusual.

"It's a vampire bite?" Esme asked. With the glass stopping any of the scents from inside the room from reaching us, it was difficult to tell.

"Yes," Leah said. "It appears to be."

"Appears? Don't you have security feeds?" I asked.

"The camera in the alley appears to have glitched," Leah said.

Esteban's expression darkened. Unhappy Old One. Just what I needed to round out my night.

"Have you called for a doctor?" Esme asked, stepping back into the fray.

"Not yet," Leah said. "Several of our staff are trained in first aid. One of them checked his vitals. They seem relatively normal. He is merely unconscious. We have an arrangement with the twenty-four-hour emergency clinic nearby, but he is in no immediate danger."

Esme just nodded. I wondered what she was thinking, but

it wasn't the time to ask. She didn't press the point that medical assistance might be required. No outside doctor meant one less person to deal with if this ended up in the Taskforce's lap, I guessed.

I didn't want to think too hard about why Esteban had an emergency clinic on retainer. But I imagined that some things that happened in a dark club required a certain degree of aftercare even if nothing went wrong. "And you're sure it wasn't an encounter between your patrons that went bad?" I asked softly.

Esteban's head swiveled toward me, those blue eyes suddenly very cold.

"What happens within my walls is consensual," he said. "This does not appear to be so." His eyes were hard. "Consensual does not end with someone lying unconscious and bleeding in the street."

I couldn't argue with that. The sorts of consensual things that went on inside Esteban's dark clubs were nothing I wanted to get involved in, but I wasn't going to judge others for pursuing what they needed to. And Esteban had never actually fallen foul of the law as far as I could tell. Sure, there were rumors about a darker side of dark. But the more I worked with him, the more I thought they were probably just rumors. Possibly fed by him for the bump it gave his reputation and the allure of the clubs to those who wanted that kind of thrill.

What went on in the clubs was already pretty deep. From what I could tell, he liked money and power and feeding on the sexual energy his clubs generated too much to risk losing it all by landing in jail or having his operating licences yanked. Or falling foul of the other Old Ones by bringing too much negative publicity on vampire behavior.

I turned my eyes back to the room. So did Esteban. We all gazed at the figure on the bed in silence.

"An interrupted attack, maybe?" I asked.

He shook his head. "Look at the wound. A vampire who means to kill, or a young one in a frenzy, can drain a human fast, and they take no care in the bite. This bite is careful. Whoever did this was in control of themselves. They didn't drain him; they didn't tear his throat out. But he was left lying in an alley. Behind my club. On a night when you are present." His blue eyes were cool. "It is not normal. I don't like it."

I didn't like it either.

Neither did Esme. "I think we should notify the Taskforce. This is unusual enough for us to be wary. And he may need… extra care."

That was diplomatic of her. "Extra care" meant containment if I was right about her line of thought. Smith had been siphoning cash from Esteban's clubs somehow. And now here was a vamp attack, carefully staged to provoke a response from Esteban. Smith and his companions seemed like the most likely culprits. If that were true, based on what happened to Rhi, he would turn at sunrise and become a plague vamp. Too dangerous to be allowed to live free.

Very bad news, in other words. And that was without considering what it meant that one of the plague vamps might be loose in the city. Or that Smith was making his next move.

Esteban looked like he was sucking on something sour. But he nodded. "Yes. I agree. Marco and I and the other Old Ones agreed we would cooperate should this happen." He smiled, though it was more baring his fangs. "Things may go differently if we catch the vampire inflicting these wounds."

I wasn't stupid enough to tell him that would be a crime. *Don't argue with the king of the dark clubs in his own domain.*

"I'll call Dan," I said.

"I will send someone to fetch him," Esteban said. "We know where he parked."

"You know where we parked, but none of your cameras

caught this"—I waved my hand at the guy on the bed—"on camera?"

"No," Esteban said. "Rest assured, I will find out why." He frowned again. "I will need you to release more of my funds soon. Rumors are spreading. You don't want me to seem weak in the middle of something like this."

"We're working as fast as we can," I said. "We've cleared another tranche of clubs and companies. That's what I was coming to tell you."

"Good. Now, I will send someone to fetch your wolf and while we wait, I will see if I can wake up our friend."

"It might be safer to leave him sleeping."

The smile appeared again, more feral than before. "If I can wake him up, I'll be able to put him back to sleep."

As Marco had with Rhianna. I shivered away from the memory, staring at the man's pale face. I hoped I was wrong about this. For Rhi, one bite from a plague vamp had been a death sentence, her loathing of what she'd become driving her to suicide. If he was infected, the best he could hope for would be life locked away somewhere where he couldn't infect anyone else and the vague hope that someday there might be a way to cure him. It would take a strong will to survive that.

Not for the first time, I wished my father was here to explain himself.

"Still, if you wait for Dan to arrive, he can be another witness to whatever happens. That will save time."

Esteban looked at me coolly. He wasn't fond of having his authority challenged, but apparently he thought I had a point. He stepped back.

It didn't take long for Dan to arrive, Leah trailing in his wake. For once, she wasn't flirting with Dan. Instead, her dark eyes were as flat as her boss's as she went to stand beside him, watching the still sleeping man. He hadn't moved in the time we'd been waiting for Dan and Leah. Just lay there, breathing.

Esme had held her tongue, waiting for Dan to arrive before trying Esteban with more questions.

Dan's lips pressed together as he inspected the victim through the glass. His scent had turned smoky, though he wasn't letting the anger show on his face. Still, the vamps would smell it as clearly as I could.

"When was he found?" he asked.

"About thirty minutes ago," Leah said. "One of our bar staff went out into the rear alley to deal with some trash and discovered him. "

"Security footage?" Dan asked.

"No," Esteban said. "It seems there was a problem with the camera."

Dan frowned at that news. "You didn't call the police?"

Esteban shook his head. "Ms. Keenan and Agent Watson were already here. They seemed sufficient for the immediate moment. He is not dead."

Not dead might not be a good thing in this case. And I wasn't sure how not dead he was. His color wasn't good, though his chest was still rising and falling steadily.

"And you have no idea who attacked him?" Dan asked.

"Not yet," Esteban said.

"Lord Esteban suggested that he might try to wake him," I said. "That would give you an opportunity to question him. Find out who did this."

Dan hesitated. "It may be better to wait. Until we can transport him somewhere with the facilities to deal with him."

"Deal with him?" Esteban said.

"This may be a random attack," Dan said. "Right now, with Dr. Smith on the loose, I'm not willing to take that chance. Not when it happened at the precise time when Ashley was here. We need to test him. Find out what we're dealing with."

"In case he was attacked by one of these…plague vampires?"

"Yes. Testing is protocol anyway in any attack. There are other things people can catch besides vampirism."

He meant human diseases. Or lycanthropy perhaps. The bite was too neat for a werewolf bite though. Esteban was frowning again.

"We will, of course, keep you informed should he provide information about who committed the attack, Lord Esteban," Dan said. "I appreciate you must be concerned about your security."

"That is not all I am concerned about, wolf," Esteban growled. "You really think this attack was intentional?"

"Doctor Smith—or whoever he's connected with—has some sort of connection to you," Dan said. "Or at least is using you as a target."

I knew Dan had his own theories about this. That Esteban had been targeted because the perpetrators were banking on him to not protest too loudly about fraud, given he skated on the thin edge of legality. But they had underestimated Esteban. Whether it was pride, or simply the territorial drive and thirst for power that had driven him to become an Old One, he turned out not to be the kind of man who would take a threat to his security lying down.

Which any sensible person should have been able to foresee. Of course, so far Doctor Smith didn't have a good track record with sensible. He'd allied with McCallister Tate who I would have been willing to testify was actually psychotic in a court of law and then Cilla, who, while I wasn't sure she was a psychopath like Tate, had clearly lost touch with reality somewhere along the way. Whether she hadn't been stable before she'd been turned or she'd been traumatized at some point, she had been troubled.

We had been presuming that Doctor Smith was in charge now, but maybe there was still a crazy vamp or two in his pantheon of accomplices. Then again, a man willing to team up with Tate and Cilla wasn't someone I'd necessarily classify as sane either.

Regardless of the reason, they'd made a mistake in targeting Esteban if they thought they'd be safe from retribution. True, the Machiavellian structure of Esteban's various business enterprises was slowing my investigation down significantly, but I knew I'd find the leak in the end. I was damned good at my job. And I had plenty of experience in understanding the kinds of corporate structures set up by paranoid supernaturals who could live for centuries.

And now we maybe had another thread to follow.

If Esteban let Dan take the victim out of here without a fuss.

"Do what you need to do, Agent Gibson," Esteban said eventually. "But please keep me informed."

Dan nodded. "I'll call one of our extraction teams. They'll take him where he needs to be to get the best care. Is there an entrance they can use that will be more discreet?"

Esteban nodded. "Leah, please assist Agent Gibson with what he needs." He turned on his heel to face me. "Shall we continue our conversation, Ms. Keenan? I assume Agent Gibson doesn't need your help with this man."

I looked at Dan, saw him frown slightly. But Esteban was right. The man on the bed wasn't Rhianna. He didn't need me to hold his hand. And if I didn't finish what I'd come here to do with Esteban tonight, I'd just have to turn around and come back tomorrow.

"Of course, my lord," I said. "It shouldn't take too long. In fact, I might be finished by the time Dan's team gets here."

Dan's expression relaxed at that, and he nodded at Esme. "You stay with Ash, Agent Watson. Make sure she gets home safely."

Home. Where Bug was waiting.

All the more reason to get through this as quickly as possible.

"I'll see you there," I said, not making it a question.

If Dan was going to organize for this man to be taken to Fort Lyman, where they'd taken Rhianna when she'd been bitten, he might need to go, too. Though, now the medical teams knew more about what to expect. So maybe not.

The person they were likely to need was Marco. But throwing his name into the mix in front of Esteban was not the best plan.

Lord Marco was the most powerful Old One in the city. But the other Old Ones didn't always rest easy under his leadership. There were factions and fighting and finessing, and one day, one of them might get the better of Marco and take his place. Esteban seemed a likely candidate to have ambitions in that direction. He and Marco had, at best, an uneasy relationship. The fact that Marco had called on one of my debts to settle an issue for Esteban said something about Marco wanting to keep Esteban happy.

Or maybe he saw it as an opportunity to get some closer insights into Esteban's operations. Not that he'd yet asked me to tell him anything specific about what my investigation had found. Because the vampires and wolves were also on the lookout for Smith, Marco got briefed when there was progress in the FBI investigation that might be useful, and I think Dan expected him to return the courtesy if he or one of the other supernaturals actually found Smith. I wasn't so sure about that. Vampire justice tended toward swift and deadly.

And, as much as I might prefer Smith suffer that fate, we couldn't let him die until we knew exactly how he'd created his plague vamps.

Chapter 8

"You're sure this is the right direction?" I asked Dan for the third time as we drove past what seemed like a never-ending expanse of farmland.

"We're heading to the coordinates you gave me," Dan said. He stifled a yawn and reached for the coffee in the cupholder. He'd stumbled into bed sometime about five, and we'd been up again at nine when one of the Taskforce team had called Dan to tell him the victim from the club had turned at sunrise.

One more plague vamp in the world.

Hardly the news we'd been hoping for, but neither of us was surprised.

But Dan had insisted that the team tasked with helping the man—his name was Trey—through his transition didn't need us to help them and that we should instead keep following the breadcrumbs my dad had left us.

I'd agreed, though in the clear light of day, the way I'd found the information seemed more like a dream. It had taken me a long time to fall asleep, replaying the image of my dad and the words he'd said over and over. Hard to believe he'd planted something so real in my mind. Harder still to believe I had no memory of him doing it. In fact, the more I thought about that part, the more it was creeping me out. I needed to talk to Marco about what kind of vamp power would let someone do that without me remembering. And how the hell I could prevent it from happening again.

I'd let Jase in and it had been fine in the end, but the thought of a vampire being able to get inside my head and leave me with no memory of it at all scared the hell out of me.

But that fun conversation was going to have to wait. Finding out what had been worth putting me through all that was the first priority. So road trip it was. Daylight road trip, despite the fact that none of us had gotten enough sleep, to limit the chance of any vampire-related interference.

But we all needed extra caffeine, and we'd already stopped once at a gas station to top up our travel mugs. The coffee tasted little better than battery acid, but it at least seemed to wake me up a little. Maybe. My eyes were gritty, and I had a headache as the result of the emotional turmoil of the memories, letting Jase thrall me, crying my eyes out, or all three.

Esme, sitting behind me in the back seat, looked alert and well rested. I was never sure how she managed it. You'd think cat shifters would need as much as sleep as their animal counterparts, but unless Esme had mastered the art of catnapping while keeping her eyes wide open, she seemed to survive happily on hardly any. Or maybe she just slept every moment she wasn't on the job.

We were heading to Kingville, a town an hour or so north of Caldwell. I'd never been there, and I couldn't remember my dad ever mentioning it to me, but that didn't mean anything. No parent tells their kid their every move.

Bug had been awake when we'd staggered out to find whatever stuff we had in the kitchen that we recognized as quick and easy breakfast while we tried to wake up. But Dan hadn't wanted to tell her where we were headed. Instead, he'd asked Pen to take Bug out for the day, and Bug seemed happy enough when we told her we had to go out of town for Task-force business but that we'd be back later in the day.

Her lack of gentle guilt-tripping me for working too hard only made me feel worse about leaving her. She was being too calm. Too nice. Bug usually told it how it was. But I wasn't going to get her to talk about how she was feeling about the fire until I got to spend more time with her. The universe wasn't helping in that regard.

Kingville was farm country. People think Washington is covered in trees but that's not true. We do agriculture as well as big old forests and mountains.

Though why my dad was hanging out in farm country, I didn't know. He and my mom met at UW when he was studying for his bachelor's degree. They'd lived in Seattle while he'd finished medical school and his fellowship for immunology. We'd only moved to Caldwell when he'd gotten the job at Synotech, when they'd helpfully built a research facility an hour out of Seattle. It made the commute about the same whether we lived in the city or not, and Dad had leaped at the chance to move back to his hometown.

"Maybe Dad was testing his theories on cows?" I said, trying to lighten the mood in the Jeep. There were plenty of cows around.

Dan's mouth quirked, but he kept his eyes on the road. "Not sure that's how vaccines work. Cows aren't people. They're definitely not vampires." He glanced at the GPS display on the dash. "We're getting close."

I scanned the area visible out the window. There was no sign of anything much other than fields, more fields, and the odd farmhouse. We'd passed through the town of Fox Hill about thirty minutes earlier and hadn't yet hit Kingville. It was small, population approximately six thousand. Definitely not a connection to any research facility that we'd been able to find.

I hoped Dad hadn't been playing some sort of elaborate practical joke on me. But then, as Dan started to slow the car in response to the GPS's chirpy message that our destination was approaching on the right, I realized he hadn't been. Because in the field we were pulling up next to was the same giant tree I'd seen in my mind.

"That's the tree," I said, not quite believing what I was seeing.

"Tree?" Esme unfastened her seat belt, leaning forward so she could look past me. "What tree?"

I hadn't had time to tell Dan exactly what my experience with Jase had been like, let alone Esme. They knew I'd seen him. That he'd given me the coordinates, but I hadn't told them everything that had happened. I was still too raw to share Tootsie Rolls and the trail through the woods. I wished Jase was with us, but Dan's point about limiting the chance of vampires following us in daylight was hard to argue with. It just sucked that sunshine also ruled out Jase. I'd sent him a text to let him know where we were going, but I was hoping he wouldn't see it until sunset when we should be safely home again, and I could tell him we'd found something.

I turned to look at Esme and Dan. "When Jase did what he did, it was like we were following a path through a forest. And then there was a field just like this one. And a tree. A giant tree. Like that one." I undid my seat belt without thinking and opened the door, wanting to get to the tree more than anything.

"Ash, wait," Dan said.

I twisted back, one foot already touching the scruffy gravel at the side of the road. "There's no one else here. No cars. I can't smell anyone else." All I could smell was grass and eau de cow shit. "And, like you said, it's not like vampires can do anything in the middle of the day."

The field was flat. As were the surrounding ones. No cars had followed us from the city. All three of us had been watching for that. Unless some vamps had somehow known where we were going and made themselves some sort of underground tunnels or mastered some sort of *Star Trek*-level cloaking device—and as far as I knew, such things didn't exist —there was nowhere to lie in wait for us.

"Doesn't have to be a vampire," Dan said.

"I don't think Smith is a sniper," I objected. Besides which, I was fairly sure he wanted me alive not dead.

"He could hire one though," Esme said. She slipped out of the car, pulled out a pair of binoculars from her backpack, and scanned the horizon.

"Well?" Dan asked.

"Ashley is right, I can't smell any people. Or vampires. Just cows. And there's nothing out of the ordinary in range of vision."

I looked at Dan. "There's no way Smith could know where we were going. There's no sign of a tail."

Dan looked unhappy, but he nodded. "Okay. But we'll go across to the tree together, okay?" He got out and went around to the back of the Jeep.

"Sure." I climbed out of the car and headed for the fence. The field was empty, which was lucky. No potentially ornery stock to give us grief. Hopefully there wouldn't be an ornery landowner either. But Dan had a search warrant for the coordinates, so we were covered no matter what happened.

The three of us vaulted over the fence. Supernaturally enhanced strength is handy sometimes. Dan carried a small shovel and a metal detector. There were times when his FBI-honed instincts made me smile.

"Always be prepared," that was his motto. Though that also brought him frustrations when he couldn't control every-thing. I still wasn't sure I believed there would be anything to find, but we were equipped for digging if there was.

Dan looked at me. I took a breath, nodded, and we set off across the field.

I compared the tree to the one I remembered. It was larger, if anything, which made sense given the time elapsed since my dad had been here. If he had. I couldn't help thinking that maybe I'd imagined the whole thing and we were going to look stupid, trying to find something under this tree that just didn't exist.

But if I'd made it up, surely Jase wouldn't have experienced the whole thing, too? And it was a weird sort of situation to make up for a last encounter with my long-dead father. Not to mention the fact that if I'd been going to make that sort of thing up, I'd want to see my mom, too. Sure, the last few months had been stressful, but I hadn't reached the point of actually losing my marbles.

"Now what?" Esme asked when we reached the tree.

I stared at it. It was just like my memory. *Huge*. All three of us could have stood around it and barely spanned it with our arms. The trunk didn't start to branch until several feet above Dan's head. After that it was just a normal tree. Branches, smaller branches, twigs, and leaves. Nothing hanging from any of them that nature hadn't put there.

Disappointing. I hadn't really expected to find another envelope hanging out in the open. It hardly would have lasted for years and years. But I hadn't been entirely sure.

"Buried makes the most sense," I said. "That would give whatever it is a chance of surviving." I looked down at the base of the trunk. The beginning of the roots visible aboveground were gnarled and thick. If my father had hidden anything under one of them, we were going to need a chainsaw. And we'd have a lot more explaining to do to whoever owned the land.

Esme was walking around the tree, shaking her head. "There's a lot of ground under this tree." She paused when she got back to Dan and looked up. "And in those branches. Trunks have hollows."

Dan nodded but grinned at her. "You're the cat. You can climb to check it out."

She rolled her eyes.

"Dad would go with whatever was safest," I said. "Trunks can be damaged. Hit by lightning or whatever." I circled the tree as Esme had, trailing my hand along the bark, trying to think. Here and there were old weathered initials carved into the trunk. Not *R* and *I* for my mom and dad. But they gave me an idea. I walked more slowly, scanning the trunk closer. Low to the ground, I found a small circle carved into the bark. And within it, something that might, if I squinted hard, be a Tootsie Roll.

It wasn't going to win any awards for great art, but it looked close enough to a candy for me. Not exactly a common thing to carve into a tree.

"Here," I said, pointing.

Dan came around and peered at the symbol. "What is that?"

"I think it's supposed to be a Tootsie Roll," I said. "Dad loved them. They were in the memory as well."

His eyebrows went up, but he shrugged. "Okay. It's worth a shot. I guess we dig here." He shucked off his jacket, and I stepped back to give him room as he wielded the shovel.

It also made me smile to watch the ripple of his muscles beneath his shirt as he sank the shovel into the earth. He was being careful, but he was still a study in controlled power, easy with the actions, as though he did it every day. Werewolf coordination made everyday things a delight to watch.

"Nice work," I said to him. He grinned back at me over his shoulder.

"You two going to need a room?" Esme muttered.

"I'm just appreciating my man," I replied.

"You could appreciate me by helping," Dan said, pointing the shovel at us. "Esme, do you want to turn the metal detector on?"

He'd scraped back the moss and leaves and odd stubborn tufts of grass and loosened up the top layer of soil, clearing a two-foot square patch around the base of the tree.

"Do you think he would have used metal?" I asked. "Plastic would last longer, wouldn't it?"

Dan shrugged, wiping his brow with his forearm as he watched Esme. "Probably. But there could still be something metallic within the plastic. We don't know what he left for you. If your dad went to all this trouble, he thought it through."

He sounded approving. He would have liked my dad. They were similar in some ways. Both believed in preparation, dedication, and pursuing a cause. Dad might have given Dan a hard time at first, but he'd have been on board with anyone who loved me as fiercely as Dan did.

"You're right. He couldn't have predicted that I'd have FBI help to look for this." Or could he? Clearly the memory in my head and whatever we were going to find were my dad's paranoid version of "break glass in case of emergency." But no, he would, as Dan said, have considered all the options. Thought about what would happen if I had to come looking on my own.

Burying whatever it was with something metal seemed like a simple way to increase my chances of recovering what he'd hidden if he couldn't leave it in a more normal place.

Esme swept the detector over the ground. Nothing happened. She stopped, fiddled with the controls, and then tried again. This time it beeped.

Dan grinned. "That's a good sign."

He waved her back and started digging again, this time going more slowly, only lifting a little soil at a time.

It didn't take long before we heard the shovel thud against something.

My heart started hammering. There really was something here. I hadn't imagined it. My dad had stood here under this tree however many years ago and buried something that maybe he hoped I'd never need to find.

It didn't take Dan long to clear the rest of the dirt from around our target. He stepped away from the hole, staring down at whatever it was. The hammering in my chest turned to thumping.

"Do you want to lift it out?" he asked. "Your dad left it for you."

He stepped back so I could see what was in the hole. Something wrapped in burlap that was mostly rotted away. I couldn't see much under the layer of black dirt coating everything, but it wasn't very big.

I looked at it, not sure what to say. I wanted to know what it was, but suddenly all I could think was that my dad had held this box, too. That he must have been been thinking of me when he buried it. It hurt. I had some of his and Mom's stuff, of course. But I was used to those things, knowing they'd touched them in the past while now they couldn't. Sometimes those could catch me the wrong way, too, but they were familiar and safe. But this was something new. I would be the first person to touch it since he had.

I had to blink back tears. Dan and Esme stayed quiet, giving me the time I needed. It took a minute to collect myself.

"Here," Dan said when I nodded at him. He passed me a pair of disposable gloves, then pulled on a pair himself.

He wasn't just thinking of keeping my hands clean. The box was potential evidence.

I pulled the gloves on and reached for the box. It came free easily enough. Most of the burlap that was left fell away, just a few pieces here and there sticking to the sides of what proved to be a small metal box.

I straightened, held the box out to Dan.

"Do you want me to hold it or open it?" he asked, concern in his eyes. "Take the time you need to."

I shook my head. "Just hold it. I'll open it." I studied the box. It didn't have a lock. It was a simple small blue square tin with a fitted lid. I brushed away more of the dirt and burlap with my fingers, then tried the lid. Dan stayed quiet, but the steady beat of his heartbeat was a thread of comfort. A reminder that I hadn't lost everything when I lost my parents. That I was rebuilding my family now. That I had people who loved me.

The lid was a little stiff, but werewolf strength was handy. I got it free without too much trouble. Esme held out an evidence bag, and I put the lid into that before looking to see what was in the container.

Inside the box was another tin, this one in better condition. Once I pried the lid off that one, I found a small clear plastic container that held an envelope and a key in separate ziplock bags.

More clues. I sighed.

"Was your Dad into treasure hunts?" Dan asked. His tone held an edge of frustration, too, as though he wished this was all more straightforward.

So did I.

"He was good at hiding Easter eggs, but otherwise, no," I said. I put my hands behind my back, resisting the urge to touch. The envelope had my name on it. But until I had clean gloves, I didn't want to mess anything up.

"That looks like a safe-deposit box key," Esme said.

"It does," Dan agreed. He passed her the shovel. "Can you take this and the detector back to the car? We'll be there in a minute."

As Esme walked away, he moved closer. "Ash, are you sure you're okay?"

"I wish I knew when he wrote this," I said. My voice trembled. "I feel like it's the last thing I'll ever have of his. This is the last letter he ever wrote to me." I blinked, determined not to cry. "It's dumb, I know."

He leaned in and kissed my forehead. "It's not dumb. You loved him. You lost him way too soon. I'd worry if you weren't feeling sad."

"But I have to open it anyway, don't I?" I said. "If we want to know where the key belongs."

He nodded slowly. "Yeah, looks like it. I'm sorry, love. I'd rather give you all the time you wanted. But after what happened last night…."

I swallowed hard. He was right. There was no time to waste. I couldn't let the emotions get in the way. My dad was dead and that sucked, and I hated it, but there were other people at risk.

I held up my grubby gloves. Smearing dirt on the last thing I might ever read from my dad wasn't an option. "We have wipes and more gloves back at the car, right? I don't want to get this dirty."

Dan nodded. "Yes, we're all stocked up. But you can carry the box. It's yours, after all." He passed it to me.

It didn't weigh much at all for something with so much weight of meaning. I resisted the urge to pull it closer. "You're going to tell me this is evidence, aren't you?"

"It will be for a little while. But I'll make sure you get it back as soon as possible. And our techs can make you a copy of the letter to keep until you can have the original back."

There would be a message for me. There was no way my Dad wouldn't write me a note when he was planning this whole thing. He'd embedded one into the memory he'd left for me. No way would he have missed the chance to do the same physically.

I walked back to the car slowly, watching where I put my feet, paranoid that I might trip or fall and somehow damage the box or its contents. I passed it to Dan when we reached the fence so I could climb but took it back as soon as I was safely on the other side.

Dan opened the back of the Jeep, stowed the shovel and the metal detector, then grabbed his evidence kit. "Fresh gloves, wipes. Take the old gloves off, clean your hands, new gloves." He pulled a packet out of the bag and opened it. It was a small sheet of clear plastic. "Put the box down on this while you clean your hands. There are more plastic sheets in there, too. Spread one of those over your lap if you want to sit in the car. Rest the box on the plastic. Only touch the underside of the plastic yourself. Got it?"

I nodded. I'd had the evidence speech before. Sometimes my line of work meant I handled hardware used in a crime to get to the data I'd need to help investigate a case. I knew about gloves and the chain of custody. But I'd never been the first one to touch a piece of evidence before.

"Esme and I need to check in with the office," Dan said. "Take your time." He tipped his chin at Esme, who was waiting by the fence, and they walked back down the road, giving me some space.

I pulled off the old gloves, wiped my hands, put on fresh gloves, then carried the whole thing back around to the passenger side. Dan had left the door open for me. I got into the car with the box and managed to arrange it and the plastic sheet on my lap. My fingers trembled as I reached for the ziplock bag containing the envelope, and I had to stop and take a breath, the smell of latex harsh in my nose.

Not a particularly calming scent, but it gave me something to focus on other than the fact that I was about to read a letter from my dad. But I couldn't just sit there and breathe in latex forever.

"Get on with it, Keenan," I muttered and tried again.

The ziplock yielded easily, and I gently extracted the envelope. I understood how to handle old documents. Sure, most of my clients had digital records now, but some of them were a few hundred years old and had the ancient records to prove it. Paper gets fragile over time. Thirteen years wasn't that long in the grand scheme of things, but the letter had been buried, and I didn't want to take any chances of damaging it.

A quick scan told me it was in reasonable shape. The envelope was ordinary looking, once white, now yellowed at the edges. Other than my name, there was nothing to distinguish it from any other old envelope. It smelled very faintly of paper, but mostly of nothing. No hint of my dad at all. After so long, it had been foolish, maybe, to think there might be, but it still stung a little that his scent—if it had been there to begin with—hadn't survived. And it wasn't very thick, so I knew whatever lay inside it wasn't going to be long.

I eased the flap open, a feat made more difficult by the gloves. But apparently glue didn't age any better than scent. I slid the folded paper inside out gingerly, not wanting to tear it. It too was age stained.

Darling Ash,

If you see this, then something's gone wrong. I'm sorry to drag you into this. And I'm sorry for whatever happened. Sorry, too, for the cloak-and-dagger and the memory thing. Well, the cloak-and-dagger is kind of fun—you know I love a mystery—but I wouldn't do this to you if I could avoid it.

But this is important, and I need to keep it safe.

So, here's another piece of the puzzle. I hope you were paying atten-tion to all those long-winded stories I used to tell you about meeting your mom. And I hope you still remember some of it. Because I need you to find the fruit, and that will tell you where to use the key.

I'm sure you'll figure it out from there. You've got a world-class brain, and I hope you've never forgotten that. Or forgotten how much I love you. Because that's always been true and always will be true, no matter what's happened.

And if you're going to tell your mom about this, tell her I say 'hi' and I'm waiting.

Love always

Dad xx

The writing blurred as tears stung my eyes. I dropped the letter into my lap and swiped at my eyes with my forearm. He'd thought she'd still be here with me. Whatever he'd been worried about, he'd never expected that he and Mom might die together.

Well, at least he wasn't waiting for her wherever he was. I didn't really know what I believed about the afterlife. Vamps came back from the dead, in a way. Maybe that meant there was part of us that continued on. I hoped so.

I sniffed hard and wiped my eyes again. The meltdown could wait. It would come, but first I had to try to figure out what my dad was telling me.

Their first date. What had he told me about their first date?

They'd met in college in Seattle.

He'd taken her out for burgers, and then they'd gone for a walk, and it had all been very romantic. All normal.

Was I supposed to find whatever he'd left behind somewhere in Seattle?

Doubtful. Why bring me out here to this field if the information I needed was back in Seattle? Besides, the city seemed too obvious. Too easy for someone else who had known him to know he'd met Mom at UW, too. Or think he might have a storage unit or a safe-deposit box.

But Kingville wasn't obvious. He'd brought me here for a reason. So, what else had he told me about that date?

Burgers. Ice cream. He always joked he'd almost changed his mind about Mom when he found out she didn't like coffee ice cream, but she'd been too cute to give up on.

Especially after the way she'd devoured a double bacon cheeseburger and fries with delight.

Mom had always rolled her eyes at that part.

And then Dad would say. "But what made your mom fall for me was my excellent serenading."

Then he'd break into "Strawberry Fields Forever." Given he had a tenuous relationship with melody, it had always made Mom laugh and say, "I only kissed him to make him stop singing."

But "Strawberry Fields Forever" had been their song. He'd given her little gifts with strawberries on them every so often, and she'd kept them all. I still had a few of them tucked away in a drawer.

Was that the fruit he meant? Strawberries? I couldn't think of a better option. No other fruit stood out in the tale of that date that I could remember.

Strawberries it was. And I was going to start looking in Kingville. Otherwise, it would be like looking for a needle in a haystack back in Seattle.

———————————

Chapter 9

———————————

About twenty minutes later, we stood in the main street, and I was wondering if I—or maybe my dad—had completely lost it. There was no street in Kingville called Strawberry or Blueberry or any damned fruit. No businesses with those names. There wasn't even a berry farm anywhere in the area. Or anything connected to the Beatles. It was just your average small-town community.

"Was there something else about their first date that you can think of?" Dan asked. I'd told him and Esme why we were going on a berry hunt. To their credit, they hadn't commented on how weird this all was. Perhaps in the Taskforce you got used to weird pretty fast.

I shook, my head, still scanning the street. We were getting odd looks from a few locals going in and out of the stores. The three of us, dressed in suits, kind of stood out. "He told that story a lot. And it was always burgers and coffee ice cream and then serenading her and then her kissing him to make him stop singing. I never asked about the rest of the night because I did not need to know about what my parents may or may not have gotten up to in Dad's car or wherever after the date."

It had to be one of the three. There was a burger joint a few doors down from where we stood, but when Esme had done a quick background check on her phone, it had only been in business a few years. Kingville had no ice cream store. There was a diner, and a coffee shop, but they had no obvious strawberry connections. There wasn't a music store. And there was definitely nothing useful along the lines of "Mr. Strawberry's Magic Emporium of Information from Dead Parents."

"It has to be the strawberries." I started walking again. The town was small. Its downtown was a couple of streets full of the usual kinds of stores. Post office, grocery store, a few other food places. Three bars of varying degrees of fanciness. Clothing stores. A feed store and a hardware store. The town hall sat nearly center on one of the streets, fronted by a small paved area not really big enough to be called a square. Next to it was a tiny park with a fountain in the middle of a patch of grass. I wandered over to it while Dan and Esme did more web searching. The water in the fountain splashed happily, spilling from a bowl down a pedestal carved with plants.

Plants. Maybe berries? It was a long shot, but I crouched down, inspecting the carvings. One side had roses, the next what I thought were oak leaves. But the east side that pointed back to one of the older-looking buildings across the street had strawberry plants, tiny marble berries peeping out from beneath the familiar leaves.

"Not the most obvious clue, Dad," I muttered under my breath, but I turned back to Dan and Esme. "Let's try that building across the street."

That earned me a raised eyebrow until I pointed out the strawberries. We walked back to the building. It was old, built in a similar style to the town hall. Fancy brick and stonework. And, above the doorframe, a frieze of berries carved into the stone.

The name on the door proclaimed it to be the offices of Bill Wallace & Associates, Attorneys.

Lawyers. That seemed more likely than anything else we'd come across.

The blonde receptionist looked up and smiled as we entered the office, brown eyes curious behind big red glasses. The name plate perched on the edge of her desk said Sally Nelson. "How can I help you?"

"We're not entirely sure, Sally," Dan said. "How many attorneys work here?"

"Just the one. Mr. Wallace. It's not a big town. There's us or Daniels & Co—there's no 'Co,'" she added with a smile.

"Do you offer any sort of document safekeeping for your clients?"

She nodded. "Sometimes. A few still ask for it. The bank is expensive, and there was an issue with it in the nineties. Some people have long memories."

Dan nodded. "Okay, thank you. Do you think we could speak to Mr. Wallace?"

Her expression turned to bland reception face. The kind I recognized from Jase. The kind he made when I told him to put clients off or keep everyone out of my office for a while. "His calendar is quite full today. I could make you an appointment—"

Dan held up a hand and then pulled out his badge. "It's kind of important, Sally." He showed her the badge. "So, I'm sorry, but I need to disturb your boss's calendar just for a while."

Her brows rose and she nodded. "Excuse me one moment, Agent Gibson." She got up and walked across to a door in the right wall of the office, knocked, then slipped inside without waiting for an answer and closed the door behind her. She reappeared too fast for us to even sit down in the chairs beside the window.

"Mr. Wallace can see you now. Go on through."

"Thank you, Sally," Dan said. She smiled back when he hit

her with one of his grins. "We'll try not to take too long. I know it's a pain when people mess up the schedule."

She nodded and gestured toward the door. The three of us headed into the office. The man standing behind the cluttered wooden desk looked like he was maybe fifty or so, dark curly hair smattered with gray. He had bright blue eyes that studied us intently as we trailed in, then narrowed as Esme closed the door.

"Agent Gibson, is it?" he said. "I'm Bill Wallace. What brings the FBI to my door?"

"Your assistant said you offer storage facilities for clients," Dan said.

"Yes, that's correct. This building was a bank once upon a time. We have quite the vault. And we offer secure electronic storage as well." He raised bushy eyebrows. "Got something you need a safe place for, Agent Gibson?"

I interrupted before Dan could reply. "Mr. Wallace, my name is Ashley Keenan. My father's name was Robert Keenan. I'm wondering if he ever left something here with you?"

His expression didn't so much as flicker. I guessed he was a good attorney. I'd dealt with a reasonable number over the years. Forensic accountants rarely got involved in situations that didn't involve lawyers. I knew most of the flavors they came in. Bill Wallace struck me as the not-give-an-inch, always-on -the-side-of-his-clients type.

"Do you have some ID and proof of your relationship, Ms. Keenan?" he asked.

Fortunately, we'd anticipated this question. I had my birth certificate and the legal stuff from the probate of my parents' estate along with Dad's death certificate tucked in my purse. But I started with the easy ones and handed him my driver's license and birth certificate.

He studied it a moment and then nodded. "Those seem to

be in order. And, given your companions, I can't imagine you're lying to me."

"I also have this." I held up the key.

"May I?" He took the key out of my hand when I nodded and looked at it. "Yes, that's one of ours. May I ask why you have that instead of your father, Ms. Keenan?"

"Ashley's father passed away some time ago," Dan said.

"Ah. I'm sorry to hear that, Ms. Keenan. My condolences." He sat back down at his desk and typed something into his computer. We waited while he found whatever it was he was searching for. "All right, follow me."

He led us back out of his office to the end of the hallway and down a flight of stairs. The rest of the building had been decorated in fairly bland corporate white and beige, everything looking well used and lived-in. It was slightly startling when he opened the door at the bottom of the stairs and we stepped into a room that looked more like it belonged in the Taskforce offices or the entrance to my dad's lab. Stark white, lit so there were no shadowy corners, and watched by an array of cameras in the walls and ceilings. There was a complicated-looking keypad and screen next to the solid metal door in the far wall.

"Nice setup," Dan said.

"I take my clients' security seriously," Bill said. "My father used to work with just the old bank vault. Since he retired, I upgraded a little."

He walked across to the keypad, typed in a long sequence of numbers, and then pressed his fingertips to the screen. Lights next to the pad flared green, and there was a solid-sounding click. Bill pushed another button, and the metal door slid back into the wall.

We walked through into another, somewhat larger room. A small wooden table with four chairs around it sat squarely in the center of the boring beige-carpeted floor. One wall was filled with small metal lockers, well-polished and gleaming in the bright lighting.

Bill waved a hand at them. "Those are the deposit boxes. Your father's is number forty-two." He pointed at the box in question. "I'll wait in the outer room. You can just lock the box again when you're done, then buzz and I'll let you out."

He left us alone. I stared at the box he'd indicated, rubbing the key between my thumb and forefinger. Then I unlocked the door and pulled the box inside out, placing it on the table.

When I opened the lid, it was almost anticlimactic. The box held only three things: two portable hard drives and a smaller USB drive. Nothing more personal than that.

Dan pulled an evidence bag from his pocket and handed it to me.

"Put them in there."

I slipped the drives into it, shaking off a weird twist of curiosity and sadness. It wasn't as if I could hook them up and see what was on them now anyway. Safer to give it to the Taskforce IT geeks, who knew how to avoid doing something dumb like triggering the drives to wipe themselves. Dan took the bag, and I slid the box back into the locker and locked it.

"Okay," Dan said. He squeezed my hand, then dropped it to walk over and buzz the door. "We should ask Mr. Wallace a few more questions."

The door swung open, and we walked back out into the entry chamber.

"I see you found something," Bill said, looking at the evidence bag.

Dan nodded. "Yes. But before we go, I need to ask you some questions. Is this the only box that Robert Keenan rented at this facility?"

Bill tipped his head. "That falls under attorney-client privilege."

"Yes it does," Dan agreed. "But Ms. Keenan is the surviving beneficiary of Robert Keenan's estate. We have the paperwork to prove that. And I can get a warrant to make you provide the information, but maybe it would be easier just to skip all that?"

"I promise my father won't sue you for breach of privilege," I said. "Neither will I. We need to know if we have everything my father left here."

I could almost feel the wheels turning in his head. Definitely a lawyer. A good one. But it seemed he was also a good guy, because he nodded once and then said, "It was just the one box. Would you like to see the paperwork, Agent Gibson?"

Dan passed the evidence bag to Esme. "Yes I would."

"And I'm guessing there's no way you're going to tell me what this is about?" Bill asked.

"No."

Bill shrugged. "All right. I'm not going to argue with the FBI. Let's go back to my office."

Once we were there, it didn't take him long to find the deposit box agreement. He showed me the scanned document on-screen. It was definitely my dad's signature. The contract he'd signed was a twenty-year rental for one deposit box, paid in advance, which I guess was why Bill hadn't known my dad was dead. It was dated about three months before Tate killed my father. Of course, there could be other agreements, but I couldn't think of any reason why he'd be lying to us now that he knew my father was dead. If there were other agreements, he'd have to find me as next of kin when they expired anyway.

"He seemed like a nice guy, your father," Bill said as he was showing us out of his office. "I'm sorry for your loss, Ms. Keenan."

So was I.

* * *

I didn't say much as we climbed back into the car. Esme pulled out her phone and headphones and started checking her emails. I could hear the faint pulse of music from her headphones but appreciated her giving us some semblance of privacy. I wasn't entirely sure what to say. A million questions whirred in my head about what we were going to find on the hard drives, but I couldn't seem to settle on any of them.

Dan nosed the car out of the parking space and back onto the highway to Seattle. He glanced at me from time to time but, like Esme, seemed to have decided that I needed some time to process.

The silence in the car almost made it worse, and I was just about to ask him to talk about anything at all when my phone rang.

Unknown caller. I answered it anyway. I sometimes had potential clients who managed to get my cell details somehow even though I tried my best to funnel everything through the office.

"Ashley Keenan," I said, trying not to sound like I didn't want to take the call.

"Ms. Keenan. Enjoying your road trip?"

My spine went cold. I hadn't heard Smith's voice for a while, but it wasn't one I was ever going to forget. "What do you want?"

Dan's head twisted toward me, frowning.

"Smith," I mouthed, and his mouth went flat. He yanked the wheel, and we arrowed across two lanes of traffic to hit the exit we'd been about to pass.

"Now, Ashley, is that a polite way to say hello?"

"I'm polite to people who deserve it."

"Ah," Smith said.

His voice sounded tired, I thought. I'd never heard him express much emotion other than when he'd been trying to soothe Cilla and talk her out of killing me, back when they kidnapped me.

"What do you want?" I repeated as Dan pulled the car over to the side of the road. Behind me, Esme had pulled out her headphones. One bonus of shifter hearing, no need to freak the psycho on the other end of the phone out by putting him on speaker.

"I was merely saying hello. Interesting that you've chosen to leave town today. I would have thought you wanted to spend time with your aunt while she's visiting."

Rage flared through me. "If you touch my aunt, you're a dead man," I snarled. And it was close to an actual snarl, the wolf beating beneath my skin, ready to burst through.

"Your aunt is fine," Smith said. "But we need to talk, Ms. Keenan."

"Well, that's easy," I said. "Turn yourself in and we can chat all you want."

"You think that's what you want, but trust me, it's not. You have something I want, Ms. Keenan, and I suspect you'll find out I have skills you need. But clearly you need a little time to think about it. And I'm sure your pet FBI agent has a trace on this phone. So, we'll talk soon. Enjoy your drive."

The phone went dead in my hand.

I swore under my breath. Dan was already dialing his phone, calling in to the Taskforce to see if they could trace the call.

I called Bug, fingers trembling.

"Ashley?" she said, sounding normal. "Are you on your way back?"

I took a deep breath, hoping my voice would be steady enough to speak. "Yes," I managed. "We'll be there in about two hours."

"That's good. I've been cooking with Pen. Your freezer needed stocking."

I smiled at that, relieved that she sounded normal. "Thanks, that sounds wonderful. Hey, Aunt B?"

"Yes, dear?"

"Stick close to the house, okay. And don't answer the door for anyone."

"Is everything okay?" Her voice sharpened.

"Yes, for now. But I just want you to be careful. The agents will take care of any deliveries and that kind of thing. You just hang out with Pen. Did you make snickerdoodles?"

"Of course. And brownies. I hope you're all hungry after your outing."

"There's always room for your cooking," I said. My stomach actually rumbled at the thought, despite the fact that talking to Smith had left me feeling vaguely ill. "We'll see you soon. Love you."

"I love you, too."

I ended the call. Dan was off the phone, and he shook his head as I lifted a brow at him.

"It wasn't long enough," he said. "Best they can do was that he's in Seattle. If he wasn't routing the call."

"No, I think he's somewhere in the city," I said. "He knew we were out of town. He knew Bug was there. If he's not there himself, then he has eyes on us."

Dan's response was an annoyed rumble. I understood. The Taskforce had my house and office watched. If Smith had people watching me, too, then the FBI team should have spotted them by now. "Esme, call in, make sure the team has eyes on Ashley's aunt. And Jason."

Esme nodded and shoved her earpiece into her ear as she started dialing.

"Do you think he knows? That we found Dad's stuff?"

Dan shrugged. "Probably not. I feel like he would have tried something more than a phone call if he knew."

"He said he needed something still. Do you think this is connected to what happened at the club?" My heart was pounding, anger and grief and fear warring in my gut. Smith was back. Fuck. I knew it was what we wanted, but it was also terrifying. I might have won the first round, killing Tate, and

I'd survived the second round because I'd escaped . But Smith had escaped that one, too. This time I couldn't afford to lose.

"Yes," Dan said. "We just have to figure out how. But we're not going to know anything more until we find out what's on these drives. I know today has been a lot, but everything is under control for now. Bug's safe. Jase is safe—"

"He is," Esme confirmed. "We have eyes on both of them. And it's daylight. Smith might have vamps at his disposal, but they're not doing anything until after sunset."

"Esme's right," Dan said.

"If you tell me to relax, I might have to punch you," I said. Esme was right about the vamps, but Smith was clever. He'd worked with shifters in the past. We couldn't rule anything out.

"Not relax. But just breathe, okay? You can't do anything more until we get back to Seattle."

* * *

When we got back to the Taskforce, Dan and I headed straight for the tech department. Dan apparently had a particular geek in mind as he led me through the cubicles. The name plate on the one we stopped at read ADRIA RYAN. The woman seated on a silver balance ball, headset on, and squinting at a bank of monitors as she typed furiously was tiny, with dark skin and bright green eyes, her close-cropped curls an unnatural shade of red. She pulled off her headset as we stopped and killed the monitor display with a keystroke before turning to us with a smile.

"Agent Gibson, what can I do for you today?"

Dan handed her the evidence bag. "We need to know what's on these drives."

Her head made soft jingling noises as she studied the bag. Somewhere among the multiple sets of earrings in her ears were some tiny bells.

"These are old," she said, twisting the bag around to get a closer view.

"They're at least thirteen years old," Dan agreed. "But they've been in a deposit facility that seemed to have a fairly stable environment for most of that time. But I need you to get whatever's on there off ASAP."

She nodded. "Shouldn't be a problem." She raised the bag to the light, peering at the contents. "I don't see any rust or water stains, so they should still work. The stick, at least. The hard drives might be trickier. Those are more temperamental. Do you know if they're encrypted?"

"Not for sure, but I'd be surprised if they weren't. My— the man who hid these was cautious," I said.

Adria nodded. "Most people who hide drives away for decades are. Or paranoid." Her gaze dropped to the ID badge around my neck. "Keenan. You're the civilian helping out with the case Agent Gibson is running."

"That's me."

"And you knew the man who owned these drives?"

I looked at Dan. He shrugged as if to say it was up to me how much I told her.

"He was my father."

Adria's brows lifted. "Okay. Well, maybe you should hang around for a bit. If I need to guess at a password, you can fill me in with some pertinent details."

"It isn't going to be 'password' or his birthday. Or any of our birthdays. He worked in medical research in secure facilities for most of his career. He knew how to do security."

"I'm sure he did. But sometimes some background helps." She pulled on a pair of latex gloves, cleared a space on her desk, and laid out another sheet of plastic she pulled from a pack near the box of gloves before opening the bag and easing the drives out. "Do you need these checked for prints?"

Dan shook his head. "No. I'm sure they belonged to

Ashley's dad. We're more interested in what's on them than who touched them."

Wallace had assured us that no one had accessed my dad's safe-deposit box. Without demanding thirteen years of security footage, there was no way to know whether he was telling the truth, but without the clues my dad had provided, I couldn't see how anyone else would have worked out where he'd hidden them.

And clearly, Smith—the only one who mattered at the moment—hadn't found them or he wouldn't still be trying to convince me to hand my father's research over.

Talking about Smith made me remember he was out there. And that Bug was home waiting for us to get back. "Actually, I have some other appointments today that I can't shift. But I'm happy to help." I rummaged in my purse and found a business card. "Call my cell if you have questions." I put the card down on her desk away from the drives.

She shrugged, seemingly unfazed. "Okay. Well, let's go through the first step and see if we can at least get these powered up." She turned to a cabinet and pulled out a black plastic tub packed with a vast array of neatly bagged cables and chargers. Impressive organization.

"What happens if they won't power up?" I asked as she flipped through the bags, found the one she wanted, and plugged in the first drive.

"Then I pull the drive and we see what we can do with that."

She connected the plug to a power socket. A small green light blinked into life on the drive. We all let out a breath.

"Okay, it's alive," Adria said. "Now comes the fun part. We hook it up to an isolated computer and see what's what." She turned back to her cabinet, extracted a laptop, fired that up, and hooked up the drive.

Adria's fingers danced over the keyboard as she studied the screen where various alerts, graphs, and other stuff I didn't understand flashed. "Okay, this is more than your basic encryption." She shot me another assessing glance. "You weren't wrong about your dad knowing his stuff. I may be calling you after all, Ms. Keenan."

"Call me Ashley. But yeah, he worked on lots of experimental projects, and he always said he had all sorts of NDAs and things when I asked him too much about what he was researching. I guess he learned to guard his data well."

Adria looked at Dan. "If this has to do with medical research, you're going to need someone who can understand whatever is in here. I can find you the data, but I can't tell you what it means."

Dan nodded. "Already on it. Esme is looking into who we might be able to use. You just get the info for us. We'll take it from there."

"Okay. I'll call you when I've got this baby cracked open."

Chapter 10

BY THE TIME I pulled into my driveway, the two things I wanted most were a shower and a nap. Adrenaline crash can be a bitch. I was burning the candle at both ends too often, and even werewolf stamina needed a break now and then. It was another week or so until the full moon, so I hadn't yet gotten the weird rush of energy that came a few days before that. But before I could sleep, I wanted to check in with Bug.

I only had to follow my nose to find her in the kitchen, still cooking. She looked up as I walked in, smiling at me. I didn't recognize the navy pants and a bright blue sweater she wore. Maybe Pen had brought her some clothes? We'd gotten her some basics, but there hadn't been time for an extensive shopping trip yet.

"Do I need to send Dan a new list of groceries to bring home later?" I joked, taking in the impressive number of bowls and utensils neatly arrayed over the countertop. My cherry red mixer was taking up pride of place on the counter, and the scent of lemon filled the air.

"I already put in an order," Bug said, cracking an egg into the mixer's bowl. She looked better than she had the day before. More color in her face. Maybe normal things like cooking and hanging out were exactly what she needed. Of course, I'd feel better if the hanging out part could be with me, but in the meantime, if she and Pen were getting along, I'd take it as a bonus.

"Pie?" I asked hopefully, watching as Bug zested a lemon. Her lemon meringue was legendary.

"Lemon and poppy seed muffins," she said. "You didn't have enough lemons for pie."

Darn. I should have stocked up. "That's okay. How about I make some fresh coffee while you finish those off?"

Muffins didn't take long to mix. I fired up the coffee machine and pulled out mugs while Bug poured batter into muffin tins and slid them into the oven.

By the time she'd finished, I had two lattes ready to go. I'd given mine a double shot. Something I would pay for later, but I couldn't sleep just yet.

Bug joined me at the kitchen table. I studied her, sipping coffee. She looked better, but there were still dark circles under her eyes her makeup couldn't quite hide. "How was your day?" I asked.

"How was yours?" she countered.

"Long so far," I said. I stalled, sipping more coffee. Dan had said I could tell Bug the basics if I wanted. Not about the case, but that we'd found something Dad had left for me. He was her family, too, after all. She deserved to know something about what was happening.

"Are you going to tell me what you were doing? You look nervous." She stirred sugar into her latte.

That was the problem with relatives who'd known you all your life. It was hard to fool them.

"We went to find something that Dad left for me."

Bug's teaspoon stilled. "I thought you'd been through everything he left you and didn't find anything?"

"We did," I said. "But he left me a message. One I didn't know about until one of the vampires who worked with

Smith…found it." I couldn't tell her it was Rhianna. She didn't know Rhianna had become a vamp.

"But that was weeks ago," Bug said, looking startled. "You didn't mention this to me before. Why did you go looking now? Has something happened?"

"It's hard to explain," I said. "It's all caught up with the case, so I can't tell you everything. The vampire could tell there was a message but not what it was. I got away from them before they could do anything more to me to force the issue. And to find out what it was, I had to let someone back inside my head." I looked down at the table, gripping the mug too tightly.

"And that's hard for you," Bug said.

"Yes. At first, the advice was to wait. My counselor thought I needed some time before I tried. We had other avenues to explore with the case anyway, but then we hit some walls. I tried again after you visited, but I freaked out when the vamp tried to thrall me. So we decided to wait again. But then…."

"Then my house caught fire," Bug said. "And you got worried enough to try again?" She reached out and patted my hand. "I wish you wouldn't put yourself in harm's way because of me."

Yeah, well, that wasn't going to happen. I'd always put myself in harm's way to keep her out of it. She was only in danger because of me. "Do you want to talk about that? About the fire?" I asked. "I understand if you don't. But it might help if you do."

"I'm not sure I can say anything both of us don't already know," Bug said. "The situation isn't good. The attack stirred up all the old feelings in Caldwell."

I nodded. "And they know I'm a werewolf. So it doesn't matter that I killed Tate or that I stopped those vampires, I'm one of the bad guys."

Bug shook her head sharply. "It matters to me. And it

matters to a lot of people. But there will always be people who let fear rule their choices, and some of them live in Caldwell, unfortunately."

"They're so scared they tried to burn down your house?"

"We don't know that yet."

I grimaced at her. If we were going to talk about this, there was no point lying. "I think we both know Kenny is going to find out that the fire was deliberately lit. Maybe just to scare you rather than hurt you, but that's beside the point just now."

"Well, it worked," Bug said. She bit her lip, something I'd rarely seen her do. "I've never been scared in my own home before. Worried, yes, at times when I had problems, or when you were in trouble. But never scared."

"Dan and I are going to fix it," I said. "I promise."

"The problem is that doesn't immediately make me feel better. Not when you're dealing with things that are dangerous. Both of you have been hurt already."

"We're careful," I said. "Werewolves are tough."

"Vampires could kill you though."

"They haven't succeeded so far," I said. "So far the score is vampires nil, Ashley and Dan several." Not that I liked having deaths count as victories. But when it came to vampires who were trying to kill me, not to mention unleash a plague on the world that could kill everybody, I'd take their deaths over mine. "So, don't worry about that. And anyway, Smith is human."

"That makes him worse than the vampires."

"Yes it does. But I think I can take him in a fight."

"I don't want you going anywhere near him."

"I won't unless I have to," I said. "But that brings me back to what we were doing today. Dad left me a message. And yesterday I asked Jase to help me find it. This time it worked. The message was about how to find some hard drives he left. Today we went and retrieved them, and now the FBI have someone extracting whatever is on them. I have to assume it's something to do with his research. Maybe it'll shed some light on what the hell has been going on."

I studied Bug a moment. "I know we've asked you this before, but you're sure he never said anything to you before he died? You haven't remembered anything more?"

"No," she said. "He didn't. There were times when I knew he was stressed about work. And yes, maybe just before Tate, it was one of those times. But I never knew why. I don't know if he ever even shared anything with your mother. If he did, she never told me."

"Sometimes you can be too good at keeping secrets," I said.

"Well, he was just doing his job. Those agreements he had to sign seemed draconian. He took them seriously. And sometimes keeping secrets is a good thing. I know you can't tell me everything, but obviously these vampires want something. Something not good for the rest of us. That can't go on. Or it won't just be my house that's on fire."

"I know." I sighed. "That's why we have to stop them… why we *will* stop them."

Bug smiled at me. "If anyone can, it's you and Daniel. He's not the kind to give up, that one."

I rolled my eyes at her. "You don't have to give me the pro-Dan speeches anymore, Aunty. We're bonded. It's pretty much a done deal."

That made her smile. "The two of you have come to terms, then?"

"We're getting there. And neither of us is going to quit." That much I knew. Dan and I might fight and lose our balance occasionally while we worked all this shit out, but neither of us was anywhere near the point of giving up. Even when one of us did stupid stuff.

"Do you want another cup—" My phone rang before I could finish the question. "Hold on."

I stood and grabbed my phone off the counter. Another unknown number.

My stomach twisted. "Ashley Keenan."

"Ms. Keenan. I'm glad you made it home safely."

The back of my neck began to prickle. He knew where I was. He was watching me. Or had someone watching me.

"I have to take this," I mouthed at Bug and walked out of the kitchen, heading down to my bedroom. Where my purse was. And the gun I carried in it. "What do you want, Doctor?" I asked when I was happy that Bug wouldn't be able to hear me.

"Just wondering if your journey gave you any more time to think."

"About what exactly?

"About us helping each other out."

I tipped my purse out onto the bed and made sure my gun was within reaching distance. He probably wasn't outside my house—we still had a detail watching us—but better safe than sorry. My Taskforce panic button was there, too. I rubbed the shiny black disc between my fingers. But I didn't press it. Not yet. I needed to keep Smith on the line. See if there was a chance this call could be traced. "Like I said, we're happy to help. All you have to do is turn yourself in. You'll get all the help you need."

"Was that a joke about my mental state, Ms. Keenan?"

"Your mental state is not a joke, Doctor. You sided with psychotic vampires. You've created a strain of vampirism that could wipe out humanity. That's not the act of a stable man. If you want help, then you need to prove there's a shred of humanity left in you. Turn yourself in."

"You don't want me to do that."

"Why not?" I closed my eyes, trying to focus only on what I could hear, straining for any background sounds that might offer a clue about where he was. Wind, I thought. Maybe birds. Outdoors, definitely. Then, in the distance, I heard a kid yell, "Mom?" Was he in a park? That didn't exactly narrow down the options.

"Who do you think is keeping the vampires you fear under control?"

Under control? When one of them had attacked the man outside Esteban's club? Or had Smith ordered that? Was he fishing for information now? Seeing what I knew about the club? Or trying to find out what had happened to the victim, maybe?

"You haven't done so well at controlling them so far. Besides, you could bring them with you."

There was no response. Instead, the call ended, leaving me with nothing but silence. And a lot of confusion.

I dialed Dan.

"Smith just called again," I said when he answered.

Dan cursed under his breath. "What did he want?"

"Same thing. Said I needed him."

"He might be right about that," Dan said. "I was just calling you."

That was never a good thing. "What happened?"

"Two things. First, Adria got through one layer of encryption on your dad's drives. Most of the files are still locked, but what's not seems to be medical research data. Esme is narrowing down options for who might help us. Someone independent. I don't necessarily want to hand this over to the military until we understand what it is. Adria's still working on the other drives."

I could understand his hesitation. My dad had offers to work for defense companies a few times. He'd turned them down. He'd told me he was never certain his work would be used the right way. He might well have been right. Smith was proof that some people will always give in to the wrong impulses. And technically, I supposed the data belonged to me. "And the second?"

"There was another bite victim," Dan said.

"Another one?" I glanced out the window. It was only three in the afternoon. "The sun's still up."

"Yeah, well, it's not exactly clear what happened. The guy was left in an empty warehouse. He has a storage unit in the same complex. The security cameras show his car arriving at the storage unit parking lot earlier today. But then there's a glitch. A guard found him not long ago. Maybe they didn't count on there still being some regular security check-ins."

In other words, if no one had found him until tomorrow, whoever discovered him might just have been stumbling across a plague vamp. A hungry, newly made, lacking-control plague vamp. "Is he unconscious?"

"No," Dan said. "That's the other miscalculation. He's awake. Esme and I are heading to the hospital soon to see if he remembers anything else." He hesitated, and I wondered if he was waiting to ask and see if I asked to come, too. But I didn't want to leave Bug alone again. Not now.

"Tell me more about Smith." In the background, I could hear Esme talking. Probably getting someone to try to trace Smith's call.

"He seemed…off," I said.

"In what way?" Dan asked.

"Well, I told him he was a psycho and that he should turn himself in. And he said we needed him to stay in charge of the vamps. Then I said he should bring them in as well, and he just hung up."

"That seems normal for him. He calls you, then hangs up before we can trace him."

"Yes, but he likes to get in the last word," I pointed out. "This time it just went dead. I know it's weird, but it was like I hit a sore point or something."

"Calling him names?"

"I don't think that's it. I've called him names before. It never seemed to bother him. I was wondering if it was about the vamps."

"Well, they can't have turned on him or he'd be dead. Or a vampire himself," Dan said.

"I think he was outside when he called." I stared out the window, trying to put my finger on what had bothered me about his call. "So I don't think he's been turned. But what if one of them got away from him? I mean, these attacks, they don't seem like him. Cilla isn't running the show anymore. She's dead. So other than trying to get to me to find out what Dad left behind, he has no need to let his vamps randomly attack people. In fact, it seems counterproductive. It can only make the FBI work harder to bring him in. But if one of his plague vamps got loose… well, that might be enough to push him to get back in touch with us."

"Two attacks in two days," Dan said. "You might be right. None of the plague vamps can be very old. A few years, maybe less. They still seemed to be experimenting when they took you the first time. Even if Cilla was part of the picture from the beginning, they can't have made any of them back when your dad was killed. Especially if they have to drink fresh human blood. I guess they might not have the same reaction Rhi had, of course. But finding enough real blood to feed a bunch of vampires is tricky. You can't order that much from a blood bank and not have it set off some red flags. So however many plague vamps there are, they have to be young. Which means poor impulse control, if they're like normal vamps."

We had no idea if they were like normal vamps. Rhi hadn't been. She'd woken starving and crazed. And allergic to artificial blood. That probably wasn't the usual reaction. There had been other vamps with Cilla, and they'd seemed sane. For a given value of sane that meant under the power of a vampire who clearly wasn't. Rhi's reaction to being turned was partly because of her past trauma. Or so I'd always assumed.

Maybe it had been because of her also having mind

powers immediately, too. Jase was considered a very early developer when it came to that, and he had been a vampire for nearly eight years already. Vampires have the seeds of all their abilities when they're turned, and some abilities ran stronger than others in certain lineages. But the powers developed slowly for whatever reason. Just as well. By the time a vamp's powers got strong, they'd adjusted to their new life and vampire society well enough to not do something stupid with them.

"Poor impulse control might lead them to attack random humans," I said. "But leaving a victim outside Esteban's club seems deliberate. Either that or very, very clueless. But clueless wouldn't involve taking out the security system cameras, would it?"

"You think one of them got loose and has a plan of their own?" Dan asked.

"I don't know. I mean, logically, if they're like Cilla, the plan should be to unleash themselves on the world. But that would mean biting as many people as possible, not one a day. So, what do they want?"

"Maybe the same thing Smith wants," Dan said. "We don't know why Smith wants your dad's research. But if one of these plague vamps has lived with him for a few years, they'd have to know something about it. Maybe there's some disagreement between Smith and the vampires about what should happen next."

"An average vampire isn't going to understand the type of research my dad was doing."

"Smith and Cilla were smart. Smith is clearly a doctor or scientist of some kind," Dan said. "And there are other vampires with medical backgrounds. The ones who work with the supernatural hospitals. Therapists and such. Maybe Smith and Cilla made themselves a tame researcher." He paused. "You know, that's not something we've ever looked at. If there have been other staff at the companies who've resigned or vanished besides men who might meet Smith's description. I'll get Ramirez to start looking into that."

"I can access the files from here, too," I said. "I don't want to leave Bug alone."

"No," Dan agreed. "Stay there. We've already increased your detail. But if this attack turns out to be another plague vamp, I think it would be a good idea if maybe you and Bug and I moved to a safe house for a while. Somewhere more controlled. Mercer takes too long to get to if we need back up."

"And your place backs onto a massive park. Lots of places for vamps to hide out."

"Agreed," Dan said, sounding unhappy. He loved Ravenna Park. It was also heaven for a werewolf who didn't have enough time to get to the Retreat as often as he should. He made it for the full moon most months. Every month since I'd changed. But that wasn't the norm for him. He tried to get in some social time with the pack when he could, but his job involved long hours. Being able to change and get some time in the park after dark to run and give his wolf some freedom was precious to him.

But he'd give that up to keep me safe.

It should have made me happy. It did in a way. But it also made me mad. Another way our life was being screwed with thanks to Smith and his games.

"I'll ask Bug. I'm not sure she'll agree. I'm not going to force her."

"Wait until I get home. We can try together. I'm nearly at the hospital," Dan said. "We'll see what this victim has to say. Decide after that. Stay inside, okay? I'll come home after I'm done here."

"Have you heard anything more from the base about last night's victim?" I asked.

"He's stable. He doesn't remember much so far. Marco is

going to talk to him tonight. See if he can help his memory along."

"And he's definitely not a normal vamp?"

"No. His blood work looks like Rhianna's apparently. There have been some people studying her sample, but so far they haven't learned much other than it's different." In other words, they didn't yet understand what Smith had done.

"Who's doing that research?" I hoped he wasn't about to say "the military." Rhianna was taken to Fort Lyman after she was bitten and turned. Prizing information back out of military hands was never fun. But I assumed someone had been smart enough to pass this stuff on to the actual experts in the Department of Health. They were the ones in charge of the vaccines.

"Colonel Morgan has one. The NIH has one, too, as I understand it. Right, we're here. I have to go."

Chapter 11

THE PHONE RANG AGAIN ALMOST IMMEDIATELY.

I reached for it, half expecting it to be the unknown number again and Smith's cold voice in my ear, but instead I got Marco's Italian lilt wishing me a good evening.

"Hello, Lord Marco," I said cautiously.

"Ashley, cara, how are you?"

"I'm fine." *Why was he calling me?*

"I am on my way to the base to speak to this new vampire," he said. His tone was light as always, but there was a hint of something steelier underneath it.

"That's kind of you," I said. Especially for him to be leaving before dark. Old Ones didn't need to sleep during the day, but there was still an element of risk going out in daylight. Marco had shielded cars, but accidents could happen.

"I have been informed there has been another attack?"

Informed by who, exactly? The vamp grapevine? I doubted Dan would have told Marco yet. Not when he hadn't yet interviewed the victim himself. "That's something you would have to ask Dan about," I said carefully. Giving out FBI case information was not something I wanted to do. Not even to Marco.

"Your Agent Gibson is a difficult man to contact sometimes."

"I just talked to him," I said. "Try him again now and he might be free."

"And why was he calling you? To tell you about the latest attack, perhaps?"

"We were discussing what we're going to have for dinner," I said firmly. "My aunt is visiting."

"Visiting after her house was set on fire," Marco said. "Ashley, you know I know about what is happening here. Why are you being evasive?"

"Why are you asking me questions to which you already know the answers, my lord? I'm not trying to be rude, but I'm not allowed to convey FBI information—should there be any —to outsiders. You have to speak to Dan."

"The situation is getting too serious for such trivialities," Marco said.

I'd like to see what he would do if one of his people gave away confidential information. But I couldn't actually argue his point. The situation was getting serious, and we would be in even deeper trouble if the latest victim also became a plague vamp.

"You need to talk to Dan," I repeated.

"Have you spoken to Doctor Smith?" Marco said. "Has he reemerged now that there is a development in the case?"

I sighed. "That's something else I'm not at liberty to discuss, my lord."

"I will take that to be a yes," Marco said.

"That's up to you."

"You sound upset, cara."

"I'm not upset, my lord." I *was* upset, but not at him. Just tired of the whole situation. After months of this case, I wanted it over. I wanted a normal life back. I didn't want to walk around worrying about the people I loved every second of every day.

"Doctor Smith is still after the information he believes you hold, I would imagine. Especially if he is losing control of his creations."

"You think he's lost control?" My focus sharpened back on Marco, my stomach clenching. "What makes you say that?"

"Because I do not understand his strategy if this is not the case. I see no benefit to him in letting these vampires out to attack people. If it is you and your information he wants, he has shown in the past he is capable of arranging to get it without drawing even more of the wrath of the FBI down on his head."

"Thanks for the reminder." I bit my lip, feeling sick. Marco agreed with my theory. Thought Smith had lost control of one or more of his plague vamps. "Say one of them is acting on their own. What good comes from them attacking people one by one? If they wanted to increase their numbers, they would be doing more. They're in the same position as Smith, just drawing attention to themselves that can't be helpful." I focused on the view outside, trying to calm my nerves.

My bedroom window looked out over the yard. Where it was a fine and sunny day. Birds were singing in the trees. The usual sounds of the neighborhood rose around me. No one was going to attack my house in broad daylight. But I wanted the conversation to be over so I could go sit with Bug again. Though it might take more than muffins to make me feel better. "I don't understand what they would be trying to do."

"They may not have a choice," Marco said. "They are young. The young hunger. And if they have always been with Smith since they turned, they may not be good at fending for themselves."

"The attack at Esteban's wasn't just random," I said. "They made sure his security system didn't capture them. You know Esteban. He's got his clubs locked down tight, and his surveillance is expensive. That takes some skill to hack."

"Ah." Marco said. "Lord Esteban neglected to tell me that part. As did your wolf."

Damn it. That was a mistake. I'd assumed Marco already knew the circumstances of the attack if he'd been asked to speak to the victim. But it wasn't as though it was a vital piece of information. The damned vampire grapevine would have told him sooner or later, and I couldn't see Dan getting upset that I'd let something that small slip. "I'm sure Dan just forgot. It seemed more important last night to find out whether the man had been attacked by a plague vamp than how whoever did it got away."

"Your wolf needs to consider both angles. It is important to consider your enemy's plans as well as to deal with his actions," Marco said.

"It's also important to know who your enemy is. And right now, we don't. Which makes it hard to know what they're planning. I hope you're successful in your attempts to help the victim remember tonight, my lord. The FBI can only do so much to keep the news of what's happening under control. If there are many more attacks, it's going to get out. Even if nobody knows the vampires are infectious, a spate of attacks is going to cause trouble."

"Human trouble," Marco said. He sounded almost weary. He'd been a vampire before the vampires and werewolves had come out of the darkness and made peace with the humans. Back then, vampires were slaughtered if they were discovered. And it wasn't as though humanity had immediately adjusted to the fact that supernaturals were real and everyone had welcomed them with open arms. Marco had witnessed more than his fair share of human-led violence.

"Yes," I agreed.

"Which may make what happened to your aunt's house seem tame in comparison," Marco said. "So, we need to know how to deal with them. Which returns us to Doctor Smith."

"Who still eludes us all."

"I know. The man is clever. But if one of his vampires has gotten loose, then he is running out of time. So, has he contacted you?"

He wasn't going to give up. "I can't confirm that."

"Just like you cannot confirm that Jason may have succeeded in assisting you with the problem of what your father left for you?"

"How—" I cut myself off. I couldn't ask how he knew that. That would be confirming that it had happened.

"Jason is having discussions with me about his powers. And how to use them. Last night when he came to me, I asked how you were, and he was very vague. He is not usually vague about you. He has quite strong opinions about the danger you have put yourself in of late."

"He does?"

"Of course. He is your friend. He worries. Which I imagine is how you persuaded him to try to find what was in your head. That was foolish, cara. Jason is young still, inexperienced. He is powerful, and will grow stronger, but letting someone into your mind is not without its risks."

"I know that, my lord. I've done it several times now." My tone was sharper than wise. After Tate had taken me, when I'd been worried that he'd left some sort of seed of thrall in my head that might make me susceptible to him if he took me again, Marco had looked for me and freed me. The experience hadn't been pleasant. I'd been traumatized and scared out of my wits to let another vampire in. But he'd been kind. He hadn't hurt me, and he'd taken some of the fear away. He'd offered to take the memories away, I remembered. Just like someone had taken away the memory of however my dad had managed to leave his message in my head. Clearly a vampire had helped him.

But who? Was it a common vampire power, to remove a memory totally? All vampires could thrall people and make them compliant in the moment. And memories of a thrall could be foggy. But they still existed.

I should ask Jase. Marco would know, but I didn't want to let him know too much about what my dad had done. Not yet. Not when I wasn't even supposed to let him know we'd found something.

"Including with Jason?" Marco asked.

"That's another one of those things I can't confirm, my lord."

"Ashley, you are making this conversation difficult."

"Then hang up and have it with Dan, my lord. He's the one with the authority to tell you what you want to know."

"But he is not the one who needs to hear this message first. Your wolf is not always fond of me to begin with."

He had a message that Dan wasn't going to like? Fuck. Whatever it was, I doubted I'd like it either. I gripped the phone tighter. "And what message is that, my lord?"

"That if Jason was successful, then perhaps the easiest way to draw Smith out and end this matter is to offer him what he wants."

"And what is that?"

"You."

* * *

I sat for a long time after Marco ended the call. Had he really suggested I should dangle myself in front of Smith as bait?

My body screamed a very clear "no" at the thought. My brain wasn't that happy about it either. But it couldn't quite let go of the idea that, crazy as it was, maybe it would work.

The thought still made me want to throw up. I locked it away before I made myself ill. We weren't that desperate yet. We had new leads to follow. We had some of my dad's data, and we'd have the rest soon enough.

I sent Dan a message to let him know Marco called. He

didn't call back, so I assumed he was still busy at the hospital. I went back into the kitchen and ate Bug's muffins and chatted and tried to pretend everything was just fine.

I don't think she believed me, but she was pretending everything was fine, too, and didn't call me on my nonsense. It probably wasn't the healthiest way to deal with the situation, and my counselor would no doubt lecture me about avoidance if I ever told her about it, but for the afternoon, it was going to have to do.

I needed to be able to function, so I couldn't wade into the emotions swirling around us yet. If I did, I might just drown.

Bug returned to her cooking, and I set my laptop up in the kitchen, doing some client work and continuing my analysis of one of Esteban's companies. I'd been working on this one for a few days already, and nothing had come up that made me think it was the source Smith had been using, so after a couple hours reexamining the data, I added it to the cleared list.

By the time Dan returned from the hospital, I'd made a small dent in the work that had piled up, and Bug had stocked every inch of my freezer. We'd both called it quits and made a pitcher of martinis. Usually we'd drink on my back patio, but given Dan's warning to stay inside, we'd taken them into the living room and were making plans to restock Bug's wardrobe, with something soft and soothing playing in the background.

Bug told us no in no uncertain terms when we raised the subject of going to a safe house. Dan and I tried to argue, but when she started to look wobbly, I pulled him away to the kitchen.

"She's upset," I said. "I don't want to upset her more. Let's give it a bit more time. Let her sleep on it."

He nodded. Which made me wonder what, if anything, he'd learned from the guy at the hospital. If it had been something that implicated Smith, and he thought we were really in danger, he'd be hauling us off to the safe house, no matter what objections Bug might have.

But I wanted to keep things normal for Bug, so I parked my curiosity and made dinner. Bug took herself to bed early, claiming the martinis had made her sleepy. I suspected she didn't want to be drawn back into a conversation about maybe relocating and let her go.

Dan cleaned up the kitchen and was yawning by the time he joined me in the living room. The trip to Kingsville this morning had thrown off our schedule. We both still had work to do, but if he felt like I did, then trying to power through another six hours or so until the time we'd normally call it quits for the night wasn't going to be fun.

I wanted a nap before I attempted anything requiring much more brainpower. I patted the sofa beside me, and Dan sat. I let myself yawn, leaning against him.

"Don't do that or we'll both be asleep before we know it," he said. But he slipped his arm around me and tipped his head back to rest on the back of the sofa.

"Would that be so terrible?" I snuggled closer.

"There's still work to do."

"There's always still work to do." I slipped my hand under his shirt so I could touch his skin, brushing my fingers over the muscles of his stomach. "But you know what they say about all work and no play."

He laughed. "I'm not sure I'm good for much play right now."

His skin was warm under my fingers. I could convince him if I wanted to. But curiosity got the better of me. "Did you learn anything at the hospital?"

"Other than a generic description of a vampire with dark hair and blue eyes, no. The guy was at the warehouses to put some stuff in a storage unit he rents down there. There are some covered walkways between a couple of the warehouses, and he was on one of those when a vamp stepped out of a doorway and grabbed him. He doesn't remember much after that. I think he was thralled fast."

"And he's infected?"

"It's looking that way." Dan glanced at his watch. "I guess we'll find out at sunrise. The hospital sedated him, and the team from Fort Lyman are picking him up. Marco's going to talk to him once he wakes up."

I sighed. Marco wasn't going to like that.

"Marco called me earlier. He seems upset about these attacks."

Dan tensed. "He left me a message, but I was busy. What did he say?"

"Tried to get more info out of me about the case. I told him he had to speak to you. But he said he thought maybe Smith wasn't in control anymore, too. That maybe some of the plague vamps are out."

Dan grunted. I took that to mean he still hadn't made up his mind about what he thought was happening. "Did he have any useful ideas about how to catch them?"

I hesitated, pulling my hand free.

"Ash?" Dan sat up a little "What did he say?"

"He said they would be young and hungry. He doesn't know what their agenda might be, so better to focus on Smith."

"We've been focused on Smith for months. It's not getting us very far."

"Yeah, well, he had an idea about that, too."

"Which was?"

"Give him what he wants. Me."

"What the hell?" Dan growled. He sat up straighter, forcing me to sit up, too. His silver eyes flared as he stared down at me. "We're *not* using you as bait."

"It might work. Especially if he thinks we've made some progress on the case. Which we have."

"We're not handing your dad's data over to him either. I'm not giving him anything."

"If the plague vamps are out, or some of them, then

Marco's right. And Smith. We're going to need his help. He created them. Makes sense he might know how to cure them."

"There are easier solutions than a cure," Dan growled again.

Supernatural justice, he meant. Let the vamps deal with them their own way. Which was a measure of how exhausted he was getting, too. Because usually he was all about following the law.

But then he shook his head and slumped back against the sofa. "If only it was that simple. But some of them are innocent victims. Maybe not the ones who've stuck with Smith all this time, and not whoever is behind these attacks, but the men attacked this week are. A cure would give them their lives back."

"No one's ever cured vampirism." It was something my dad spoke about as the holy grail. But every company he'd worked for was focused on refining the vaccines to protect humans from vampires, not in offering an out to a vampire who'd changed their mind.

"No," he agreed. "I think we're talking about a cure for the infectious part. If they're not a danger to everybody, then they can just live their lives like normal vamps."

"So we do need Smith."

"That doesn't mean we need to hand him you," Dan said. "Hard no on that plan. Besides, we don't even know what's in your dad's data yet."

"There doesn't have to be anything useful in it to make him think there is. We could fake him out."

"Bait and switch still requires bait," Dan said. His expression was as stubborn as Bug's when she'd refused the safe house earlier.

I didn't think I was going to win the argument. Not yet. But I had the horrible feeling that Marco was right. To get to Smith, we were going to have to lure him out.

"Stop thinking about it," Dan rumbled.

He was right. There was no answer just now. Until we knew what was on those hard drives, we wouldn't be able to work out what the best play was. Marco would have more information from the new vamps in the morning. For now, we should focus on what we *could* do. But I didn't want to get back to work. Not just yet. I wanted a distraction. This day had been too intense already.

"How about you give me something else to think about?" I moved fast before Dan could react, swinging a leg over to seat myself in his lap. And then I kissed him. Hard and hungry. Feeding all that frustration and adrenaline into the one thing I knew would make me feel better.

Dan.

It was always him.

Solid ground and safety and pleasure and happiness all wrapped up in one person. He'd become the center of my world again so fast that sometimes it scared me. Because I'd lost the center of my world before.

But this time I was hanging on. And if I needed to lean into the bonds between us, to hold us together even as every-thing else we were dealing with tried to pull us apart, then I wasn't above using a little old-fashioned sex to do it.

Despite his protests of being tired earlier, Dan's reaction was fast. His hands closed around my waist, pulling me tighter against him, and we made out like crazed teenagers. He was hard under me, and I pushed into him, wanting him in all the places I was aching. Pleasure pushed everything else away. Made the world just Ash-and-Dan again.

"Perhaps we should take this to your room?" he said. "Don't want Bug catching us."

"Well, it wouldn't be the first time she caught me making out with a boy on the sofa," I said, grinning down at him.

His eyes, dark with pleasure, sharpened. "Is that right?" His voice was an amused deep rumble. That tone was one of my favorite sounds.

"There may have been a time or two," I said.

"Well, those were boys. I'm not a boy." He rolled his hips up, pressing into me. "And I want more than just a sofa and making out."

I wanted that, too. Wanted his skin and his hands on me. Wanted his mouth on me. Wanted mine on him.

"Take me to bed," I murmured into his mouth.

It was all the encouragement he needed. He stood, raising both of us off the couch with no effort at all. The benefits of sleeping with a werewolf. I still found the sheer power of his body thrilling. Even though I knew I had strength equal to his in many ways, I liked that he could pick me up and carry me away when that was what I needed.

And I needed it now.

We kissed as he carried me through the house. He knew the way, knew how not to bump into anything. We'd done this many times now. Each time it felt new. The sex could be wild, but beneath it all, my heart always knew it was home with Dan.

We made it to the bedroom, and Dan had just kicked the door shut when his phone began to ring.

Chapter 12

"Fuck," I said.

"Hold that thought," Dan said, equally frustrated. He let go of me and walked a few steps away, pulling his phone out of his back pocket and scowling.

Damned phones. Always interrupting us. Sometimes I fantasized about living for a year on an island with no technology. Just me and Dan. Maybe Bug and Jase in huts far away from ours so we could visit but not see them every day. No interruptions. Just a year of peace. With cocktails in coconuts and Dan in tight swim trunks and hot steamy nights—

"Adria," Dan said. My imaginary castaway beach fantasy vanished as my attention snapped back to him. "What can I do for you? Or is it what have you done for me?"

Adria's voice was muffled, but I caught something about "cracked" and "more encryption."

My pulse sped up more than it had from Dan's kisses. Had she done it? Had she broken the encryption?

"Great," Dan said. I could tell he was trying to sound pleased, but there was still a rough edge of frustration thrumming beneath the words. Adria was human. Hopefully she wouldn't be able to hear it.

"That's great work," he added. "We'll come into the office. You can explain it to us then."

"What?" I asked as he ended the call. "What did she find?"

"She got past another layer of the encryption. According to her, she found 'a whole lot more science crap.'"

I sat down on the bed abruptly. All this time. All this time we'd been trying to break this case open and find a new lead, and now we were doing it. We were going to have all my dad's research. Maybe there really was an end in sight.

"Ash?" Dan said. He came and sat beside me. "Are you okay?

"Yes. It's just…I think I was starting to believe that this was never going to end."

He put an arm around me, pulled me in a little. "It will end," he said. "But we're not there yet. Adria said some of the files are still encrypted. She's still working on those."

"It's a start though," I said. "If Dad's work can help reverse whatever Smith has done, it's a start."

He kissed the top of my head. "Yes it is. So we need to get into the Taskforce. See what Adria found. Then we can work out what to do with it."

Right. We needed scientists.

"Did Esme find some contacts?"

Dan nodded. "Yep. We have a few based on what our science guys could make of the initial data dump Adria found. I'll get them to take a look at some of the new stuff, and we'll make a final choice then. I don't want to yank anyone away from their work too soon."

"Okay." I ran a hand through my hair and tried to bring my brain fully back to the case from happy-kissing-Dan-sex-soon world. "I can't say I love her timing."

He looked down at me, his silver eyes still darker than normal, and smiled ruefully. "Rain check?"

"Definitely."

* * *

Adria sat behind Dan's desk and typed a series of rapid commands, her bright orange nail polish flashing as her fingers flew over the keys. "I'm dumping this into your secure server, but I've added some extra security checks, too. I'll explain those later, but I figured you probably didn't want anyone getting their hands on this who shouldn't have it."

"No," Dan agreed. "That would be bad." He fiddled with the cuffs of his shirt as he waited for her to work her magic. He had good hands, my wolf, the scars on his wrists from Tate's silver cuffs fading fast. Even though I was keen to learn more about what Adria had found, there was still a large part of me that wished we hadn't been interrupted back at the house.

"Do people often try to hack the FBI?" I asked, trying to make myself focus on Adria and not Dan.

"You'd be surprised what people try for funsies," Adria said, eyes intent on the monitor. "But for cases with this level of clearance, we lock shit down extra tight as a matter of policy. No snooping even from inside the office. People sometimes let curiosity get the better of them. Even people who should know better."

And sometimes, even FBI agents could be corrupted. I didn't think it was likely that Smith had someone inside the Taskforce, but it was a niggling worry in the back of our minds. We hadn't found any signs that anyone in the FBI was helping him, but he'd still managed to stay one step ahead of us a lot of the time.

I glanced at Dan. He didn't seem overly concerned by Adria's words. If he'd been worried about a mole, he would have told me before now.

"Okay," Dan said. "Can you give me a rundown on what you found?"

"Like I said, it's science. There's a bunch of what look like academic papers. Or maybe drafts of academic papers. I ran a search on some of the phrases and couldn't find any matches in any published journals. And then there's a lot of data I don't understand. Research findings, maybe? And a few random files. Images, mostly. I haven't checked those out yet. I haven't gotten into the last database of files yet. That stuff is buried under a lot of security. Maybe that's the notes explaining the rest. I'll keep working on it." She looked at me. "Your dad really wanted to make sure people didn't just stumble into this stuff. I looked at his file and yours for some clues, but so far, nothing."

"I told you he wasn't going to use birthdays for his passwords," I said.

"No," she agreed. "But people have an unconscious tendency to use bits and pieces from important dates and events and connections, even if they think they're being secure. Words or phrases, too. Can you think of anything that might help?"

"I can try," I said. "I don't know how much help it would be. He loved the Beatles. Grunge music. The Mariners. And Tootsie Rolls." I remembered them leading me through the path. But I didn't think he'd use anything like that for a password.

"You two go and talk about it," Dan said. "I'm going to talk to the science guys and see what I can do about finding the right people to help us understand what this means."

* * *

I spoke to Adria for about thirty minutes, then headed back to Dan's office. "Any progress?" I asked.

"Science guys have the latest info. They'll make a recommendation from Esme's short list." He swiveled his monitor toward me. "Do you want to take a look? See if any of this stuff makes sense to you?"

"I doubt it will," I said. "My dad used to give me the 'immunology for dummies' version of what he did, but I topped out at senior biology and chemistry. Not my thing. I like numbers, remember? Data analysis I can do, but I can't help with the science."

Dan tapped the screen. "Plenty of numbers in this. Lots of statistics."

"Okay, but they're not going to be useful unless you understand what the numbers relate to. And I doubt it's financial." I peered at the screen. Dan had the window open with a list of folders. One of them was labeled "Images." "Did you look at any of the pictures yet?"

He shook his head. "No. Do you want to take a look now?"

"Why not?" I doubted there'd be any photos in there—the images were more likely to be scans or maybe pictures from his research—but who knew?

Dan nodded and clicked to open the image folder. The files were numbered rather than named, and my suspicions were confirmed as we opened the first one, which was a scan of a page of handwritten notes in my dad's scrawling writing. I peered at the screen. It was a couple paragraphs, and most of the words were long scientific terms I didn't recognize.

"These should probably go to your scientists," I said.

"Yep," Dan said. He clicked through the files. More handwritten notes, a couple scanned printouts. And a few pictures that looked to me like microscope slide images. Dad had taught me to use a microscope as a kid and how to prepare something on a slide. He'd even once shown me pictures of the Stoker variation and lycanthropy viruses when he'd been explaining to me how the vaccines worked.

"Definitely for the scientists," I said as Dan clicked on the last file. "You—"

I cut myself off, staring at the screen.

"That's Smith," I said, voice going too high on the last word.

Dan peered at the screen, twisting his head. The man in the image was younger than the man I'd met, and he had more hair—dark hair—and he was grinning, turning back to face the camera. He was seated on a sofa next to a woman with dark hair and a pale blue shirt. I couldn't see anything of her face, but it was definitely Smith. Why had my dad included a picture of Smith with everything else?

"Are you sure?" Dan asked. He'd only ever seen the composite image that Bug and I had worked on with the FBI forensic artist after we'd gotten free from Tate.

"Yes. It's him. It needs to be aged up, but that's him." I started to grin. "Holy crap. We have a picture of him." I'd been excited that we might be able to figure out what Dad had been working on. But now we had a picture of Smith as well. It was like Christmas Day.

Part of what had held us back in our hunt for Smith was our lack of an actual photo of the man. No one who looked like the FBI image had turned up in any of our searches of companies Dad had worked for. With a real photo, the FBI could start searching their databases of faces and CCTV from the city and do all sorts of things they couldn't do with just my memories and a fake name.

Dan grinned back at me. "He can't hide from us now."

It was late by the time we were ready to leave the Taskforce.

I'd downed one too many coffees, riding the buzz. We had a picture of Smith. We had nearly all my dad's data, *and* we had a picture of Smith. I knew we should go home, should attempt to sleep, but I didn't want to. The detail had checked in and let us know the house was quiet just as we were packing to leave. Bug was safe.

"Why don't we go to Moxie, grab a drink?" I said.

Dan paused from shoving stuff into his laptop bag. "A drink? You don't want to go straight home?"

I shook my head. "Too much coffee."

"It's late."

"It's late, and we deserve a break," I said. "This is a victory, today. We have my dad's research. Let's celebrate. Just one drink."

He held up his hands in surrender. "Okay. Just one. We still have plenty of work to do."

"I know. But not tonight," I said. "C'mon, Dan. Buy a gal some booze. Who knows, maybe you'll get lucky."

"Maybe I want you to buy me a drink," he said, but he was smiling now, and I knew I'd convinced him.

"I will buy you all the drinks you want," I said. "As long as it's somewhere with fancy chairs and soft music and ridiculous bar snacks."

"That sounds like Moxie," he agreed. Given his choice, he probably would have chosen one of the bars the Taskforce frequented. They tended to be more low-key. Moxie was a gossamer confection of a cocktail club that Aunt B and I had discovered on one of our girls' days out, and Dan and I had been there a few times. It was elegant and whimsical and sexy, and it might just be what both of us needed.

* * *

It didn't take long to reach the bar. We parked only a block away and held hands as we walked to the door, Dan's thumb subtly stroking my wrist. My skin tingled in response. One drink and then I was going to set my sights on a different kind of entertainment, maybe.

We were halfway down the short velvet-clad staircase that led into the bar when Dan's phone beeped.

"Not again," I groaned, seriously contemplating grabbing

the damned thing and drowning it in the nearest champagne bucket.

Dan pulled out the phone and glanced at the screen. "This won't take long." He tipped his chin toward the bar. "Go. Order me a drink. I'll be five minutes." He turned and headed back up the staircase.

I continued into the club, trying not to feel annoyed. There were two empty stools at the hammered bronze bar, and I slipped into one of them and reached for the cocktail menu. The bartender was young and cute and smiled at me when I ordered two cucumber gin fizzes. He filled a dish with what looked like acid green popcorn and slid it toward me.

"Candied wasabi kettle corn," he said. "It'll go well with the cucumber in the drinks."

It sounded like an odd combination to me, but I'd never had a bad drink here, so I was willing to give it a whirl. I tossed a piece into my mouth and bit down, letting the hit of heat and sugar take the edge off my mood. It was odd but good. I smiled and nodded at the bartender.

"Told you," he said and went back to making drinks.

He was fast, and I was staring at the cocktails before I had time to eat much more. I sipped mine. Delicious. It slid the tension out of my spine, and as I took another sip, I glimpsed Dan coming down the stairs.

His eyes met mine and I smiled, arching my back a little, teasing him.

His gaze went dark, and even through the myriad smells fogging the air in the bar, his scent hit me.

Oh, but he was wild tonight, my wolf. I could feel the heat in him, prowling under his skin and setting a shiver over mine like the lightest brush of silken fur. A shimmer of sensation that made me want.

Want whatever he wanted.

Because I knew it would be good.

The loose stride as he walked toward me was easy, fluid.

To me it spoke of what he was, and I was surprised that none of the humans around us seemed to sense the beast that stalked through their midst.

Maybe they did. Maybe for a few of them, their skin tingled with shifter buzz like mine had when I was still human. But if they did, I had no time to notice their reaction.

I was too focused on him. On heated silver eyes fixed on mine, and the smile playing around his mouth. He'd pulled his tie off and unbuttoned his collar. Deep blue suit. Stark white shirt, rumpled now after his long day.

Rumpled Dan was maybe my favorite Dan of all.

At least when he was rumpled and hungry for me as he was now.

I shifted on the stool, feeling an ache starting between my legs.

Fierce, as it always was between us. Two sparks that made flame.

I sipped the silly cocktail, the sour and sweet liquor sliding easy down a throat gone dry.

I didn't need the buzz of liquor. Not when there was Dan. But it took a lot of alcohol to give a shifter any real high, so it was really just a distraction.

Which Dan knew.

His smile widened as he reached me. He grabbed the drink waiting for him, took a swallow. "Nice," he said, putting it back.

I looked him up and down. "Not bad," I agreed.

"Only not bad?" Silver glinted at that, his eyes going brighter, the wild wolf tang of him rising around me.

"I'm not a girl who's easily impressed," I said, grinning back at him. I tossed back the rest of the cocktail, licked my lips to catch the last of it. And to see what he would do.

A wolf knew a challenge when it saw one. And this was my wolf.

He stepped closer, between my thighs, his legs pushing

mine apart, making me glad for the darkness of the bar as my skirt rode higher.

"I'll have to try harder, then," he said, and then he kissed me.

Not the sort of polite public kiss we usually stuck to. No. That wasn't the mood I'd read. He wanted. And he took my mouth like he was going to have satisfaction there and then.

Wild and hard and urgent. His tongue slipped against mine, and I forgot that we had any sort of audience as the taste of him flooded through me, better than any liquor ever invented. Stronger, too.

The spark flamed, and I moaned and pulled him closer.

It wasn't until his hand was sliding down to my butt and I heard a long low whistle from somewhere behind us that I remembered we had an audience.

I pulled my mouth free, stared into eyes now all dark pupil thinly ringed with silver. Did I look as dazed as him?

I hoped so.

But we were going to have to wait just a little bitbit longer.

"Better," I said, working a little for the teasing smile when my wolf was now all need and haste and hunger that just wanted more of him.

"Just better?" One dark eyebrow quirked. "We'll see about that." His hand curled through mine, and he tugged me off the stool. I obeyed, willing to follow him wherever he was taking me at that point.

He led me back through the bar, the music pulsing through me and emphasizing the need somehow. A primal rhythm that made the wolf want to howl and the woman want to drag him into a dark corner.

We reached his car, parked a little way down the street, spotlit by a streetlamp about ten feet farther on but otherwise dark. He pushed me against the passenger side door and kissed me again, this time tugging the waistband to my shirt up a little so he could slide his hands over my skin.

I forgot where we were again, careless of the rain misting down around us. It would take more than rain for my wolf to care while Dan had his hands on me. Luckily this time, he seemed to remember before I dragged him into the back seat. He pulled back, hit the button on his keys to unlock the door.

"Buckle up." Another spine-tingling grin.

"Oh, I plan to."

It didn't take long to reach my house, though each minute keeping my hands to myself so as not to distract him in the rainy night felt far too long.

But as soon as he pulled into my drive, I undid my seat belt, pushing the door open. I ran for the front door, through the pelting rain, knowing his wolf would be unable to resist the chase. We half tumbled through the front door, giggling and dripping, hands tugging at clothing while we tried to kiss and not fall over.

"Aunt B," I hissed as Dan reached for the zipper at the back of my skirt.

He grinned down at me. "We can be quiet."

"We can be quiet once we get to the bedroom," I said. Aunt B was a solid sleeper, but good sleeper or not, I wasn't having sex in the living room when she could just wander in, searching for a midnight snack. Or a 5:00 a.m. snack, rather. Which for her might be breakfast, given her tendency to be up with the sun.

I grabbed Dan's tie and tugged. "This way."

"Bossy," he said, but he followed as I led him toward the bedroom at the back of the house. Far away from the guest room that was upstairs.

"Sometimes you need to be taken in hand," I said, grinning at him as I closed the bedroom door.

"Ash, you can take me any way you want me," he said, eyes dark and intent.

"Good. Take off your clothes."

I watched him as he undressed. He wore his suits well—

hell, he wore most clothes well—but I would never grow tired of the sight of him naked.

Werewolves have fast metabolisms so we find it easier to stay in shape than humans. But Dan worked at staying really fit. He ran—both in human form and wolf—saying it was the easiest way to fit in exercise around his schedule, but the Task-force had a gym, and he worked out when he could. More than I did.

It showed. He was sculpted muscles beneath lean flesh, strength and power in every line of his body. The moonlight coming through the window kissed his skin, making him shadow and light, his silver eyes bright as he watched me watching him. I hadn't even taken off my shoes and he was naked and waiting for me.

Heat roared through me, but I made myself wait. Let the anticipation build higher.

"See something you like?" he said. He let his hand drift down to his cock, which was hard and ready for me. He wrapped one hand around it, and my knees weakened.

"Definitely," I managed, the word a little too close to a moan.

"What are you waiting for, then?"

"Maybe I'm just enjoying the scenery."

"The scenery gets even better up close." He stroked himself again. "I promise you'll like it."

I smiled at him, feeling the sharpness of it. The wolf wanted her mate. "I'm sure I will," I said. "But I want to watch you do more of that."

I nodded at his hand.

A shiver ran over his skin.

"Show me what you want," I said softly.

He stroked himself again, his moves fierce. His eyes didn't leave mine, even though I could see his breath speed up and his muscles begin to tremble as he continued.

I toed off my shoes and started to unbutton my shirt. Slowly. "Don't come," I said. "Wait for me. Don't stop. But don't finish."

His response was more a grunt than a word. But he obeyed and watched me as I slowly undressed for him. The need in his face, the longing for me made my breath catch as it always did. It was still astonishing that I had him back. That we'd found each other again. That he was meant to be mine.

I wanted to remind us both that was true. After the last of my clothing fell to the floor, I walked to Dan. Wrapped my hand over his. He stilled, breathing fast. The gold of his skin was flushed with red across his chest, and the rapid thump of his heart echoed mine.

"You're killing me here," he said.

"Oh, but what a fun way to go," I said, squeezing slightly so he groaned. With my free hand, I pulled his head down to me and kissed him. First his lips because I wanted the taste of him in my mouth, but then I trailed kisses down his throat. He moaned again and his head fell back.

Trust.

I pressed my teeth into his neck. Not biting but claiming. He was mine. I was his. Sometimes he was in charge; sometimes I was. That was how it would work with us. We were a pair. Equally matched.

He rumbled a pleased noise as I lifted my head. Then apparently he'd reached his breaking point, because he swept me up into his arms, and before I could catch my breath, I was on my back on the bed with Dan over me, kissing me madly.

I didn't object. I was aching for him.

He pressed his teeth into my neck, gently as I had done to him, and I growled softly and wrapped my legs around his hips. "Less biting, more——"

He cut off the words with his mouth. He was so hard

between my legs, pressed against my clit, giving me shivers in all the right places. I gasped, the sensation mingled with the memory of him standing there, stroking himself. The heat bloomed and burned through my skin, and I shifted beneath him, trying to find the angle where I could have all of that hard and ready inside me.

"Please," I murmured against his lips. "Please, Dan."

"I thought you wanted to enjoy the scenery."

"Fuck the scenery," I muttered. I tried to move my hand down to encourage him, but he caught my wrist, pinning my hands above my head.

"Show me what you want," he said.

I arched against him, feeling the slide of wetness against him. "That. You. Us." I arched again, and he smiled.

"Well, if you put it that way." He pulled his hips back and then pushed them forward, and just like that, we were one again.

Together.

Bound by this magic we could create between us.

Dan started slowly at first, teasing me, keeping my wrists pinned as he moved, driving me wild. He knew me too well now, knew exactly how to make me crazy. He kept up the same steady, sure pace until I was writhing beneath him, begging him for more. And then, when I was on the edge of desperation, he unleashed his strength and gave me what I wanted. What we both wanted.

Took us down into the place where it was pure instinct and need, where the animal and the human met. Where the bond between us lived. And pulsed between us as the pleasure built.

"Mine."

The word seemed to shimmer around us, filled my ears. Filled my heart. I didn't know if he said it or if it had been me. But it didn't matter. The only thing that mattered was that it was the truth. He was mine, I was his, and there was heat and pleasure and his skin slick against mine, his heartbeat in my ears, his liquid silver eyes burning into me until I couldn't hold on any longer, and the orgasm that ripped through me stole my breath and my mind.

Chapter 13

THE NEXT TWO days were quiet. No attacks. No calls from Smith. I wondered if he'd somehow regained control over the vampires. If he'd ever lost it. Dan wasn't convinced. The FBI were running image searches based on the photo we'd found —the original and an aged version—but so far Smith hadn't popped up anywhere.

Which was disappointing, but the breathing space gave Dan and Esme time to secure some scientific expertise to help figure out my dad's data. Which was why Esme and I were walking into a Taskforce meeting room to meet one of them and find out what he'd determined so far from my father's research.

"Ashley, this is Professor Felipe Medina. He's a consultant to the NIH. And knows a lot about the vaccines," Dan said as I entered. "Professor, this is Ashley Keenan."

I studied the man as he rose to greet me. He was darker skinned like Andy with earthy brown eyes. But his hair was more gray than black, with several near-white streaks at his temples. On him, it looked good. Silver fox territory. Very white teeth flashed as he smiled at me.

"Señorita Keenan. Roberto's daughter, no? You have

grown up." His accent was definitely not American. Spanish, maybe. Or South American, perhaps, but I didn't know the accents of that part of the world well enough to pinpoint it to a country.

"You knew my father?" I said, startled. Dan had failed to mention that part when he told me he'd found someone he thought would help. But Dan, too, seemed surprised. So perhaps he hadn't known.

"We crossed paths a few times," Felipe said.

"You're an immunologist?" I asked.

"These days more of an epidemiologist," he said. "But I started in immunology, many moons ago. The vampire vaccine was something I was involved in for quite some time."

He looked past me toward Esme, eyes lighting as men's often did when they spotted her. "And this is?"

"My colleague, Agent Watson," Dan said smoothly. "She spoke to you on the phone."

"Hello, Professor Medina. It's nice to meet you in person," Esme said.

Felipe tilted his head, expression slightly puzzled.

"Something wrong?" she asked.

"No." He shook his head as though shaking off a memory or a temporary thought. "Nothing is wrong." He waved at the long table, which was scattered with papers and several thick binders, a laptop open in front of the central chair on the right-hand side. Rather than a coffee cup, there was a dark green metal travel cup with a straw sitting by the computer. I recognized the smell. Maté. Definitely South American. I'd tried it a few times on a trip to Argentina to deal with a vampire's estate. Bitter but powerful. I hadn't acquired the taste but could see why people did.

"Come, let us all sit down," Felipe said, sitting back down in the chair near the laptop.

We arranged ourselves across the table from him. Dan told me Felipe had been briefed on the basics of the case. He knew there was a more infectious strain of vampirism emerging and that the man we thought was responsible was interested in my father's research. For a man who had only recently learned about a potential plague of vampires, he seemed perfectly at ease.

He looked over at us and smiled. "Now I feel like I have been called to the principal's office for a scolding. So fierce, the three of you. But I understand. You have been working on this case for some time, I am told."

"Yes," Dan agreed.

"And now you have Roberto's research. A brilliant man, your father, Señorita Ashley. I always followed his publications with interest after he left the university."

I raised my eyebrows. Dad had never talked much about publishing his research. "I thought most of what my father worked on was confidential. The pharmaceutical companies always seemed to tie him up in nondisclosure agreements."

"True. But he was a clever man, your father. He published in other areas not so directly related to his research. The companies knew they were lucky to have him. I remember when I visited him at Synotech. We were talking about—"

"You worked with Dad at Synotech? You didn't show up on any of the records." I had nearly memorized Synotech's employee roster for the entire time my dad worked there at this point.

"Well, I wasn't an employee," he said easily. "More like a visiting fellow at a hospital. I had temporary privileges with your father's lab, but Synotech didn't pay me. It was only for a month and quite some time ago now, so I can't see any reason they would have a record of me."

Damn. We hadn't thought of that.

"Hang on," I said, looking at Dan. If Felipe had spent time at Synotech, there was a chance he'd met Smith. Maybe. "You might be able to help us with more than the research." I took my phone out of my pocket and pulled up the photo of Smith. "Do you know who this man is?"

Felipe took the phone from me, frowning down at the screen. "Is he somebody important?"

"Yes," I said shortly. "He's the man who created the plague vamps."

Felipe's expression tightened. Maybe he wasn't as calm as he was acting. He brought the phone closer, peering at the screen. "It was a long time ago that I was at Synotech. But I have a good memory for faces. Though I meet many people in my work." He squinted at the photo. "You don't know his name?"

"He goes by Doctor Smith. Nothing more than that. It's not his real name as far as we can tell. Not unless he got someone to do a very good job of scrubbing his records from existence."

"Smith does not ring a bell," Felipe said. "But there is something familiar about him. Do you think he worked with Roberto?"

"We're not sure. He knew Dad, but we haven't found any record of him working at the companies Dad worked for. He had a girlfriend." I wasn't sure if that was the exact term for their relationship, but it would do. "Her name was Cilla." It was an unusual enough name that perhaps it would be enough to jog his memory.

"Cilla." He pursed his lips. "Let me think. I do not think I have met many women with that name. Where did I go with Roberto?" He snapped his fingers suddenly. "There was a baseball game. Or softball, perhaps? I am not entirely clear on the difference. There was a man there, with a very beautiful woman. Her name was Priscilla. I tried to flirt with her, but she seemed sad."

"Do you always flirt with other people's girlfriends?" Esme asked.

"Flirting is enjoyable, Agent Watson. I do not mean

anything by it, and I do not press." He tilted his head at her and bared those white teeth in a grin that was very attractive despite the fact that he was probably thirty years older than me. "Do you not enjoy flirting?"

She gave him one of her ice-queen looks.

"You are not South American, I think," he said. "Which is strange. Because from the sensation I get from you, you are a cat shifter, no? You feel different to Agent Gibson and Señorita Keenan here. They are wolves."

"You feel shifter buzz?" I asked, startled.

"Yes," he said. "My family has connections to one of the oldest tribes of jaguar shifters in Argentina. Distant connections. I am not a shifter myself, but I am sensitive to them. Which has come in handy a time or two." He smiled at Esme again. "You feel like a jaguar. But you do not look like any jaguar shifter I have ever met."

Esme didn't look like most people. And she didn't answer his question. "I think we're straying off topic. You remember a Priscilla. Do you remember the name of the man she was with?" she asked.

"It was a long time ago. Let me think." He rubbed his forehead, muttering under his breath.

I caught mine. My dad used to do the same thing, and the pang of remembrance was sharp, the encounter with him in my memories so fresh. I waited, hardly daring to move in case I interrupted Felipe's train of thought, willing him to remember. If he did, then we might actually find out who Smith really was.

But a smile flashed back over his face. "Yes. Yes. He had a strange name, too. One of those odd names you Americans have where last names are first names, too. It started with a *B*. Bryson? No. Baxter. That was it. I am sorry, I do not remember the rest of his name. I believe he was a researcher, too, but I am not sure what field. But he was playing for a different team, so I do not think he worked with Roberto directly. Red. He wore red. And Priscilla had a red scarf. Red must have been his team colors."

Synotech's softball uniform had been purple and silver to match their logo.

I tried to remember if any of the companies we'd been talking to in our attempt to identify Smith had red logos but came up blank. But someone at Synotech would know about the softball games. They'd been a fixture when Dad worked there. They had a regular league and family days. I'd stopped going regularly as a teen but had been to plenty when I was younger. They'd been fun and popular, so probably hard to cut out. Even if the league was no more, there'd be records. I remembered pictures on the walls around the Synotech head-quarters. Photos of the teams and other company events. We should be able to work out which company wore red easily enough.

I grinned at Felipe, resisting the urge to bust out a quick chair dance of victory. "That's very helpful, thank you."

He looked pleased. But he tapped the stack of binders. "Don't you want to know about the more interesting part of the puzzle?"

My fizz of excitement dulled a little. Dad's research. I did want to know. "What did you find?"

Felipe sat up straighter, suddenly looking very professorial. "The data is complicated, so this is my preliminary analysis only, yes? Most of it tallies with the small parts I knew about his work. Your father was looking for ways to make the vaccines more effective and safer. He was pursuing a path related to examining how the virus—the Stoker variation was what he was mostly focused on—replicates itself in the body and how the body changes in response to it."

"That much we know already from the information Synotech gave us," I said.

"Yes, so Agent Gibson told me." Felipe tapped the pile again. "A lot of this agrees with that path of research. But there are some unexpected directions in here. There is information about hormonal impacts of the virus—that is a common thread of vampire research, trying to understand how vampire physiology changes—but in particular, your father was looking at estrogen."

"Estrogen?" I said. "Female vampires don't reproduce."

"No, but estrogen plays other roles in the body. It helps with healing. It impacts the heart and blood. Affects bone strength. These are things that change in vampires. Maybe that is what your father was interested in."

"Maybe? You can't tell?"

"Not yet. There is a lot of data in here but no detail on what your father was thinking. Agent Gibson tells me there are files still being decrypted?"

There were. Adria had called me twice more to tell me my dad had a brain like an evil hacker to come up with the protection he had, and why wasn't I in IT if he'd been such a genius? I told her I'd had no idea he was a computer genius. Which left us wondering if he'd had help designing the security over the files. She thought she was making progress, but running decryption programs wasn't like it was in the movies. It took time, so we just had to wait.

"Yes. But without that information, what is your best guess about what he was looking into?"

"As I said, he wanted to make the vaccine more effective, less harmful. The reason the vampire vaccine is troublesome is due to the extent of changes wrought in the vampire body by the virus. Werewolves experience a number of changes in their biology, but they remain essentially human at the core. Accelerated versions of human, perhaps, if you ignore the ability to change forms. In vampires, the changes are more drastic. In trying to stop the virus making those changes, we can trigger reactions that are harmful without meaning to. That is why some people have unfortunate reactions to the vaccine. And, of course, there is the magical element to it."

"You believe in magic?"

"Do you not? We live in a world with vampires and shifters, Señorita Keenan. I come from a part of the world where my ancestors had many rituals and mysteries. What we know of the Stoker Variation and lycanthropy cannot be fully explained by science alone. Technically, both viruses should kill us. They overwrite our DNA, alter our bodies extensively. Change us in a manner that we have not yet managed to fully unlock despite many years of intensive research. Vampires and werewolves heal fast, but we do not know how the viruses manage that. If we knew, we might be able to leverage it to help us in other ways. And werewolves can have children. Children who carry the strain within them even if it does not activate until they reach certain stages of human development." He smiled at me, triumphant.

"Sex hormones again. In epidemiology, we look at how diseases are spread and how to prevent that spread. Once the first vaccines were developed for the supernatural viruses, our focus shifted back to the normal human diseases. We do not have mass outbreaks of vampirism or lycanthropy these days." He frowned then. "Or at least we have not for a long time. It seems there is a new threat, if you cannot stop this Smith-Baxter person. But no. I am straying off the path. You have me here to talk about the immunology, not the disease control.

"So, there are some paths of research here about looking at how reproductive hormones might alter under the impact of the virus and whether there is a protective mechanism that could be used in the vaccines. Reproductive hormones trigger many changes in the body, and I think your father might have been looking at whether they could have a preventative role in stopping the vampire virus taking hold. In blocking the changes somehow. I am not sure yet. The data in these files is mostly related to his main field of work. This theory of his seems to have been in the early stages. He was working with some experiments, but there is not a lot of data about the results."

Reproductive hormones. It wasn't exactly what I'd expected to hear, but it was teasing at the back of my mind. Then it clicked. "Professor, is it possible that you could find a vaccine—or a treatment, perhaps—that allowed a vampire to be changed but remain fertile? Or perhaps to regain fertility?"

His mouth dropped open before he caught himself and snapped his teeth shut. The initial shock on his face turned to curiosity. "*Regain* fertility? That would be hugely complicated. Vampire bodies just do not work like human ones do. It does not seem likely to be something your father was working on."

"But if we understood the way the reproductive hormones worked with the virus, could the virus be modified? Make it more like lycanthropy in some way? Could you have a fertile vampire?"

He frowned. Sipped some of his maté. Then shrugged. "I suppose in theory it is possible. But it is not likely. If it was a simple change, it is likely the virus would have mutated over the years to allow it. After all, viruses like to survive. And they change and adapt. But this one has not altered to allow vampires to reproduce sexually. Which suggests it would be very difficult to achieve." He tilted his head at me. "Do you think it was one of your father's goals?"

I shook my head. "No. Not that he ever mentioned to me. He just said he wanted humans to be safe. He didn't think we'd ever have a perfect vaccine—and I don't think it was his goal, because that would wipe out the vampires, perhaps—but he wanted the vaccines to be safer. But Doctor Smith—Baxter —I think perhaps he is interested in it. Or at least Cilla was. Could you make a more infectious strain of vampires if you were trying to mess with the virus to make vampires fertile?"

Felipe's frown was more severe this time. "The answer to that is yes, Señorita Keenan. That is the danger with changing a virus, as it is difficult to predict the outcome. Particularly when the virus is something with such a far-ranging effect as this one. It is why we try to deactivate them or block their effects with immunology rather than fighting them with new live versions of themselves. It is too unpredictable. We have learned the lessons that our friends in biology learned trying to introduce foreign predators into a system to control a bug. They almost always just create a new problem. As it seems this Baxter may have discovered."

"How easy is something like that to reverse or cure or whatever?" Dan asked.

Felipe spread his hands, shrugging. "A difficult question. It would depend on exactly what was done. If we had samples of the new virus, then it becomes slightly easier."

"We have samples," Dan said. "Which means you need to remember all those secrecy forms you signed yesterday. I'm going to introduce you to Colonel Morgan at Fort Lyman. He can provide you with samples. Do you think you might be able to offer an opinion and see if there's a connection to Robert's research?"

"Possibly. If the military have the samples, why not give them the research?"

"Well, for one thing, it technically belongs to me, or perhaps Synotech," I said. I wondered about that. Synotech hadn't, as far as I knew, come chasing after missing pieces of my dad's research after he died. Either they already had this information or this was stuff Dad had been working on independently. We were maybe going to need some legal advice as to who owned the intellectual property if there was something useful in all the data, but that was less pressing than knowing what we were dealing with to begin with. "I want to understand the implications before we take any more steps."

Dan nodded. "We're being cautious. I'd rather have an independent opinion for now."

"You do not want the military deciding to experiment themselves?" Felipe asked.

"I'm not sure I can immediately think of a military application for infectious vampirism," Dan said. "But, as I said, caution for now. If I can get you a sample, can you give me an opinion?"

"Yes. Or, if I cannot, I can recommend someone who can," Felipe said. "Because a more infectious vampire is very bad news indeed. And if this Baxter, whoever he is, has created such a thing, then he is very bad news as well. You need to find him. Bring him in alive. Bad news or not, he may be the only one who can help undo what he started."

* * *

Once the professor had gone back to work, we dove into the new information he'd unwittingly given us. I knew quite a few people at Synotech now, and the CEO's executive assistant, Hannah Lo, had been there forever. She'd known my dad, and she knew everything about the company there was to know.

A quick call to her, and my heart nearly stopped at first when she told me there wasn't a team with red shirts in the intercompany league. But when I asked if she remembered Felipe and whether there might have been a team around the time of his visit, she laughed.

"Oh yes, Professor Medina. He made quite an impression around here. He was a terrible flirt, but very nice. Handsome. Do you know him?"

"I've met him. And he's still very good-looking and a terrible flirt. He said he went to a game with my dad when he was visiting and that one of the teams wore red shirts. Do you keep records of the league games?"

"We might not have all the names, but the schedules used to go in the company newsletter back in the day. These days it's just on the intranet, but I have the files for the old newsletters. And I know we have pictures. Let me do some digging for you and I'll call you back."

"Thanks."

I was grinning as I ended the call.

We were finally on the right path. We were going to find Smith and stop all the chaos.

I'd barely had time to email Dan to tell him Hannah was looking into things when she called me back. Dad had always said she was the most efficient person he'd ever met. Apparently he hadn't been exaggerating.

"Red shirts were a company called WishLife," Hannah said. "They only played for two years. They moved their facilities here for a couple years but then made a better deal in another state and moved again. I've found a few pictures. Tell me where to send them."

I reeled off my email address and thanked her profusely, making a mental note to send her all the flowers and chocolate, and hung up.

Dan got a warrant for WishLife's employee records, and we had them a few hours later.

In the meantime, I'd done some digging around on their corporate site. They were not a big company, but I was surprised to find that, rather than being involved in the fertility game, they were firmly focused on research and treatments for childhood cancers.

Which was a very worthy field of research, but one that made me wonder exactly what had happened to Smith to make him go from "save dying children" as a life's mission to "create deadlier vampires." Something had gone very badly wrong, and I couldn't help feeling that thing was Smith meeting Cilla.

Once we had the employee records, it didn't take long to find him. Baxter Edward Harris. He'd worked for WishLife for about five years around the same time my dad had been at Synotech as a researcher. He'd moved with them from California when they relocated the company to Seattle. And he'd resigned about six months before Tate went on his spree in Caldwell.

Convenient timing. Was that when he started to get dragged into whatever was going on? There was no way of knowing that yet. But the important thing was that we had a name and now a date of birth and a social security number. Which would make tracking him down easier.

I left Andy and Dan to do that part and went back to Esteban's company records, looking for new clues. Whoever was siphoning money off his company had to have made an initial contact somehow. Most likely with a dummy company or a real one who'd actually provided some sort of product or service and used that to slip into the system and start their scam.

The thing I'd found over the years was that people doing this kind of thing weren't often that subtle about it. Particularly those who weren't the hardcore organized criminals or scammers who started off intending to commit massive fraud, those who got sucked into fraud via an addiction or something going wrong in their lives that drove them to do it. And one way they tended to mess up was in how they named the companies they used to do stuff. They thought they were being clever, but there was often something subtle that linked back to them.

I pulled up the vendor lists for the companies I hadn't yet cleared for Esteban. He didn't just own dark clubs, he'd spun that money off into other businesses that were less controversial. He owned a number of commercial buildings downtown and more scattered throughout the suburbs of Seattle. He'd started buying in other cities as well. His portfolio included a leasing company and two construction companies and a majority share of the security firm who did most of the work for his clubs. I wouldn't have wanted to be the other partners there at the moment. With ongoing fraud and now the security cam hack, there had to be some uncomfortable conversations happening.

And then there was a web of other small businesses that seemed random, though I suspected he invested in ideas that his employees brought to him, or maybe he rewarded employees who did well for him with some seed money. And his clubs and holding companies. And he had a stake in a couple of financial and investment firms. Those were locked down tightly enough in their security that I doubted they were the source. But they were complicated enough that I hadn't yet cleared them.

I started a search for all the versions I could think of Baxter and Harris or combinations of those letters and the various streets from the home addresses WishLife had provided for Smith, letting it run while I went to make coffee. By the time I got back to my desk, I'd found a possible connection: Traxbet Inc, who'd sold six months of cleaning services to one of the commercial buildings Esteban owned seven years ago. I started digging.

After so many months, this was the fun part. When the might of the FBI and their investigatory powers could go to work. Between their access and my know-how, we had Traxbet's entire corporate history unearthed in short measure. Registered by a Harris Smith. Sadly, it seemed to come to a dead end about five years ago. As did the identity of Harris Smith. But it was a start. I could follow the threads. Companies were hard to kill. They left traces even after they were shut down. And what I was more interested in was what they'd done before that stage.

I got ready to dive deep into accounting geekdom and found myself grinning at the computer. Luckily no one could see me in the small office I'd been sharing with Andy. But before I could really immerse myself, Dan knocked on the door.

"Did you find something else?" I asked.

"No, but we need to tell Marco what we've found out about Smith. His real name. See if that helps shake something loose. I thought maybe you might want to be the one to do the honors."

"You don't want to do it?" I asked, puzzled.

"You're the one with the debt," Dan said. "This might help."

Ah. That made sense. Dan was being strategic. "He's not going to forgive my debt because I tell him this."

"I know, but we want to keep that relationship working well."

I raised an eyebrow. "I wasn't aware it wasn't. Marco and I are fine."

"Well, then, you'll be even more fine," Dan said. He tipped his head toward the door. "So, let's go."

A man in a hurry, it seemed. "We're going to Marco's house?" I asked. "Why?"

"Because he's an Old One, and he's done us several favors in the last few days dealing with our victims. He gets a visit and a thank-you."

I wasn't sure what was really going on, but I didn't think that was the whole story. But either way, leaving the office was probably a good way to get an early night by our standards.

Dan and I talked tactics for trying to find out more about Smith as we drove, and by the time we reached Marco's, we'd come up with several good ideas.

Marco's security team let us in the gate, and we parked near the front door. I always found Marco's house somewhat unsettling by moonlight. Darkness turned the Mediterranean arches and vines to something that offered too many hiding spots for things that went bump in the night. My wolf was far too aware that there were many vampires close by and many hiding spots they could use.

And I was far too aware that the last time I was here, I'd

done something foolish. I tried to quell my nerves as we were shown into Marco's office.

"Agent Gibson. Ashley, what a pleasant surprise." Marco's expression was quizzical as he greeted us, green eyes glinting in the light of the many lamps around the room. He was wearing a fine wool sweater in a deep shade of green that played up those eyes, and dark gray pants, and tan shoes I was willing to bet were handmade Italian leather. His outfit probably cost more than Dan's Jeep.

Dan nodded at him. "Lord Marco, it's good to see you. And good of you to see us on short notice."

"I am always happy to help the FBI. You know that, Agent Gibson."

I resisted the urge to add "for a price." We were here to make nice. And I wanted Dan and Marco to get along. As long as I owed Marco a debt, it would be better if they could be civil.

"Which we appreciate, my lord," Dan said. "But perhaps this evening we can help each other."

One of Marco's dark brows lifted. "Oh? Do you have some information for me, Agent Gibson?"

Dan angled his head to me.

Right. He wanted me to tell Marco the news. I still wasn't sure why. "We've discovered Doctor Smith's real name. It's Baxter Harris. He was a medical researcher—a doctor, so that part is real."

Marco frowned. "That is not a name that is, as you say, ringing any bells."

"Maybe it will with someone. You can get the word out to whoever is looking for him."

"Do you know anything more? Clearly the man has changed his identity. Perhaps more than once."

I rattled off what we had learned. Smith's—it was too hard to start calling him Baxter in my head—date of birth and where he'd been born. His college and schools. Places he'd worked during medical school and after he'd qualified.

Marco took notes. "Thank you. That may be useful." He smiled. "Perhaps with this information, this will be over soon." He rubbed his chin thoughtfully, and the gesture made me think he was tired, perhaps. Vampires didn't really show fatigue much, and their stamina only grew as they got older. It was worrying if Marco was feeling the strain of the current situation, too.

"How were the men you were helping?" I asked. "Are they doing…okay?"

"They are doing better than your friend, if that is what you wanted to know," Marco said. "One of them showed a mild reaction to the artificial blood, but with treatment, he seems to be able to tolerate it."

That was a good thing. Rhianna had been allergic. She'd had no option but to drink real blood. Not good if you were a vampire who would turn humans with a single bite.

"Both of them are still somewhat distressed," he said. "It is a bad thing, this way of turning. The change is hard even for those who have chosen it. To have all disrupted without choosing is wrong." His eyes narrowed. "But you both know something of that."

We did. Dan had been bitten by a werewolf in the line of duty. But he'd been the one who'd bitten me, hoping to prevent Tate from turning me. His gamble had paid off. But I knew he sometimes struggled with the fact that he'd turned my life upside down. But I'd made my peace with it. I wanted him. I loved him.

I smiled at Dan, touching his hand briefly. "It was an adjustment for both of us," I said. "But it's good now. Hopefully these men will come to terms with it as well."

"I hope so," Dan said.

"Will they be released from the military base?" Marco said. "It is not the best environment for a newly turned vampire. I am sure the soldiers mean well, but they look at them like specimens, not people. Your Colonel Morgan is too much the scientist, I think. And that is not necessarily a good thing, as we have learned."

"Smith is a scientist, yes, but I'm not sure he got into this for science—"

I stopped as the door of Marco's office opened and a vampire who looked like he'd maybe been in his late thirties when he turned walked in. He wore a sharply cut dark gray suit with a white shirt. The sort of thing Dan wore to work. Professional. Something about him gave me a similar vibe to the Taskforce agents. I'd have bet he was ex-military or ex-law enforcement.

My suspicions were confirmed when Marco introduced him as his head of security, Pietro.

"My lord, my apologies for interrupting," Pietro said, "but we've had a ping on the security system for that car we spotted on the way back from Fort Lyman. The same plate just registered driving down this street."

Dan's mouth flattened. "You were followed back from Fort Lyman?" he asked. "For how long?"

"Not all the way from the base," Marco said. "My driver assures me of that, and my cars are equipped to record their surroundings. But at some point, back in the city, my driver told me he thought a car was following us. He managed to shake it off after a time, and we came home."

"And you didn't want to share this information?"

"It is not an unusual thing, Agent Gibson," Marco said. "I am who I am. Sometimes people act foolishly because of it. Youngsters trying to tail the vampire. Or actual problems because I am an Old One. But as you can see, I am still here, and I am well protected."

Dan nodded acknowledgment, but he didn't look happy. "Still, right now, that's a concern. Whoever attacked those men was able to infiltrate Infradark and evade detection. You need to be careful."

Marco shrugged a shoulder. "I am always careful. We will provide you with the license plate information, Agent Gibson. You can do with it what you wish."

He sounded vaguely annoyed. But I didn't know whether it was with Dan or with whoever had been following him.

Pietro nodded. "I'll send you the plate and the image of the vehicle, Agent Gibson. We'll spot it if it returns. Our surveillance coverage of this street is comprehensive."

I was sure it was. In fact, I wouldn't be surprised if Marco owned a good chunk of his street. But Esteban's security system was extensive, too, and it had been undermined.

Marco nodded, his expression easing. He focused back on me as Pietro left the room. "And you, Ashley, are you well?"

"Should I not be, my lord?"

"You let a young vampire into your head," Marco said. "I merely wanted to make sure you were not feeling any unwanted consequences."

"I trust Jase," I said. "And no, I haven't felt anything unusual."

Marco smiled. "It is good to trust your friends. I did not mean to imply that Jason would do anything deliberate that would be counterproductive. But he may do so accidentally. As I told you before, he is strong, but he is inexperienced."

"I haven't noticed anything," I said. "Is there anything in particular I should look for?"

"It is not entirely easy to say. I would say if you are having any recurrent memories of the experience that make you uneasy, it might indicate a problem. But your instincts will guide you, perhaps. I could check, if you are troubled."

He had done that after Tate. But my experience with Jason hadn't left me terrified like Tate had. Upset, yes, but that had been about seeing my father, not having Jase in my mind.

That part was easy. "No, my lord. I think I'm fine. But I'll keep it in mind. You are clearly a good teacher."

"He is a good student. And it helps that his abilities are similar to my own."

"Is that because he's from your lineage?" I asked, curious.

"It sometimes works that way," Marco said. "But vampire abilities are not always straightforward. Some of us develop talents that cannot be explained by our sires. Lord Esteban, for example. The vampire who sired him did not share his ability to manipulate emotions as he does. And while I have known some vampires in the past who had similar talents, his is the strongest by far. We do not know why these oddities occur. But it proved useful to him. As Jason's talents will to him, I hope. Though he has more freedom to decide in these times."

"These times?"

"In the past, before we revealed ourselves, vampire society was far more violent. Out of necessity. There could not be too many of us in any one place or it would draw attention. The kind of attention we did not want. Therefore, the strong ones took power and made sure there was a degree of control over who was siring and how we lived. Of course, that meant that when a new vampire was found to have strong talents, they usually had to challenge their sire or leave and fight for power somewhere else. Not conducive to a peaceful existence."

I studied him. He looked not much older than Dan, so it was hard to believe he was speaking of his own experiences over the centuries. His eyes sometimes gave him away, showed the age he carried. And the power. But right now, he looked almost…regretful.

"Your Jason will not have to fight for power unless he chooses to," Marco said. "His talents will bring him success if he wishes to use them, but he will not be forced to fight for his survival."

"Not forced, but you are teaching him how to use them anyway?" Dan asked.

"That is a protective measure. To stop him hurting anyone accidentally," Marco said. The words were a little too smooth. Marco might be speaking of more peaceful times now, but the truth was he still had his power base to defend, and it was entirely likely that he would use Jase to his own ends if the need ever arose.

I hoped it didn't. Because I would protect Jase if it came to that.

"I see," Dan said. I thought maybe he felt much the same as me.

"Does Niko share Esteban's talents?" I asked.

Marco shook his head. "Not that I know of. He is pretty, of course, and charming when he wants to be. But no, I do not think he has dazzled Jason with any psychic interference. Just the old-fashioned way."

"He is pretty," I agreed. "They do seem to enjoy each other. And Jase is smart."

Marco nodded. "Yes. He and I have discussed the complications of him being involved with Niko when Niko's loyalties are firmly tied to a different lineage. But we will leave them to work it out. If something goes wrong, it can be dealt with."

"I keep an eye on Niko," I said. "He's not getting any information about the case from me or Jason." It made me feel better to know there was little chance of Niko seducing it out of Jase the way Esteban might have been able to. "Wait, you don't think Esteban might be able to get to Jase?"

Marco shook his head. "Not without Jason remembering that he had. Esteban does not have much ability to cloud a mind. To be able to erase a memory rather than just the fog of thrall or a temporary distraction to get away is a vanishingly rare skill."

Well, here was an opportunity I hadn't expected. I'd been

going to ask Jase about this, but if Marco was in a sharing mood, I wasn't going to let the chance slide. "How rare?"

"Rare enough. I can do it, after a fashion. That is why I offered to ease your memories of Tate. I might not have been able to make you forget entirely, but I could fade the emotions connected to the events. Make them feel distant, if you will. There are a few others I know of who can do this, too. I have heard rumors of those who can do more. But I have never met one." He smiled ruefully. "Or maybe I have, and I do not remember. Such a skill would be kept hidden, I think. It would be dangerous in the hands of someone with bad intentions."

My father had clearly found someone. "Would you do the same for a child? A teenager?"

His headshake was decisive. "I would not. Well, perhaps I would be moved to ease a trauma, but no, I can think of no other reason to interfere with a child's mind. It would be too easy to inflict harm. We have taboos around the young for good reason. They are off-limits to turn. Off-limits to feed from at all. "

Well, I guess that ruled Marco out as the vampire who had helped my father. I knew it was illegal for vampires to turn anyone under twenty-one. Their taboos on turning children were so strong that they'd actually insisted on that being written into law when the first agreements between humans and supernaturals were struck. It was the reason why children weren't vaccinated against Stoker's either, because there was a risk they would turn. But I realized I'd never really questioned why that was the rule. If there was a deeper reason beyond it just seeming wrong.

"They do not adjust well, cara. Teenage minds do not seem to cope with such a drastic change. And even for the few who do adjust, it becomes more difficult to remain trapped in a teenage body as you age. In past times, it was harder for a child to do anything independently. Perhaps these days a teenager might be able to pass for older and not have so many issues with that side of things. But even if that were true, it is too risky. As I understand it, it was rare for a vampire made too young to not choose the sunlight eventually, if they were not killed by others."

I bit my lip. Was that why Rhianna had coped so badly? She was still young. Only just twenty-one. But it seemed pointless to ask. I couldn't go back and change what happened to her.

Marco shrugged, shaking his head. "And even if that were not the case, missing children were too likely to incite the humans against us in the past. Foolish to put yourself at risk when there are so many adults around to feed from."

Well, that was clear, if somewhat creepily pragmatic.

"Is it possible a vampire with that kind of power could have gotten into Esteban's club?"

Marco frowned, expression darkening. "Anything is possible. They would have to be very strong when so many who work there are vampires and shifters. Generally, our powers do not work on vampires the same way. I can command someone in my lineage, but it would be difficult for me to cloud Esteban's memory. And Esteban's shifters would be well trained in shielding." His frown deepened. "But a vampire with such powers might explain why these two new victims have little memory of what happened. It could, of course, just be the trauma. Or the result of the change that has been imposed on them so suddenly…but it could also be an influence."

"Would you be able to tell? If you—" Dan stopped and waved a hand in the air. "—looked or whatever it is you would need to know?"

"That would depend on how good the vampire responsible is. There may be signs. There may not."

"Would you look?" Dan asked. "I know we've imposed on your time a lot lately, my lord, but—"

Marco dismissed his objections with a flick of his hand. "Of course, Agent Gibson. You know our interests are aligned on this issue. If there is a vampire who is both infectious and powerful in this way, then the problem is more urgent than we have considered before. Especially if they have now decided that they are out to cause trouble." He turned to me. "How are your shields, Ashley? You should be careful."

"My shields are strong," I said. "Maybe too strong."

"In what way?"

"Well, they have kept several vampires out so far. Even when I'm not trying."

Marco looked startled. "I see. Well, normally I would say that requires some assistance from your Alpha, but perhaps right now, stronger is better than not. Do you want me to try? I am stronger than most vampires you are likely to encounter."

I took an involuntary step backward, and Dan rumbled a growl. I made myself stop. Held up a hand. It wasn't a pleasant idea, but Marco was right. If I could resist him, I should be able to resist most vampires.

"Sure, let's try." I met Marco's green gaze, picturing the moonlight and the glass around me.

He stared at me for a moment, eyes narrowing. Then he reached out to touch my cheek, murmuring, "Let me in, cara."

I braced myself, waiting for the rush of green wind in my head. But nothing happened. I blinked.

So did Marco. He stepped back. "Impressive. You have learned well."

I didn't think learning had much to do with it. At this point, it was instinct born of trauma. But I'd worry about that problem later, if I wanted to. After all, I wasn't planning on letting any vampire back into my head ever.

Chapter 14

I CHEWED over what Marco said as we drove home, glancing in the rearview mirror every few minutes, wondering if someone was following us as well.

"Nobody following," Dan said after the fifth time I checked. "I'm paying attention. I gave the license plate to the detail on your house. They'll run the recent footage and let us know if the same car has been anywhere near us."

He was right. I was being paranoid. But it was hard to shake off the anxiety. "Who do you think would be following Marco?"

"Like he said, it's difficult to know. You can stop freaking out."

"If someone is casing the house, then I want Bug moved somewhere safer. She can't go home yet."

"No," Dan agreed. "But she was clear earlier that she didn't like the idea of a safe house."

We'd had a report from Kenny earlier in the day. Bug's house wasn't safe for her to live in until it was repaired, and the insurance company needed to authorize repairs. To do that, they needed to finish their investigation. Kenny had sounded frustrated that no one on her street had noticed anything prior to the fire. And no one in the town was admitting anything. The rumblings about supernaturals seemed to have died down. Which either meant they'd gotten what they wanted and chased Bug out of town or they were lying low before making their next move.

Or, a little voice in my head was insisting, it hadn't been someone in the town but someone targeting Bug specifically. Either to get me interested or…well, I couldn't really come up with another reason.

"We can ask her about the safe house again," I said. I didn't want to push her into it. Not if I was just jumping at shadows. But maybe she would change her mind now that she'd had some time to get used to the idea.

"Do you think she'll agree? Unless you're going to spend your time there with her."

Which I couldn't do. Not all day, every day.

I sighed. "I can't do that. We have to work."

"We can talk to Ani and see if she minds Bug hanging out there during the day," Dan said. "Someone is nearly always home at their place, and it would take some serious balls for anyone to attack the Alphas' house to get to her."

It felt like I was farming Bug off to strangers. That I couldn't keep her safe. The wolf wanted to snarl at the thought. My pack had to be safe.

"Anyway, we might just be jumping at shadows," Dan said. "Marco draws attention for all sorts of reasons. It might have nothing to do with this—"

He stopped as his phone pinged. He hit the hands-free, frowning. "Gibson."

"Dan, it's Andy."

"What's up?"

"I just had a message from IT. They found a gossip blog that had a post up about vampire attacks. Rumors at this stage. They're shutting it down, but just thought you should know."

Fuck. We didn't need media attention on top of everything else.

Dan shook his head, and his knuckles tightened around the steering wheel before he said, "Thanks. Keep me posted," and ended the call.

"That's not good. We're running out of time," I said.

He shot me a look of frustration. "Yeah."

The Taskforce had done a remarkable job of covering up what had happened. There'd been some news coverage about the vamp attack in Caldwell, but it had been chalked up to a random incident. Young, out-of-control vampires, etc. Dan and I had killed them all, and there'd only been one human fatality, so the story had gone away relatively fast. Partly, I assumed, due to the media companies cooperating with the FBI considering the sensitivity of the case. But if some less obliging sources got hold of what they thought might be a huge story—like, say, plague vampires—and started publishing, the mainstream press would jump on the bandwagon, and there'd be no keeping the genie in the bottle after that.

I took a breath. "Okay, so we keep after Smith. If we can get him, then, hopefully, all of this will go away."

"Only if we can take him and his vampires. We don't even know how many there are. Especially if there are two factions now."

I didn't want to think about that possibility. Instead I crossed my arms and stared out the window, rehashing what I'd learned about Traxbet and trying to come up with another angle to find out more about Smith. I wanted to start with the company that hired Traxbet for a start. But that would have to wait until tomorrow.

When we turned onto my street, the boring white van the FBI detail used flashed its lights at us. Dan pulled up beside it and wound down his window. It was late, and all the houses on the street were dark, so there wasn't much risk of anyone seeing us.

"What's up?" he asked.

Agent Sato, who was new to the Taskforce, had a serious expression. Then again, he almost always had a serious expression. His default mode seemed to be intense. Many vamps were. "We ran that plate number. There was a car with that number reported stolen five days ago."

My stomach sank, my jaw clenching. Stolen car made it less likely that the "following Marco" part was random.

"Well, that isn't entirely unexpected," Dan said, glancing at me before he turned back to Sato.

Sato nodded, his fingers tapping the steering wheel lightly. "There was something weird in the report. The guy who owns the car says he was doing a late grocery run. He pulled up at his local mall. Parked. But then he has a memory gap. He found himself walking back out of the mall without anything he'd wanted to buy, but thirty minutes or so had passed. At first, he thought he'd just forgotten where he parked his car, but then when he couldn't find it, he went to the police. There's footage of him parking, talking to a guy in a car parked next to his, and then they both walked into the mall. The other guy came back out and drove off with the victim's car."

"And he has no memory of that?" Dan said.

"None. Doctors checked him out, but there's no sign of any injury or anything like a stroke that might explain it." He shook his head. "I mean, the guy must have been thralled, but the memory wipe is unusual. He wasn't bitten. He was just escorted into the mall and left there. Maybe under orders to wait a certain time before he left if he was thralled."

Dan frowned. "Wouldn't he still be thralled if that was the reason?"

"No, so that's weird, too. It's like he just forgot."

Mind powers. Marco had mentioned mind powers. And the victims had gaps in their memory, too. I suppressed a shiver. A vampire who could take control of people and make them forget all about it? That was something out of my nightmares.

I gritted my teeth against the fear. This was all just speculation. And I knew how to defend myself.

"Did we get an ID on the guy who went into the mall with him?"

"No. He wore a baseball cap and sunglasses. Didn't look up at any cameras. He knew what he was doing."

Dan rumbled annoyance. "But there's been no pings on that plate here?"

"Not so far. Not on any of the Mercer Island data we have."

"Good," Dan said. "I want a real-time alert on it. That car isn't to come anywhere near Ashley's house. Or mine. Or anyone else connected to the case. We need to warn Seattle PD. Tell them to up whatever efforts they have to find the car but not to let their officers approach the vehicle. The last thing we need is whoever it is preying on a cop."

"Yeah," Sato agreed. "We'll let them know the car has been involved in some suspicious activity." He nodded at me. "You two have a good night."

That didn't exactly seem likely.

* * *

My sleep was uneasy, fragments of Smith and Tate and my dad filling my dreams. The full moon was getting closer, which often made me feel itchy and full of energy, but usually full moon dreams were good ones. Filled with running in the moonlight, being with my pack. Being with Dan. Not fear. Dan looked equally tired when we stumbled down to the kitchen before midday and silently made coffee.

"You heading into the Taskforce?" I asked.

He nodded. "Do you want to come with me?"

I glanced toward the living room, where Bug was reading.

She would have already been up for hours. "I really want to spend some time with Bug." But I also really wanted to look for Smith some more. The FBI's databases would make that a lot easier. But I didn't have remote access to them. If I wanted to look at them, I had to go in.

"Pen already told me she's happy to spend as much time with her as you want."

"It's not what I want, it's what Bug is comfortable with," I pointed out. I hated the guilty feeling in the pit of my stomach. I'd always worked hard, but I'd always tried to prioritize time with Bug when I could. Losing the rest of my family taught me to make the most of the time I had with people. But now it wasn't just me having to choose between work and Bug. It was choosing between what could be life and death for a lot of people and Bug. Selfishly, I wanted to stay with her, but my conscience wouldn't let me do it.

"It's up to you," Dan said.

I sighed. "It's really not." Then I went to tell Bug that she'd be spending another day without me.

* * *

When we reached the Taskforce, I settled down to search for Baxter/Smith through his corporate trail. I still felt like Traxbet might be a good thread to pull on, so I sent Esteban an email, asking if he would be happy for me to visit the management company who hired them and talk to the people there, see if anyone could tie Traxbet closer to Smith before I settled down to continue my analysis.

I'd only been working for an hour or so when Dan interrupted me.

"Felipe is here," he said.

I looked up, frowning as I tried to pull my thoughts out of corporate paper trails. "That seems fast."

"It is fast. I'm not sure whether he has questions or if he's here to tell us some bad news. Either way, we should find out." He leaned against the doorframe, waiting for me to close down what I was working on. His expression didn't fill me with hope that he thought it would be good news. I shut down my laptop fast.

Felipe was pleasant and smiling as we joined him in the meeting room. The stack of files and folders he'd piled on the table seemed to have grown, but he didn't look stressed. His pink shirt and light gray suit were a stark contrast to the black and navy the agents and I wore. He shook hands with all of us, grinned at Esme and told her he liked her suit, and then waited as we all settled around the table. His apparent good mood made me more hopeful that he'd made some progress.

"I wasn't expecting to hear from you so soon, Professor," Dan said, cutting through the small talk.

"I was not really expecting to be back so soon either, Agent Gibson," he said. "But from my initial scanning of this data and the information we have, I am not sure how helpful I can be."

Crap. That wasn't the news I wanted. Judging by everyone else's faces, it wasn't the news *any* of us wanted.

"What does that mean, exactly?" I asked.

Felipe shrugged, the movement fluid, nearly as elegant as Andy or Esme. I wondered exactly how close in his family tree those jaguar shifters he mentioned were.

"So far, I cannot see anything revolutionary in it. There are some interesting techniques and ideas, but from my understanding, they are pathways that have been followed since your father's death and mostly dismissed as not useful. It does not mean there is not anything on here, but I wanted you to know that if you were hoping for a cure, I am not sure this will offer one." He tilted his head at me. "I am not entirely sure what Baxter or anyone else would make of this. He may, of course, have had a problem that he thinks one of those pathways might solve. Maybe Roberto had a new insight into the virus that helps him somehow. But, of course, I will study the data more. I may be missing something. Or there may be a missing piece. Has your IT department made any progress with the final files? The ones that were not yet unencrypted?"

Dan shook his head. "Not that they've told me. I can check." He tapped out a message on his phone, I assume asking Adria for an update. But I couldn't imagine that she wouldn't have told us already if she'd found something.

"Maybe there will be something in what remains," Felipe said. "So far what I have looks like a continuation of Roberto's usual work to refine the vaccines."

"He always said he couldn't perfect it, but he could improve it," I said.

Felipe nodded. "Yes. There is no perfect vaccine, but we can strive for it, anyway. I understand that urge. In my work, we always seek the best and safest cures and approaches to disease management. Better ways to beat these threats we face. But, in short, there is nothing in here that explains the changes evident in the samples of the virus from your victims. Nothing obvious, at least. But what we do is not always a fast business." He ran a hand through his hair, rumpling it. "Without something more to go on, I cannot tell you why Baxter or Smith or whatever you wish to call him might want this."

"There's nothing in there about fertility?" I asked.

"A little on hormone pathways and how the virus might interact with them. But one of the other experts I talked to says nobody has had much interest in those. You understand that the focus of the research being done is on making the vaccines better, not on changing the virus itself."

"No money to be made in building a better vampire," Andy quipped.

Felipe shook his head. "Well, not from a civilian point of view." He frowned at Dan. "It is not possible to say what your military might be doing, of course."

"Colonel Morgan told me he's shared all their results with you," Dan said.

"In military speak, that may mean merely the results he is allowed to share," Felipe pointed out.

Dan shrugged. "Not much I can do about that unless we find evidence they're holding something back. An infectious vampire doesn't strike me as a weapon the military would have a use for. Not an obvious one, anyway. Too risky."

Felipe didn't look any happier. "Which leaves us with something of a dead end. The vampires themselves are not calling for change to their condition. There are those among them who are wealthy enough to fund research if it was something they wanted, but they have not."

Esme narrowed her eyes. "Difficult for them to make a case for altering themselves that humans wouldn't be threatened by," she said. "The peace between the races holds largely because of equilibrium. Humans breed faster and more. Vampires can only turn those who are willing. Werewolves try not to bite people, and not all their children inherit the virus. If the humans thought the vampires wanted to shift that balance…well, I don't need to spell out what would happen. The Old Ones are well aware of this. And the taboos in the vamp community against turning children are strong for reasons."

"Okay, so the vampires don't want this any more than we do," I said, trying to bring the conversation back to the data. "So, let's concentrate on what's in front of us. Felipe, you need more time, or more information, to figure out what the connection is between what's in here and what Smith might have done to create the plague vamps, right?"

He nodded.

Dan's phone beeped. He glanced at the screen. "Adria's still working on it. She says it's hard to give a time frame, but soon."

"Soon" seemed to be a somewhat flexible concept in geek

land. Adria had been telling us "soon" for a few days now. Not that it was her fault. What she was doing was complicated and required time. Time we were running out of if rumors were starting to circulate.

"Well, barring her succeeding or you bringing me your Doctor Smith to explain himself, I am afraid this is going to be a long, slow process, Agent Gibson. Science takes time," Felipe said, lifting his hands in a "what can you do" gesture.

"We'll get you more resources," Dan said. "Tell me who and what you need."

Felipe lifted a brow. "The people and things I need are not cheap, Agent Gibson."

Dan's smile was tight. "This case has a large budget, Professor. I'm sure I can swing what you need. Stopping a plague of vampires is a priority."

Felipe nodded. "Of course. I will send you a list." He lapsed into silence.

No one spoke immediately. Were the others all feeling as deflated as me? I'd been so buzzed just yesterday thinking we could catch Smith. Maybe we still could, but he was only part of the problem. The plague vamps were the other. We could catch them, too, but we needed the science to cure them.

My phone buzzed to life. I raised an eyebrow at Dan, and he gestured for me to pick it up. I took that to mean the meeting was about to be over anyway.

I grabbed the phone without looking at it and hit Answer.

"Why is Felipe Medina in town?" Smith's voice growled in my ear. For once he didn't sound cool and in control. In fact, he sounded out of breath.

I shoved down the instinctive recoil of fear his voice invoked and focused on listening. Where was he? Why was he out of breath? But this time I couldn't hear anything distinct in the background. Not even the sound of a car engine.

"Who?" I asked, stalling. I put the phone down on the desk, switching to speaker. Dan sat forward, and Esme clapped a hand over Felipe's mouth when he opened it as though he was going to ask what the hell was happening.

"Don't play games with me, Ashley. Professor Felipe Medina. Renowned epidemiologist, former vaccine researcher. Seen entering the Taskforce building yesterday. Did you find Robert's research?"

Dan made a little rolling gesture with his hand. Keep him talking. Right. I knew that.

I nodded but focused on Smith. He definitely sounded out of breath. Worried. Angry. Maybe this was the time I would be able to keep him talking, distract him from paying attention to the time.

Keep him off balance. That was the key.

"Why would I tell you that?" I asked. "I don't know who your Professor Medina is. But the Taskforce deals with all sorts of specialists. You're not the only game in town, Smith." I wasn't going to tell him that I knew his real name. Not yet. He might run. And Felipe said we needed him. I had to keep him talking.

"I will be the only important game soon if you don't come to your senses," Smith said. "I need Robert's research."

"Tell me why," I said. "Is there a problem with the vampires you've created? Tell me what's happening. Maybe we can come to an agreement."

There was a long pause. Too long. His breathing was still loud, but he wasn't talking. Long was good. Long gave Dan more time to track the call. But it also gave Smith time to lose his nerve and hang up. I needed to keep him on.

"What's happened?" I repeated. "Are you in danger? Are you hurt?"

He laughed then, and the sound wasn't pleasant. "Would you care if I was?"

"I care about finding a solution to the problem you seem to have created," I said. "And you keep telling me we need you to do that. So yes, your health is important."

"But if you didn't need me, you'd just kill me? Like you did Tate?"

"Tate was trying to kill me. He tried to kill Dan. It was self-defense."

"That's an easy excuse."

"Well, we all find ways to justify our actions, Doctor. That's how we live with our choices in the end, isn't it?"

There was another long pause. I strained my ears, using every scrap of ability that my werewolf hearing gave me, trying to pick up anything else that might give us a clue where he was. There were no other voices in the background. Just a low rush of something that might be air conditioning or heating.

"Tell me if you need help," I said impulsively. "I understand that things can get out of control. Can spiral. If something has happened, then we can make a deal, maybe." Across the table, I saw Dan clench his jaw, but he didn't interject. Esme was leaning forward, listening as hard as I was.

He laughed then and it wasn't a happy sound. More incredulous. The sound of someone who definitely wasn't in a good place and knew it. "You don't know what you're stirring up. If you give me the data, I can fix this."

"Fix what? You haven't told me what's changed. Talk to me. Maybe we can help you."

"I—" He broke off as a car engine roared to life in the background. "We're all going to be out of time," he said, and the line went dead.

Dan was typing something into his phone. A fierce grin bloomed over his face.

"We got him that time," he said. "Probably a burner, but we can do a search on the call records and see where it's been."

Chapter 15

JASE WAS STANDING WITH NIKO, just outside the building where Esteban's building managers had their offices. I smiled as I drove past them. I hadn't seen Jase in person since he'd found the memories in my head, even though we'd talked. The two of them looked happy and cozy, chatting in the moonlight, Niko laughing at something Jase said. Laughing, his face was even more spectacular. I didn't necessarily trust him yet, but he made Jase happy, so I was going with it. Happy was important.

I was looking forward to spending a few hours with him doing the things we were good at rather than trying to stretch my brain around science I didn't fully understand. After Felipe left, I'd dived deeper into Smith's corporate trail, but Traxbet still seemed like the best lead. It was definitely the only business I'd found so far that had a direct connection to one of Esteban's companies.

Whoever helped Smith cover his tracks was good. But I was better. I'd already found two other small shell companies leading from Traxbet and was on the trail of the next level beyond those. This was my version of hunting down my prey, and I wasn't letting go now that I had fresh scent to follow. Especially after Felipe's verdict on my dad's data.

Esteban had replied to my email, pleased I had a new lead. He'd arranged for Niko to meet me here, to smooth my way with the owners—on paper—of the firm. Niko, as I had learned as we'd worked together over the last few months, was good at getting people to do things they didn't want to do. His personal charm and the fact that he worked for Esteban were a formidable dual arsenal, and he wielded both without a hint of self-consciousness. Even though most of the businesses we'd visited during the investigation tried to do some form of grandstanding when we first arrived, with Niko to smooth the way, most of them ended up cooperating faster than they would have if it had been just me and Jase.

And while a management company might be a more respectable business than a dark club, in my experience, supposedly respectable corporations could get just as squirrely about allegations of fraud as less respectable ones. More so sometimes because they were so damned worried about their reputations. But if the owners of this company were willing to have an Old One hold a significant financial stake in their business, I was hoping that reputation wouldn't be as much of an issue as it might be elsewhere.

I pulled the car into a parking spot about a block down the street and climbed out. It was busy for a Wednesday night, lots of people around, which made navigating the crowd of pedestrians slow. Most of them were headed in the opposite direction. Where were they all going? Out to dinner or going to the theater or whatever drew people into downtown these days other than working ridiculous hours. Having a real life. Something I didn't.

I couldn't remember the last time I'd seen a show or even gone to a damned movie theater. I hadn't even managed dinner with friends for months. Other than pack dinners. Which I didn't arrange. And even before I'd been bitten, my schedule had made regular catch-ups tricky. Of course, lots of people who offered services to supernaturals worked strange hours, too, but most of the crowd looked like they were relaxing, not commuting.

Relaxing. What did that feel like? When was the last time I'd just chilled out for more than a few hours? I was actually looking forward to the full moon, when I could go to the Retreat and run until I forgot all the human problems. But that was still days away.

Tonight, maybe I'd get to have coffee with Jase and Niko after we finished our work. That was as close to socializing as I came. And doing that would mean less time with Dan or less sleep, which might equal less time with Bug in the morning. I needed a damned clone or something. Or just to catch Smith and get my life back.

I'd nearly reached Jase and Niko when a car came speeding down the street. Too fast for downtown. Too fast for anywhere. My hackles rose as I spun to track it, registering out of the corner of my eye that Jase had turned to watch it as well.

That was a mistake. The car was only a distraction. Because as it vanished around the block, three men came vaulting through the crowd, running fast and too smooth, nearly vanishing into the small patches of darkness between the storefronts.

Vampires. Coming for me. But not careful about who they took down in the process. Several people fell in their wake, and the humans started to scream and run, increasing the chaos and making it hard to spot the vamps.

"Ashley!" Jase yelled, and suddenly he was next to me. Niko appeared on my other side. I had a gun, of course, but I couldn't shoot into a throng of panicking humans.

The first vampire broke past the edge of the crowd with a leap, landing only a few feet away, his teeth bared in an expression that might have been a triumphant grin or a snarl.

He apparently didn't have any qualms about firing in crowded places, because he pulled a gun from his pocket and lifted it. Aiming not at me but at Jase. Mistake. By the time I heard the shot, I had already shifted, leaping toward him.

He hadn't expected a wolf. His eyes went wide with shock as I landed, my front paws hitting his chest and my teeth closing around his neck.

"Jason," Niko cried.

I didn't look around. The wolf didn't waste time when she was focused on her prey. Part of me knew I should keep the vampire alive to be questioned, but that was lost to the part that knew the only way to take out the threat was to make sure it didn't rise again. Vamp blood, hot and acidic, filled my mouth as I ripped the vamp's throat out with one quick bite and used the motion as he fell to push and leap again, trying to locate the other two.

Where were they?

Attacking Niko and Jase.

Thankfully not with guns. But the four of them were fighting, moving at speeds I couldn't have followed in human form. Niko was a whirlwind of practiced savagery. I could tell he was trained to fight. Knew what he was doing. The vamp he was tangling with was losing ground. But the one focused on Jase was holding his own. Jase was favoring his right arm, blood blooming on his sweater.

Did that fucker with the gun hit him?

I sprang back toward them just as Niko gained the upper hand with the vampire he was fighting, closing his hands around the man's head. One fast twist and the vampire's neck cracked with a sound the wolf heard all too clearly. The vamp collapsed. I didn't know if he was dead, but even a vampire couldn't heal a severed spinal cord fast, so he was out of the picture. The vamp Jason was fighting landed a punch to Jase's injured arm that sent him reeling backward, his eyes wide and shocked.

Niko and I reached them at the same time. I was behind the vamp and went for his hamstring. He snarled and tried to turn as my teeth tore through the back of his thigh. Mistake. Both because his leg crumpled and because it gave Niko the opportunity to repeat his neck-snapping trick. Which he did with an expression of cool efficiency that made me wonder exactly how many times he'd done it before.

But just then, I couldn't resent his skills. Not when he might have just saved Jase's life.

I nosed at Jase, scenting too much blood that was definitely his. After scoping out the surroundings with a practiced scan, Niko herded us back toward the building, guiding Jase to sit on the steps.

Jase didn't protest, and Niko pulled a knife from his boot and sliced Jase's shirt sleeve off, fastening it into a makeshift bandage around his shoulder.

Deadly, beautiful, and practical.

I was beginning to like him more.

Jase was paler than usual—which meant he was approximately the color of weak milk, given he was pale to start with —but he was still conscious. In the distance, sirens wailed. Clearly some of the humans had called the police and the paramedics.

My panic button was back in the jacket that had most likely been shredded when I changed. And I wasn't shifting back just yet. There could be another attack. Not to mention, I'd be naked in the middle of downtown with a whole bunch of law enforcement and possibly even media about to turn up. Not going to happen.

I nudged Jase's hand again. Then nosed his jacket pocket, where he usually kept his phone. *"Call Dan."* I knew Jase could hear me in this form. Not all vampires could. Niko didn't react, so maybe he couldn't.

He nodded, pulled out his cell phone with his good hand,

and said, "Call Daniel Gibson," in a voice that was remarkably steady.

When Dan answered, Jase told him what had happened and where we were. Then he ended the call, tried to stand up, and fainted.

Niko caught him and eased him back against the door of the building. I followed them, whining with worry, but turned to face the street so I could see if anybody else decided to try something. Nobody had emerged from inside to offer any assistance. I might need to have words with Esteban about that. But all down the street, doors to cafes and other stores that had been open when I'd arrived had shut, lights turned off. That was only sensible for humans when gunfire was involved, really. In their place, I probably would have done much the same.

"Do not worry, Ashley," Niko said. "There is not enough blood for the bullet to have hit anything vital." I glanced back at him. He bent down to put a finger on Jase's neck, checking his pulse, then stroked his face. "Jason, caro, wake up."

Jase's eyes were fluttering open. I bounded back to his side and licked his face. He flinched and muttered, "Ew, wolf spit." I did it again.

"Gross," Jason said, eyes all the way open now. "Quit it, Ash."

"You are awake, caro," Niko said. "Good. Hold on, I suspect there will be paramedics aplenty any moment now."

"I'm not that badly hurt," Jase said.

"You *fainted*," Niko said with a roll of his eloquent brown eyes.

"Only for a moment."

"You fainted," Niko said again, and his tone was so worried, I grinned, wolf style. He clearly cared about Jason. That probably shouldn't have made me happy because he was who he was, but it was better than thinking he was purely pursuing Jason because he'd been ordered to do so.

"I'm fine."

"You have a hole in your shoulder."

"Yes, it hurts." He peered down at me. "You didn't tell me it hurt this much being shot."

"You didn't ask." Wolves couldn't really shrug, so I just made a rumbling noise and licked him again, relieved. He was a vampire. He'd heal. The fact that he was awake was a good sign that there hadn't been anything weird about the bullets.

I glanced back down the street. The three vampires were lying on the pavement, and beyond them, knots of people surrounded others lying on the ground. A few of them seemed to be alive, judging by the intent expressions of those helping them. But two were clearly not, the onlookers crying or shocked.

Fuck.

This wasn't good. This wasn't feeding from someone and leaving them to be found. This was a purposeful attack. And worse, it had been aimed at me.

What the hell was going on?

I didn't have too much time to ponder, as Dan's Jeep came barreling toward us about ten minutes after Jase's call. He pulled up in the middle of the street, leaving enough room for other vehicles to get around him, and climbed out, moving fast.

"What happened?" Dan asked as he reached us. He squatted beside Jase, eyeing the bandage. "Gunshot?"

Jase nodded.

"Bad?"

"The bleeding is slowing," Jase said.

He could tell that? Was that a vamp trick?

Dan looked skeptical. He reached for the knot Niko had tied.

"I think the bullet went straight through. I'm fine." Jase was trying to sound tough, but he hissed when Dan moved the bandage away.

"Hurts, huh?" Dan said. He looked at the makeshift bandage, then told Jase to lean forward so he could look at the wound.

"Yes," Jase said. "Stop poking me." He twitched away from Dan as Dan loosened the bandage.

"Don't be a baby. You're a vampire. You heal fast." Dan peered at the wound, frowning.

"I'll heal faster with a mouthful of werewolf blood," Jase snapped, "so don't push me."

Dan straightened and grinned. "Yeah, I'd like to see you try." He tightened the bandage back into place. "I'm sure the paramedics can give you some blood to help things along. You probably don't need to be sedated, so you might just have to suck it up for a few hours. But it's a lesson. Don't get shot."

"I don't intend to," Jase said, shaking his head. "And there was very little risk of me getting shot or anything like it until you showed back up in Ash's life."

"Yeah, well, not much we can do about that now. Things will get back to normal eventually."

I doubted it. Even if we caught Smith and wrapped this whole business up, there was still an unescapable fact that Dan was in a dangerous line of work. I shivered and a whine escaped my teeth, and his head snapped back to me. "Ash? Are you hurt?"

I whined again, shaking my head, but my teeth were chattering. Shock, I guessed. Dan couldn't hear me while he was in human form, so I couldn't answer him.

"What happened?" Dan asked Niko as he took a seat beside Jason and gestured for me to come sit with him.

I did. If anyone was going to react weirdly to a werewolf downtown, it would be useful to be seated beside a Taskforce agent.

I leaned in to Dan. He was, as always, warm like he was wrapped in a heated blanket. But I wasn't shivering because of the cold. No, that was the vampires and the guns. And Jase with a freaking bullet wound in his arm. The tremors ruffled my fur. Jase had his eyes closed, leaning back against the door. I couldn't smell much fresh blood on him. The acid of vamp blood stung my nose, but most of it was coming from the bodies behind us rather than Jase.

"A car came along the street," Niko said when Jase didn't answer Dan. "Dark gray. Sedan. I did not see the model." He frowned at that. "I think maybe they took the badge off. There were no plates either."

"You're sure about that?"

"My lord pays me to pay attention, Agent Gibson. You may take my word for it." He pointed up at the security camera above the door. "And if not, you will see when you check the cameras."

If the vampires hadn't taken them out of commission again. So far, they'd done a pretty good job of getting around any surveillance.

"Go on," Dan said.

"The car turned the corner. It was a distraction, I think. Meant to stop us seeing the vampires. They came for Jason and Ms. Keenan and me. One of them had a gun. Ms. Keenan changed and attacked the one in the lead, but he shot Jason. She killed him." Niko smiled approvingly at me. "Jason and I fought the other two."

"Are they dead?"

"Yes." Niko's tone was blunt. "It was self-defense. They clearly intended to kill us. Or take us. I was not going to let that happen."

I whined agreement at that. I wasn't going to be kidnapped by bloody vampires again.

Dan's hand skimmed soothingly down my side.

"I have no issue with what you did," he said. "It just would have been useful to question one of them."

"I will remember that should the occasion arise again," Niko said. But there was a certain stubborn look in his eyes that suggested he thought acting first was the better plan. I didn't like the chances of any vampire who tried to hurt Jason around him.

That made me like him a lot more than I had before. I made an approving rumble in my throat.

"Don't you go getting bloodthirsty on me, too," Dan said, tugging my left ear gently.

I rumbled again.

Niko grinned at me.

"All right, so we have three dead vamps to deal with," Dan said.

"I think there may be some dead humans as well," Niko said. "The three were not careful when they were moving through the crowd to get to us."

Dan stared back down the street. Paramedics were working among the humans now. "I can see that. This isn't good." He stared at Niko. "I expect you'll be telling Lord Esteban about this?"

"Yes," Niko said. "He will want to know. He is unhappy with the situation as it stands." He looked down the street. "And I do not think it will be possible to keep this incident quiet, Agent Gibson." He tipped his chin in the direction of the vampires. "There will be press here soon. And people have their cameras out."

That got a grimace from Dan, but he didn't look surprised. The other two attacks had been secluded. This was not. Now it would be damage control. We just had to hope that the vamps hadn't bitten anyone on their way through the crowd. "Do you recognize any of the vampires?"

Niko shook his head. "No. I have a fair head for faces, but I do not think I have met any of them before. I will take photos, and my lord will make enquiries."

"Jason?" Dan asked.

Jase opened his eyes. "I didn't recognize any of them either."

The vampire population of Seattle was sizable. They liked the gloomy Washington weather, I figured. It didn't necessarily mean anything that neither of them recognized the vamps, but I didn't like it all the same. This was connected to our case. I leaned harder on Dan.

"When you say they were careless with the crowd," Dan said, "did you see them bite anyone?"

"No," Niko said. "They were just rough. A vampire's strength unguarded can be a fatal blow." He looked back up the street, frowning. "It is reckless to behave so."

If I'd been in human form, my brows would have lifted. I didn't think Niko would have too many scruples, working for who he did. But apparently I'd been wrong.

"I agree," Dan said. "Which is why we're going to find out who those three vamps are. Take your photos. Show Lord Esteban and ask that he spread the word. I will be very grateful for an identification." Which meant he wasn't expecting them to have any ID on them. The vamps who attacked the memorial service hadn't.

Niko nodded and stood. "I will take photographs now and speak with my lord. Then I will go with Jason to the hospital."

"I don't need a hospital," Jase said.

"You were shot, caro," Niko said. "You go to the hospital, and when a doctor says you are fine, I will take you home and look after you."

I made a noise that was as close to "Awww" as a wolf could manage.

Jase opened his eyes and looked down at me. "Don't encourage him."

"I'll always encourage people to take care of you." I grinned a wolfy grin at him, then rose and put my front paws on Dan's legs, stretching across him to lick Jase's face.

Jase tried to dodge, but I was too fast. "Quit it with the wolf spit, Ash," he said, wiping his cheek. "Wolf spit has no magical healing powers. Keep it to yourself."

I licked him again and he laughed, then winced.

"Ash, get down, please," Dan said. "We need to get to work. You'll have to come back and check out this firm another time."

I dropped back down to all four paws on the ground, angling my neck to look up at the building doors, lip curling in frustration.

I knew Dan was right. Even if Jase hadn't been hurt, the area was going to be swarming with law enforcement for some time, and the steps where we sat would be considered part of a crime scene. Plus, if I changed back to human form, I'd have no clothes. So no getting one step closer to Smith tonight. Which made me frown, or as near as the wolf could.

Was it a coincidence that there'd been an attack just as we'd closed in on this new lead?

Part of me didn't think so.

I whined softly, and Dan looked down at me.

"Tell me at the office," he said. But he glanced back at the building, and I could tell his thoughts were running in the same direction as mine.

Chapter 16

I'D NEVER TRAVELED in Dan's car as a wolf before. The Jeep was roomy, but it was still kind of awkward. Though better than trying to change forms in the back seat and dress in one of the spare outfits Dan carried in the back for both of us.

I lay on the back seat—the Jeep wasn't tall enough for me to sit—and enjoyed the stream of smells flowing through the window, like a smorgasbord of information for my nose. Of course, in the city, a lot of that information was gasoline and garbage and the smells of too many people together, but there were intriguing hints of so many other things, passing almost too fast for my brain to process. I understood why dogs liked car rides so much.

It was simpler as the wolf. That part of me knew I was worried and upset, but as far as it could tell, I was safe, and our mate was here, and the car was familiar, so it stayed calm. By the time we got back to the Taskforce, my adrenaline spike and crash had leveled out a little. I changed in one of the first-floor locker rooms—designed with shifters in mind—and then headed upstairs. Jase had told me the latest on the office schedule and my appointments while we waited with him for the paramedics. He'd said it took his mind off his arm to think about other things, and while I'd watched the color return to his face as his vamp healing started to kick in, I'd known he was going to be okay. Otherwise, I would have gone with him to the hospital rather than with Dan back to the office, case or no damned case.

I grabbed my phone as I walked. There was already a text from Jase telling me he was fine and to stop worrying. I texted him back a hug and told him I'd worry if I wanted to.

As I headed to Dan's office, I glanced at one of the monitors that were always playing various news channels, wondering if the attack was being covered. Then I froze as I saw Marco's face. He was standing outside his house, surrounded by media.

What was he doing? I hit the volume button.

"—no cause for alarm," Marco said in his cool but calm tone. "The people responsible for the attack are already taken care of." I noticed he said "people," not "vampires." Trying to emphasize that we were all the same.

"Lord Marco, what does such a bold attack in the middle of the city mean? Have you lost control of the vampire population?"

It was either a very brave or very dumb reporter who asked that question, and I was surprised he didn't shrivel into dust from the icy stare Marco turned his way. Not full vamp mind whammy—Marco was too aware of his position and responsibilities to try to intimidate a reporter that way—but it was definitely scathing.

"No," he said shortly. "No more than the government has lost control of the situation when anyone commits a crime. There will always be people who do not wish to be good citizens. And those of us responsible for the safety of the city will always act to curtail their ambitions in that direction. You may rest assured that the vampires of Seattle want nothing more than to live peaceably as we have done alongside the shifters and the humans for many years now. Do not try to fan the flames of fear. You do no one any service if you try that."

I couldn't see the reporter's face, but he didn't ask a follow-up question. There were several more who asked slightly less direct versions of the same question before Marco called the conference to a close and went back inside.

I turned the volume down, my sense of calm fading. This wasn't good. The press was going to turn this into the kind of disaster we were trying to avoid if they continued on this path.

Damn Smith. He was putting us all in danger. And I'd been attacked again. Anger curled through me.

I went to look for Dan. I found him in his office, talking to Esme and Andy.

"Marco was just on TV," I said to the three of them.

Dan lifted a brow, not looking too concerned. As the head vampire in Seattle, Marco did, of course, make public statements from time to time. I imagined Ani or Sam would, too, if there'd been an incident with a rogue werewolf.

"What did he say?" he asked.

"That the perpetrators had found justice, essentially. The reporters were hitting him pretty hard on whether this is a sign of vampire troubles. One asked him if he'd lost control."

"Ouch." Andy winced. "That's not good."

"No," I agreed. "If the press decides to stir this up into 'vampires gone wild,' we're in trouble. We don't need reporters sniffing around looking for links to other recent incidents."

Dan shook his head. "We've got the reports of those attacks locked down."

"Someone will start digging," I said. "Some dumb reporter is going to decide this is good clickbait and get into it. And they might find someone willing to talk. A lot of people work for Esteban. And I'd imagine the security guard at the warehouse has friends. One of them might decide cash for a story is a good deal."

"I know," Dan said. "We're already on it. Talking to the

media outlets to keep the hype to a minimum. But we can't put the genie back in the bottle. Besides, people need to know to be careful."

"Once this blows up on social media, there's not going to be any stopping the hysteria," I said. "All those idiots out there talking up nonsense on those sites aren't going to be listening to the FBI or anyone else calling for calm. Even if they don't know about victims this week, this is another seemingly out-of-the-blue attack like the one at the memorial service. That's two attacks, not that far apart. That hasn't happened for years. People will get angry."

"I know," Dan repeated. "But we'll deal with it, Ash."

He didn't say to calm down, but he was skating close to it. Somehow that only put me more on edge. I could smell that he wasn't as calm as he was pretending to be either.

"Do you think Smith did this?" I asked. "It's a pretty big coincidence that someone tried to attack me just as I was closing in on Traxbet."

"I agree. But it's too early to make that call. And it depends on what's moved him back into action."

I thought about Smith on the call. He'd definitely been worried. Scared even, perhaps. About something like this happening?

"If it's not Smith, if it's these hypothetical other vampires he's lost control of, I don't get why they'd still come after me. What can I do for them?"

"Maybe they want the same thing Smith wants," Andy said.

"Then why break away from him? That makes no sense." My voice was a little too loud, and I bit back a breath. Perhaps my adrenaline rush hadn't settled as well as I thought.

Dan held up a hand. "Ash, we don't know the answers. We're working on ID'ing the vampires, and maybe that will help. We'll put things together and go from there."

I knew he was doing things the right way, the only way he

could, but I wanted more answers. And I had an idea about how I might get them. An idea I wasn't sure Dan would like.

"We could try talking to Smith again," I said. "We have his number from earlier."

"It's a burner phone," Dan said. "It pinged as being in Georgetown. But then it went dead. He'll have ditched it."

"Maybe. Or maybe he's been too distracted. Before he hung up, there were car sounds. If those other vampires are trying to get to him, then maybe he's on the move. And maybe he wants to talk to me. He's human. If his vamps—or some of them—have mutinied, then maybe he's starting to realize we're his best chance at coming out of this whole mess alive."

"He's been very careful up until now."

"And now things are unraveling. Or escalating or whatever the hell is happening. It's worth a try, isn't it? If there's no answer, then we've only wasted a minute." I stared at Dan. "He can't hurt me just talking on the phone, Dan. It's safe."

He grimaced but nodded. "Fine. If you want to try, then call him."

I blinked. I'd expected more of an argument.

I looked at my phone. Smith's number was still in the list of recent calls. All I had to do was hit Call and I'd be speaking to him again.

I hit the button on-screen before I could stop and think myself out of doing it. To my surprise, there was a ring tone.

And then "Ashley?"

"Hello, Baxter," I said. I wasn't going to mess around anymore. He needed to know we were on his case. Maybe he did already if he was behind today's attack.

"I take it you did find something from your father, then?" he said. I had to hand it to him. He was cool in a crisis. If my knowing his real name was a shock, his voice gave no sign of it.

"I don't need that to find out who you are," I said.

"It's taken a long time."

"Yeah, whoever you got to wipe your identity was good. But not quite good enough."

He didn't rise to the bait. "Is there a reason for the call?"

"Maybe I just wanted to chat." Across the table from me, Dan shook his head. Meaning "Don't be snarky and make Smith hang up."

I took a breath. He was right. If Smith hung up and ditched this phone, then we were back to square one. "I'm calling about what happened downtown."

"Downtown?" He sounded surprised.

I frowned. Was he acting, or did he genuinely not know what had happened?

"There was a vampire attack. People were hurt. Just like they were in Caldwell at the memorial service."

"Caldwell was different," he said. "They were only supposed to take you."

"They came after me. People are hurt. Vampires are dead," I said. "So not that much different."

"Dead?" he said sharply. "Who is dead?"

"Three vampires," I said. "They underestimated me."

He sucked in a breath. "Three?"

"One of them pulled a gun, Baxter. He was going to shoot me. He did shoot one of my friends."

"May I trouble you for a description?"

"Are you going to tell me who they are?" I countered.

"Just tell me what they looked like, Ashley."

I offered the description of the three vampires. There was a small chance he'd tell me their names.

"All dark-haired?"

"Yes," I said, and I heard him blow out a breath. Was he happy or sad about that fact? "Is there someone else you thought might be involved? Someone behind these attacks? If you tell me, then we can help you. Unless you were behind the attack and you're just a very good actor."

"I don't want you dead, Ms. Keenan. I want the information you have."

Right. He wasn't going to answer my question. "Which you will never get if I do die, just to be clear."

"I understand that," he said. "But if things are escalating, it would be better for both of us if there's a deal to be made."

Better for him. I'd be happy with just bringing him in. But trying to take him by force carried a degree of risk. What if something went wrong and Smith died? If Felipe was right, we needed Smith to figure out what he'd done to the virus. We had to bring him in and keep him alive.

So maybe he needed to think we were willing to trade. Get him to meet with me. How did I get him to agree to that? And how far would Dan let me push the boundaries to lure him in? He hadn't wanted me to be bait, but maybe we were now at the point where we were out of options. If there was truly a group of rogue plague vamps out there and they were willing to escalate the situation to get whatever they wanted, we'd run out of time to catch Smith the old-fashioned way.

"All right. But if it wasn't you behind the attacks, then obviously you're no longer in charge of all the vampires you used to control. Or all your plague vamps, at least."

"Was someone bitten?" He sounded worried.

"No. Not tonight. But it won't be long until it happens. Not if the same person was behind today's attack who was involved in other recent attacks. So, Baxter, who is it? Who's doing this? Tell me and we can maybe help you. Because I'm thinking if they're after me, they might just be after you as well."

"I...." He hesitated.

"If you want to make a deal, then you have to start with some honesty," I said sharply. "So, I'll ask you again. Who is the vampire behind these attacks? And don't pretend you don't know. If there's someone else out there making plague vamps, then we have a bigger problem, and I have no incentive to help you. So, your choice, Baxter. You can help us, or you can stay quiet. And, well, that's the end of any chance of a deal."

For a moment I thought the phone had gone dead. That he was choosing whatever insane version of loyalty he was practicing rather than getting what he wanted. I gripped the phone tighter. He had to make the choice. If he wanted help, he had to offer something in return. Hopefully stubborn wouldn't outweigh self-preservation if I was right about his vamps being out of control. I held my breath, waiting for the answer.

"His name is Lancaster. Mitchell Lancaster."

I resisted the urge to do a fist-pump. "And that's a real name?"

"Yes." There was a weight of something I thought might be sadness behind the words.

"All right. Mitchell Lancaster. That's helpful. I take it he worked with you?"

"No. He worked at Synotech. But he was one of Cilla's friends."

That made sense. All of this seemed to circle back to Cilla and Smith—no, Baxter—in the end. Love—or love combined with guilt—sometimes was a force for destruction.

Across the table from me, Dan was listening, but his fingers were already typing. Sending Lancaster's name out to be searched for.

"Thank you," I said. "That will be helpful. Now, you said you wanted to make a deal. So let's work out if that can happen."

"I gave you what you wanted," he said, the words half a snarl.

"You did. But you might want something I can't give you," I said. "I'm not a miracle worker. But we could meet. Discuss it. See if we can come to terms."

"I'm not sure that's a good idea."

"Because of Lancaster?"

"Yes."

"We can meet in daylight. He hasn't made a move in daylight yet." At least not that we knew of. Not one that had left any evidence—or bodies behind.

"I suppose you think we should meet at your FBI head-quarters? Where it's *safe*."

The sarcasm was so heavy in his tone I could almost see the air quotes around safe. "No," I said, and Dan glanced up at me, eyes narrowing. "I don't expect you to do that. I still think that might be the best approach, but we can find a neutral meeting place if you prefer."

"No FBI."

"No." That was a lie. There would be a team watching me. There was no way Dan would let me do this alone. But I was hoping I could convince him to let me talk to Smith for a while before they moved in. "But you have to understand that the goodwill only goes so far. If you try to screw us over, then the deal will be off." And he would be carted off to prison faster than he could say "vampire." Where, if he chose not to cooperate, I wouldn't shed a tear if Dan sicced a whole team of vampires on him to thrall him and get the information we needed.

"How about the Geiger Hotel?" It was one of the boutique hotels where Bug often stayed. It was smaller than the big chain hotels, and I knew the layout. It had a down-stairs lounge bar that was busy enough that Smith would feel safe, but not big enough that the Taskforce wouldn't be able to keep an eye on me. "Do you know it?"

"Yes," he said.

"Good," I replied. "Then tomorrow, 2:00 p.m. I'll see you there."

I hung up. Then looked across to Dan, whose jaw was clenched. "Okay, yell at me now."

He threw up his hands. "I can't yell at you. It's a crappy plan, but right now, I can't think of a better one.

That wasn't the reaction I'd been expecting. "That's it?"

"Unless you think you can call Smith back and convince him to turn himself in after all, yes. We don't have much time, and we have an operation to organize. We need to get agents into the hotel and set up an observation room before Smith or anyone else who's on his side can get anywhere near the place."

Esme and Andy were already typing things into their laptops.

"Okay. What can I do?"

He shook his head. "For now, nothing. No, wait. You can run the searches on this Lancaster guy. Find out some background. We need to know who we're looking for."

* * *

With a name and a former employer, it didn't take long to find photos of Lancaster. He was younger than Smith and Cilla. Only a few years older than me. He looked like your typical slightly geeky guy. Sandy blond hair, blue eyes. In the employee photo we got from Synotech, he looked awkward, as though he wasn't quite at ease in his own body. He was wiry, I thought, though the photo showed him in a lab coat and only from the chest up, so I didn't get a good sense of his height. He didn't look like an evil genius who would team up with the likes of Tate, Smith, and Cilla, that was for sure.

But then again, Smith didn't look evil either. He was cold and detached, and that had been my main clue when I'd first met him that maybe he wasn't entirely normal, but he didn't look like a mad professor. That was the problem with human monsters; sometimes they hid themselves quite well. Tate had been a different story. He looked wrong somehow, even in photos. Nothing behind his eyes but the soul of a predator.

But Mitchell Lancaster looked normal. He could have been a neighbor or the Little League coach or the nerdy guy talking about the latest in cold brew in a coffee shop.

The only thing he really had in common with Smith was that his identity also seemed to vanish from the records not too long after Smith had. He'd worked at Synotech for about eighteen months after Smith resigned from WishLife, but then he'd quit and his apartment had gone up for sale. After that, he was smoke.

"Great, another phantom," I muttered. I looked across at Dan, who was staring at something on his screen. "I'm sending you the info now. Picture. His bio before he vanished."

Dan nodded, not looking up. "A picture is worth a thousand words these days."

"Send it to Marco and Esteban. If he's been around the city, especially if he has a group of vampires with him, then they may have been careless. Someone might have seen them."

"I'll get this out. And then you and I are going to talk about what you just agreed to do with Smith some more."

Chapter 17

SMITH WAS late for our appointment. I sat at the small table in the far corner of the lounge at the Geiger and wished I could down the martini I'd ordered. The vodka was chilled, but I was not. My palms were damp, my throat dry. I'd taken a seat with the wall at my back so I could see the entire room, and still my spine crawled as though someone might be sneaking up on me. There was at least one agent in the room, but Dan had picked someone I didn't know. That way I couldn't look at them and give the game away.

Or so he'd said during the long hours we'd spent planning how this was all going to play out. Dan and Esme were monitoring from a guest room on one of the lower floors. There were several other agents wearing hotel uniforms and moving around the building. And another in the hotel security office, watching the feeds. Dan was doing that, too, including some tiny cameras they'd set up in the room to fix any potential blind spots in the hotel's security. I was safe. Bug was safe; there were extra agents at the house. Even Felipe was spending the day at a very secure lab facility with a few other experts he'd recruited to help him. No one was going to get hurt.

But I couldn't quite convince my instincts—or my wolf—

that was true. Not when we were about to come face-to-face with the man who'd caused me so much pain. Tate had inflicted his share, but he'd been enabled by Smith. And, unlike Tate, Smith was alive. Tate might haunt my nightmares, but I'd never actually have to face him again.

There'd been times I'd feared that maybe I would never see Smith again either, that we would fail in our quest to bring him to justice. But now that I was about to face him, it was turning me into a nervous wreck.

I sipped the glass of water I'd ordered along with the cocktail and tried to remember how to breathe. I was shielding, too, even though it seemed unnecessary. Smith wasn't a vampire. Lancaster and his rogue vamps weren't going to show up. It was broad daylight outside, and the Taskforce had all the exits and entries covered. But still, I wanted to be prepared. No vamp was ever going to thrall me against my will again.

The water was cold, but it did little to ease the churn in my gut. As I took another sip, I spotted Smith standing in the doorway. Dressed in a charcoal sweater and lighter gray pants, he looked expensive, like the sort of clientele who frequented this hotel. He also looked tired. The creases in his face seemed deeper, and his pale blue eyes were shadowed with dark circles that would probably beat mine. He spotted me, and I made myself lift my hand and wave, as if he was a friend I was waiting for.

He made his way to my table and drew out the chair opposite mine. "Ashley," he said. "It's good to see you."

"I think we'll stick to Ms. Keenan," I said, fighting the urge to push my chair back, get up, and leave as his scent registered. Cologne and cool skin and the faint scent of antiseptic he'd always carried with him. And that combination was nothing but pain and death and fear in my memories.

I reached for the martini, took a quick slug.

"Day drinking?" he said. "Perhaps I'll join you."

He twisted and gestured at the bartender. A waitress headed in our direction. I declined her offer of another martini and stayed silent as Smith ordered red wine.

My hand itched as I waited, though I wasn't sure if I wanted to punch him, reach for my gun, or just get the hell out of there.

"So," he said after the waitress left, "we're here. What shall we talk about?"

He seemed remarkably calm for a man who had to know he was surrounded by FBI agents. Remarkably sure that I wasn't about to bring down the entire justice system on his head.

"Lancaster," I said. "We know who he is now. Tell me what he wants."

Smith didn't flinch. "Who can say what any man wants?"

"If you're going to fuck around, I'm leaving," I said. I only just stopped myself from adding, "and you won't be." Smith had to suspect the FBI would be nearby, but I didn't want to spook him by confirming I'd broken our agreement. "I'm not here to mess around."

That sharpened his interest. "So hostile on such a lovely day."

"It's not a lovely day. People died yesterday," I pointed out.

"And you killed them."

"Not all of them," I said. I wasn't going to apologize for killing vampires who'd been shooting at me. "Innocent bystanders were hurt." There'd been one fatality other than the vamps. A man who'd fallen and hit his head after one of the vamps shoved him. There were several others in the hospital, but they were expected to recover. Thankfully none of them had been bitten. "And no one needed to be hurt at all. What was Lancaster hoping to gain by attacking me?"

I wasn't expecting an honest answer. I didn't think Smith was going to confirm that there was a connection between him and the company we'd been going to visit.

"I'm not sure what he wanted. Perhaps he only took advantage of the situation, took a chance to create chaos. It seems to be his way."

He looked as though he wanted to say more, but he cut the words back as the waitress returned to the table with his drink.

I studied him as he tasted the wine, smiled, and nodded at her. I didn't think I bought his story. But I tried not to let that show. I was here to extract information. The question I really wanted to ask was how the hell Lancaster knew where I was going to be. Or how Smith did, for that matter. But that was another one of those questions unlikely to gain me an answer. Better to focus on what might be more useful.

"All right, let's try this. Do you think he has an end in mind?"

Smith drank again. He acted calm, but he'd already drained most of the glass. "I suspect he wants me dead. Eventually."

That had the ring of truth to it. "So he's broken away from you? Gotten out? Did Cilla sire him? Is he infectious?"

Smith squared his shoulders, shaking his head. "That is a lot of questions. I think we should exchange truth for truth here, Ashley. I tell you something, you tell me something. Have you found Robert's information?"

I sipped my martini, stalling. We'd prepared for this situation. That Smith might want to trade. And there were things I was prepared to give him, to make him feel as though he could trust me. But I didn't want to agree too quickly.

"How do you even know my dad left something behind?"

Smith's eyes narrowed. "Because Rhianna told us. Answer my question."

Okay, so he wasn't going to give much ground. I nodded. "Yes, we found something my dad left for me."

"Information about his research?"

"Yes." That was all he was getting for now. "Tell me about

Lancaster. Not the boring things. We know who he was before he vanished. Tell me how he became involved in all this."

"He was a friend of Cilla's. A data analyst. He helped the researchers crunch numbers." Smith's expression was dismissive. "He was unwell, and she offered to turn him. He agreed. We gave him the vaccine suppressant. He turned without any problems."

"Your treatment worked?"

"It's difficult to say. Some people who are vaccinated can be turned successfully anyway. Our success rate wasn't high enough to know for sure."

"So, Lancaster was the first plague vamp?"

"Is that what you're calling them?" His mouth quirked, as though he found the thought amusing.

"Isn't it what they are?" I said. "They're highly infectious. They're potentially deadly to the human race. They need to be stopped."

"You mean *I* need to be stopped?"

"Yes," I said bluntly. "You've caused enough pain and destruction."

"Progress requires sacrifices."

"Okay, that's the sort of thing serial killers and dictators would say," I snapped, then took a breath, reining in my temper. Reminding myself that he didn't have the upper hand for once. That we could take him. But also that this was my best chance to understand the situation before that happened. Once we had him in custody, he might refuse to talk. Ultimately, he could be thralled, but I wanted to hear the story from him. To see if he had a reason for doing the things that had caused so much chaos in my life.

"Back to Lancaster. Cilla turned him after your 'treatment.' Then what?"

"To answer your earlier question, no, he wasn't the first. Or, rather, he wasn't the first when he was turned."

Then something else had happened to make him infectious? When? Marco had said he didn't think the plague vamps could be that old. "So, he became infectious later? Then after him, you continued creating infectious vampires. And some of them, I'm gathering, didn't react well. Like Rhianna."

Smith sighed and gestured for another glass of wine. "I am sorry about that. But the change has always taken some people that way. It amplifies any tendencies they may have already had toward depression or…other issues."

"Like Tate?" I asked. "Or was he just a psycho before he was turned?"

"McCallister was not so…obvious when I first met him," Smith said. "Though he was somewhat unusual."

"How did you meet him?" I held up a hand. "And before you ask to trade another fact, yes, the information we found from my father contains a lot of detail about the research he was doing when he was murdered." I wasn't going to say died. It was murder. Tate had killed him. And Smith worked with Tate. He needed to hear the truth.

"Tate was the vampire who sired Cilla," Smith said.

I blinked a moment. I hadn't expected that. Though it explained why Cilla was unhinged. Being made into a vampire by a psychopath would do that to a person. "She turned voluntarily?"

He went still a moment, took too long to answer. Then "Yes."

"That doesn't sound like the whole story." I knew a little of it now, of course—who Smith was, who Cilla had been. But I didn't know the details. I wanted to understand what would make two people pursue something so dangerous. "You told me once you killed her daughter. Did she choose to turn after that?"

"Actually, it was before," Smith said. He looked down, running a finger around the rim of his wineglass as though he wasn't entirely aware of what he was doing. Lost in thought.

"Why don't you tell me what happened?" I asked softly. "If you want me to trust you enough to give you my father's work, to trust that you want to do something good with it, help me understand why you've done everything you've done." I had no intention of giving him the research. Not unless he was under lock and key and agreed to cure the plague vamps.

He lifted his head, icy gaze meeting mine. "Have you never done anything foolish for love, Ms. Keenan?"

He knew I had. I'd rescued Dan from Tate, risking my own life. I'd tried to save Rhianna.

"I haven't—" I stopped. I'd been about to say I hadn't killed anyone, but that wasn't true. I hadn't killed anyone who hadn't been directly threatening my life. I sipped my drink again, trying to think of the diplomatic way to say, "I'm not a mass murderer." I settled on "I've tried to help people I love, yes. I haven't done it by choosing something that could cause harm to a vast number of people."

"Is that what you think I've done?"

"Tate murdered my whole family," I said. "Not to mention a lot of other people. What do you expect me to think?"

"That was a mistake," Smith muttered, looking down at his glass again. His finger circled, and the glass sang a soft sad note. "He messed up."

Every inch of me went cold. I put down the glass very deliberately. *Messed up? The massacre of so many people was an accident?*

"What do you mean by 'messed up'?" I said slowly.

Across the table, Smith's head snapped up. "I…."

Cold fury slid through my stomach. "Smith. Tell me. Tell me now. By messed up, do you mean when he killed my father?"

"Ashley, I—"

"No. You need to be honest with me. Because if you mean what I think you mean, and my father died because you sent Tate to my town to kidnap him or force him to tell you something, then you being honest might be the only thing keeping you alive."

Inside me, the wolf was snarling, outraged. Wanting to defend this old wound to her pack. Wanting to hurt the intruder who had hurt what was hers. And those emotions ran through me, too. My hand flexed and itched to slide to my back where my gun was snug in its holster.

Smith straightened his shoulders. "All right. Truth. Yes, Tate was supposed to go to Caldwell and convince your father to give us some of his research."

"You sent a psychotic vampire to bully my father into telling you how to create these monsters you've created?"

His pale eyes looked sad for once. "I sent Tate. At the time, we didn't know exactly how crazy he was."

"You found out when he slaughtered thirty people."

"Yes."

"And yet you kept him alive."

"He had money. And he had leverage."

That jolted me out of my fury. Or at least tamped it a little so I could think. Leverage? What exactly was he holding over Smith? Cilla? A young vampire was easily controlled by their sire. Had Tate used that to keep Smith compliant? "All the more reason to take him out. It sounds to me, Doctor, like you thought he would still be useful to you, so you let him live." Or had been too terrified of Tate to try to plot against him. But no, if Smith had Cilla on his side, he should have been able to take out Tate easily enough. Drug him, stake him. Or drug him, tie him up, and leave him out for the sun to take. Easy enough. And no evidence to dispose of.

The fact that he hadn't suggested that meant I was right. That Cilla had sided with Tate. Which must have been a nasty shock. To have your girlfriend support the clearly deranged vampire.

"What happened in Caldwell? Why did he kill everyone if he was only there to take my dad?"

Smith shook his head. "I don't know. He only ever said that something went wrong. I don't know if your dad fought back and Tate killed him accidentally or if something else happened. But he killed him. And then he decided to entertain himself."

I wanted to throw up. Entertain himself? He'd slaughtered so many people. He could have killed me that night. It had been purely whim that he'd left me alive. Some desire to increase his enjoyment of the pain and fear he was exacting by making sure there were survivors to feel those emotions. He wanted the trauma and the terror and the grief to feed his sick fantasies.

It had been nearly a year before I'd been able to sleep without a light on and having to triple-check all the locks and have Bug sitting with me.

Tate had killed my dad, and who knew what he'd done to him before that? Or to my mom? There had been autopsies and inquests, but there wasn't much question around the cause of death when a vampire ripped throats out. I didn't know if there'd been other injuries. I'd never asked, and Bug never told me. She'd kept me away from the inquests. I'd been too broken at the time to handle them.

I could find out. Dan could get those records for me. Find out if Tate had tortured my father because of this man. My hand flexed again. I longed to hurt Smith as he'd hurt me. To give him a taste of my pain. Wanted it so badly my throat vibrated with a suppressed growl. But we needed him. I had to control myself.

"Which brings me again to why you didn't take him out. But I guess the answer to that is that you wanted what you wanted more than you cared about my dad or any of those other people."

"I cared about finishing what we'd started."

"Yeah, but you haven't done that either." I snapped my teeth shut before I could say more. In the past, taunting Smith had never ended well, and I was supposed to be keeping him here. This was my chance for answers. I couldn't let my anger ruin it.

His face twisted. "The theory was sound."

"My dad often said, 'Theories can be sound, but making them work is the hard part.'"

Smith nodded. "He was right about that. I was trying to make things better. To give the vampires a way to be more normal."

"They're not normal. They're vampires. They're supernatural creatures who rise from the dead and die by the sun."

"They're still people." He gazed at me over his glasses. "You care about one of them, at least. Your assistant. He's a vampire. Do you think he might have wanted children one day?"

The question startled me. I mean, we'd speculated that this was what Smith and Cilla had been working on, but it was still a surprise to hear it flat out. "Is that what you were trying to do?"

"Is that so unreasonable? Humans have children. Werewolves have children."

"Vampires make other vampires," I pointed out.

"That's not quite the same as having a child," Smith said. "Don't you think your assistant deserves that?"

We'd been talking about murder. Now he wanted to talk about children. I'd known Jase in college, where he'd been young and intent on having as much fun as he could have while still keeping up his grades. We'd never discussed children. He knew family was a sore point with me, anyway. And after he turned, it became kind of moot, so I'd never asked.

"Jase seems happy to me," I said. "We've never discussed it."

"He seems quite taken with his current boyfriend," Smith continued. "What if they wanted to settle down?"

"Then they'll figure something out if either of them has

paternal urges. Perhaps they'll get a pet." I doubted it. Jase had a dog when he'd turned. But Eddie had died a few years ago, and Jase hadn't wanted another dog. He said he'd realized that they lived such short lives, and he'd only have endless heartache if he kept taking them in. I didn't know if he was going to change his mind about that at some point, but he seemed happy. He had friends—vampire and otherwise—and liked his life as far as I knew. And now he had Niko. I still had my doubts about how wise that was or whether he was just heading for another heartache, but that was for Jase to worry about and not me. After the attack, I was pretty sure Niko cared about Jase, too.

"But if I can make this work, they could have a son. Or a daughter."

I shivered. The idea just felt wrong somehow. "And how was that going to work exactly? A vampire child? Would it age? Would it feed?" Would it be fundamentally messed up by the truth of how it fed once it realized it was different? Adult vampires made a choice—mostly—to turn and accepted the consequences. And that was without considering matters such as school. Vampires were nocturnal. Werewolf children were normal kids until puberty and their first change. And the packs tended to homeschool them for a year or two when that happened or send them to schools specifically run by wolves for the first few years until their control was solid. But a vampire child would always be a vampire.

"The details could be worked out," Smith said. "Humans have always found a way to make things work. They did it when the supernaturals emerged. We could find a way to coexist."

I couldn't tell if he actually believed that or whether he'd just told himself the lie so many times over the years that he might as well believe it. It didn't matter in the end.

"But it didn't work. Instead you created vampires who are a threat to everybody."

"I can fix that," he said. "It's just a matter of reverse engineering the vaccine again. That's why I need Robert's research."

"The vaccine already has issues," I said. "You think you can make one that's effective to protect humans against an even more infectious strain?" If that was what he'd been trying to do, then no wonder my dad had hidden his research well. He wouldn't have wanted to give Smith the tools to go down his path. I wondered if he'd known exactly how far Smith had gone already by the time Tate killed him.

"No. I want to find a treatment for the vampires. Make them not infectious."

Once again he'd surprised me. A cure was what we wanted, but I hadn't been sure it was his goal, too. "Is that even possible?"

"I have ideas."

I had ideas, too. Like locking him up. Like finding every one of his plague vamps and locking them up safely, too. Smith could work on a cure from prison. The government would find a way for that to happen. Vampires lived a long time. Without any hope of a cure, the plague vamps would be facing centuries in prison. Never able to live any semblance of a life. That would just be cruel. And some of them were innocent in all this. Turned by Cilla without, I had to think, any understanding of what they might become.

If that was possible. I suppressed another shiver. Damn Smith. He'd created a situation with no good ending here. Unless he could find a cure. But as tempting as it was to give the signal and have the FBI move in and take Smith now, I couldn't give in. Because we didn't have a way to control the plague vamps. Hell, we didn't even know how many there were right now. Lancaster was out there. We'd found the victims so far. Or we thought we had. There could be others. There could be new plague vamps rising who had no idea what they were and spreading the problem like wildfire.

I'd watched the contagion movies and the zombie movies. I knew it didn't take long for things to reach a critical mass and flare out of control. A vampire plague might burn itself out eventually, but only once all the humans were dead and the food source therefore effectively gone. And the humans would fight back before that. As a species, humanity was good at trying to wipe out people it saw as the enemy. But either way there would be losses and disaster. So, for now, to try to avoid that fate, we had to play along with Smith and Lancaster and however many other plague vamps there were.

"And your vampires want a cure?"

"They're not idiots. They can see the ramifications as well as you do."

"You must have seen the problems as soon as Lancaster became infectious. Why didn't you stop then and there?"

"Cilla," he said simply. "Lancaster was one of her best friends. She wouldn't let me simply kill him once we'd realized he'd become infectious."

Cilla. It always came back to her. And Smith being a guilt-ridden idiot instead of a man who owned up to his mistakes and chose to do what was right rather than continuing to enable the delusions of a heartbroken mother.

I didn't want to continue down this path.

Smith wasn't rational when it came to Cilla. For him, she was the justification for all he'd done. I wasn't sure he had ever been entirely rational. Clearly my dad had concerns about Smith, too, or he wouldn't have hidden his formula from him so carefully.

"And you need my dad's research for your ideas. Why? There's been a decade of immunology research since he died. There must be new methods you could try."

"Oddly enough, I don't have access to those either," Smith said. "And I know what Robert was working on. Your father was a genius, and I think he has what I need. He definitely went to enough lengths to keep his research away from me once he found out what Cilla wanted to try."

Because he was worried Smith was going to do exactly what he'd done. Mess with things and cause a disaster. In hindsight, my father hadn't exactly covered himself in glory either. He should have handed Smith over to the authorities if he'd been worried about him.

"You never told me exactly what happened with Cilla," I said. "You said her child died. What happened? I know you were dating when Cilla was still human. People from WishLife remember her."

"Why do you care about a woman you killed?" he asked.

"Rhianna killed Cilla," I said. "Not me." It was mostly true. I'd been thralled. Rhi had made me. But I still carried the guilt.

"Killed her because she loved you."

"And you loved Cilla. I understand that. I understand that love can lead you down—" I paused. I wanted to get the information out of him, so I had to make him feel like maybe I was sympathetic, but it was hard. Part of me wanted to hit that panic button, get Dan to move in. But I still wanted to know. Wanted to know what had led to my parents' deaths. To the man in front of me causing havoc. "Strange paths," I continued. "Tell me what happened."

Chapter 18

"CILLA and I met at WishLife. Her daughter, Aurora, had leukemia when she was ten, and that was one of our areas of specialty. She was in remission, but Cilla wanted to help our research. She was involved in some of our philanthropy efforts, raising money. Researchers always need more money. We met, and we clicked. And then Aurora's cancer came back. Aggressively. There was nothing we could do. Cilla was beside herself, naturally. Desperate to find a way to save her. And somehow, she got fixated on the idea that Aurora could be turned. That she would live on."

It wasn't such a crazy idea. It was, after all, exactly what Jase had done in the face of a similar diagnosis. But he'd been an adult.

"How old was Aurora then?" I asked.

"Seventeen."

"That's too young." Too young to be dying. That was unfair. But also too young to be turned. The courts had been clear on that, even in cases of terminal illness. The vampires insisted.

"Yes," Smith agreed. "And she was vaccinated."

"What? How?" In America, like in most countries with

239

larger vampire populations, the punishment for vaccinating anyone underage was life in prison. The penalties were always enforced, and as a consequence, it was rare for anyone to attempt it these days.

"Cilla took her to South America at one point, for an experimental treatment. She never told me exactly where. The doctors she went to were working on ways to make the immune system fight any potential recurrences of cancers. And they thought the vamp vaccine might help. It does make the immune system more aggressive, when the body accepts the vaccine. The theory was that by ramping up the immune response, you might be able to get the body to fight the cancer more effectively."

That was true. Immune systems needed to be revved up to fight off the Stoker Variation or lycanthropy. Dad once told me the boost caused by the vaccine was only a small one, but maybe even a small improvement might seem worth trying for when your child was dying.

"What sort of doctors were they?" I asked.

It was a hell of a risk giving someone younger the vaccine. And once someone was vaccinated, it increased their risk of death if they decided to chance being turned. These days it was generally only people who, like Jase, were dying who gambled with the probabilities. Or a small number of outliers who somehow became obsessed with vampires.

As far as I knew, the werewolves didn't add many people to their ranks by infecting them deliberately. I'd have to ask Dan. Most people got accidentally turned through exposure to blood or saliva of a werewolf in wolf form. Lycanthropy was contagious. Even with the vaccines, it was a risk. It was why people who became infected tended to stop living with other humans on a permanent basis. There was a risk of transmission. It was why I'd broken up with Dan when he'd been turned. Back then, I couldn't handle the thought of becoming a supernatural.

"Renegade would be the best term for them," Smith said. "But they managed to immunize her without any side effects. Which was very lucky. It could have gone very badly. They would lose their licenses if they worked here." He shrugged, as though he wasn't particularly concerned with the ethics. That didn't wholly surprise me. At this point, he had to be somewhat beyond ethics.

"Who knows, maybe they did her a favor? Maybe it took so long for her cancer to come back because she was immunized," he continued.

"I can't imagine losing a child," I said. Cilla had been crazy when I met her, but I could sympathize with the mother she'd been before she'd made bad choices.

Smith nodded, raised his glass, and drank as though chasing away a painful memory. "Yes. I tried to help Cilla, got her to counseling, etc., but she was spiraling. And Aurora was running out of time."

I could see it. A man in love. *Crazy* in love, maybe. Trying to help the person—people—he loved. I'd felt helpless when Dan had turned, my life thrown out of control, careening in a direction I didn't want and, at the time, couldn't handle.

"What happened next?" I asked gently.

"Cilla asked me to find a way to make it easier for Aurora to be turned. She knew I knew Robert. They'd met a few times. She became obsessed with the idea of his work. She said if you could make a vaccine more effective, you should be able to use the same ideas to come up with a way to turn it off as well. That they were just opposites.

"She wasn't a scientist, of course, so she didn't understand the technicalities. But she couldn't give up on the idea. So I spoke to Robert. Just about whether it was possible. We'd had a conversation once, after a few too many beers, about fertility in vampires. About why they couldn't reproduce like shifters can. In medical school, I did a rotation in a women's hospital. I worked for the fertility program for a time. I knew a bit about how we intervene for humans. But in vampires, every-thing is turned off. Their hormones are essentially nonexis-tent. So we can't use the same techniques. It was just speculation, but Robert said he thought maybe hormone pathways would be interesting to look at. But we left it at that. It was just speculation. But this time I asked him whether he thought you could reverse someone's immunization. I didn't tell him why. And he…reacted badly."

I winced. I could just imagine my dad's reaction to the idea of someone trying to do something that would effectively undo everything he'd strived for. He had a hot temper some-times—one I'd inherited.

Smith didn't seem to notice my reaction. Lost in his memories again. He wasn't really focused on me as he kept talking.

"Robert told me it would be unethical and dangerous. Even buzzed, he was so angry at the idea, I thought he was going to hit me. Which made me wonder if he'd done some research in that direction."

I didn't know why he would have. Unless he thought there was some way to understand how to make a vaccine better by understanding how to counteract it. Maybe he thought he could build in additional layers to prevent that from happen-ing. "If he had, clearly the results alarmed him," I said. "So why would you pursue it?"

"If you could go back in time and intervene to stop your parents dying—even if it meant doing something risky and stupid—would you do it? You confronted Tate to save Agent Gibson. Love makes us do strange things. As does grief. Aurora was dying. I had to try something. I made friends with some other immunologists at Synotech. And I hacked into their research. I mean, I just needed some direction to follow. You can find the basic makeup of the vaccines online. I just needed to figure out if I could suppress it somehow. Treat the immune response from the vaccine as something that could be switched off again. After all, the immunity does diminish over time. That's why people get boosters."

"What happened?"

"The process was too slow. Cilla had plenty of money. Her family was rich, and her parents died young. She set me up in a lab, but Aurora didn't have a lot of time. Eventually I had something I thought might work, and we had to take a risk. I couldn't convince Cilla to change her mind. By that time, she'd found Tate. He was willing to turn Aurora for money."

That should have been the first clue Tate wasn't entirely all there. The other vampires would kill a vampire caught turning children.

"So, Cilla paid Tate to turn Aurora?"

Smith nodded. "Aurora and her. She wasn't going to leave her daughter alone as a vampire."

That wasn't unheard of either. People choosing to turn together. Though usually it was a couple. Or siblings. I wondered if that was what Niko and Leah had done.

"Did she turn first?"

"No. She didn't want to scare Aurora. She told her I had a new treatment. That it was a trial. That it would make it safer for her to try."

I winced, trying not to imagine a teenager trusting her mother to save her.

"But Aurora died when Tate tried to turn her?"

"Yes. Cilla nearly went insane. But Tate insisted a deal was a deal. He bit her the first time the same day Aurora died. He must have thralled her. Or Cilla didn't care, thought she would die, too, and join her daughter. Tate turned her after a few weeks. Let her stay human long enough to bury Aurora. Cilla survived, and once she was a vampire, it seemed to ease her grief at first." He sighed. "But it didn't. It just changed her obsession. She wanted me to keep working. I couldn't say no. She and Tate might have killed me if I'd tried. And I wanted to try to give her back some happiness."

"You didn't want to turn, too? Once Cilla was turned, I would have thought she'd want you to join her."

He shook his head. "Tate convinced her that I needed to remain human so I could access research more easily. Move about during the day. That sort of thing. He was her sire, so he had influence over her. And, well, I knew he would quite possibly kill me without a second thought if he thought I was going against him. He used to tell me he'd do it. Then he'd promise if I was good, he'd turn me one day." He shuddered a moment. "My list of regrets is long, Ms. Keenan. Failing Aurora, not stopping Cilla. But my biggest regret is that I didn't kill Tate—or try to—as soon as I realized what he was."

After he'd committed mass murder.

It was hard to feel sorry for Smith. Tate was one of the scariest people I'd ever met, even when he was trying to be polite. He couldn't hide the monster inside, even though he tried. Smith was either stupid or had been willfully deluded if he hadn't realized sooner how dangerous the man was. The fact that Tate been willing to try to turn a child should have been a massive red flag.

"But you continued the research?"

"Yes. Tate delighted in the idea of vampires having the upper hand again. Being able to turn people at will. He wanted me to break the vaccine. And Cilla, well, once she began to recover from her grief, she became obsessed with having another child. Siring wasn't enough for her. Though she did that, too, from time to time. She wanted me to pursue that path, too. I told her I wasn't sure it was possible. That I'd try, but it would take more time. And money. Tate had money. Cilla had money, but it wasn't going to last forever. She said she'd find more. And so we continued. I worked on breaking the vaccine mostly while Tate was in charge. Not making much progress, which Tate didn't like, but Cilla managed to convince him these things take time. He knew he had to lie low after…."

"After Caldwell?"

"Yes. He knew the Old Ones would have a death sentence on him. He ventured out occasionally, disappeared for a week or two. But he always came back."

And Smith hadn't run because of Cilla.

"And then he came after me again? Because you wanted Dad's research?"

"Because we suspected he might have left you something, yes. And we were running out of money."

His casual tone was chilling. He'd been willing to destroy my life, turn me into a vampire, all to get his hands on what my father had left behind. I hadn't even known he'd left anything back then.

Smith could blame it on Tate and Cilla, but he was just as ruthless as they were. Colder even. And I wasn't going to let him touch anything of my father's until he was in jail where he belonged.

The money part was interesting. The FBI had realized Tate was active again when he'd tapped a bank account he'd left untouched for over a decade. Did Smith know that? I guess there was a limit to how much they could hope to get out of Esteban's businesses without him noticing, and maybe Tate decided the risk was worth it.

But I'd worry about the money side later. What mattered now was making sure I knew the truth before I let Dan take Smith.

"But Tate died." Worth the reminder that I'd killed him. That there were consequences to messing with me. "What happened then?" It felt like such a long time ago when in reality it had only been a few months.

"Cilla wanted to keep the research going. She was convinced there would be something in Robert's research that would help us. I couldn't convince her otherwise. And she was…persuasive. I had tried some different approaches to the pathway that led to the infectious vampires. She and

Lancaster offered to try the treatment. I think back then, Lancaster hoped I might have a cure."

"But you didn't."

"No. It didn't cure him. Or make either of them fertile. It did enhance their psychic powers."

Well, that explained Cilla coming after me. And how she could knock me out as she had at the Retreat. Thank God my shields had withstood her the second time we'd met, when she'd kidnapped me and Rhi.

"Cilla had a grip on all the other vampires. I couldn't have just walked away. They would have come after me."

That was the problem with teaming up with crazy people. You never knew when they might turn on you. Part of me should have felt sorry for Smith. What happened with Aurora and Cilla was a tragedy, if you ignored how Cilla had handled it. I could almost understand her being driven crazy by grief. I knew how dark that emotion could be.

Smith had made a bad choice, fallen in love, and his life had careened out of control. But there had to come a point where he could no longer blame that first decision. Or say he was scared. He'd kept doing the wrong thing, over and over.

I was tempted to press the panic button, call Dan in.

But I wasn't quite done.

"So, am I to assume that you and Lancaster disagreed about how to proceed after Cilla died?"

"Yes. He loved her, too. And he resented me. Once she was gone, he wanted to be in charge. And now I think he's run out of patience altogether."

"What does that mean?"

"He led a small mutiny against me. Said I was being too slow, too cautious. That I wasn't going to find a cure if I didn't get my hands on the research." He shook his head. "I'm not entirely sure he wants me to find a cure now. He likes being powerful. Likes to be in charge."

"Are you saying he's unstable? That he has some delusions of vampires ruling the world?"

"I'm saying he's dangerous. He needs to be stopped."

He wasn't the only one.

"I gather some of the others joined him when he left?" If not, he'd managed to convince more vampires to help him very quickly.

Smith nodded. "About half went with him."

"How many is that?"

"Seven."

Fourteen. Was he telling me the truth? Fourteen plague vamps to spread like wildfire if left unchecked. But not too big a number to control if we could find them. And three of them were already dead. So, eleven. Plus Lancaster himself. Unless he'd added to his number since leaving Smith and the three vamps we'd killed earlier hadn't been part of Smith's original fourteen.

"And where are the ones who stayed with you?"

"Safe, for now," Smith said. "I have them contained." He smiled at me then. "But if I don't return by a certain time, my precautions will be overridden. Then you may have seven more plague vampires looking for some entertainment in your city."

Ah, so that was his backup plan. If we took him, he'd loose the other vampires on the city. As leverage went, it was good. But one of the Taskforce vamps would be able to get a location out of him if it came to that. He could be lying, after all. But I wasn't counting on it. Smith was too smart not to have made some contingency plans.

"All right. So, we need to make a deal. We both want to stop Lancaster."

He nodded at that, hands flexing.

"And you want Dad's research."

This was the part where things got tricky. How to convince him I was willing to hand something over?

Chapter 19

I LOOKED past Smith and froze. A man had just walked into the lounge. Tall, skinny, sandy blond hair cropped short. Bright blue eyes.

If Esteban had a gangly, nerdy-looking cousin, it would be this guy. Only he didn't look nerdy. He looked fierce.

It took my brain a moment to catch up to my body and recognize the face. Lancaster. It was Mitchell Lancaster.

How had he just waltzed in without anyone from the Taskforce stopping him?

He caught my eye, grinned, and flicked a hand at me in an odd gesture.

I blinked and then smiled at Smith, wondering what had broken my attention.

Smith was sipping his red wine and watching me. Waiting, perhaps, to see what I would ask next.

Right. What was I going to offer him to keep him talking for a few minutes longer?

Smith glanced toward the bar and dropped the wineglass.

"Lancaster," he said.

I followed his gaze, saw a blond man—no, saw him *again*, I

realized, hairs rising on the back of my neck. I'd seen him walk into the bar, and then I'd...forgotten.

Shit. He'd *made* me forget.

Even as the waitress hurried over to us, towel in hand to clean up the glass, the fear on Smith's face cleared and he turned back to me, clearly having forgotten what had made him drop the glass.

I threw up my shields, the reaction instinctive. Crap. What was he doing? I racked my brain, trying to remember what Smith had said about him.

Lancaster stood by the bar, watching Smith, perfectly at ease, as though he was in no particular hurry. No one in the bar was reacting to his presence. Given there was supposed to be at least one Taskforce agent in the room with me, that was bad news.

Very bad news.

I made myself focus back on Smith, hoping like hell that my shields would hold against whatever Lancaster's power was. And if they did, I didn't need Lancaster to know I wasn't under whatever power he thought he was exercising.

Marco said some vampires could make people forget.

And Smith said Cilla and Lancaster had gotten more powerful. Fuck. Why hadn't I asked him more about that? I needed to know what Lancaster could do. But Smith thought we were talking about my dad's research. About what he needed to find a cure.

"What do you think you're going to find in Dad's research?" I asked, picking up the thread of our conversation. I slipped my hand down to my jacket pocket, folded it around the panic button. But I hesitated. If I called the other Taskforce agents into the room, who knew what might happen if Lancaster got them all under his control? None of them were vamps because this was a daytime operation, and while the shifters were all well trained in shielding, it only worked if you did it preemptively. Werewolves didn't routinely walk around with their shields up, especially not when they weren't expecting to be around vampires. Lancaster had clearly taken control of whoever Dan's agent in the room was with ease. I didn't want to give him more of them. And I definitely didn't want him to get his hands on Dan. So no, no button. No reaching for the phone in my purse. Nothing to increase Lancaster's leverage. Or make him realize I wasn't under his thrall or whatever the hell it was.

"I need to understand how to turn off what I turned on. No one was better at manipulating the virus than your father," Smith said.

The hairs on the back of my neck rose. Felipe hadn't seen anything new in my father's research. Not yet. What did Smith think Dad had found? What would happen if he got his hands on the information and it didn't contain the answers he needed?

"I see." I tried to watch what Lancaster was doing without looking directly at him.

"Baxter," I said softly. "You said Lancaster's and Cilla's powers became stronger. What exactly are Lancaster's powers?"

Smith's forehead wrinkled. "That's an odd question."

"Not so odd. Just curious. You said before that you weren't entirely sure how he got the jump on you when he attacked you. Before you escaped…I wondered whether maybe he thralled you."

Smith's frown deepened. "If he thralled me, I would be dead, I think."

"What are his powers, then?"

Smith frowned. "I'm not sure I…." He trailed, off looking confused.

Crap. Had Lancaster made him forget? Removed the memory of what he could do?

The wolf growled deep inside me. She knew danger when

she saw it. I wanted to run, but I couldn't leave Smith. What if Lancaster killed him? It was safer here. I had backup here.

At least I hoped I did.

Where the hell was Dan? If they were monitoring me, then they should have picked up Lancaster's face. Something was badly wrong.

As if to agree with me, the lights in the lounge suddenly flickered and went out.

"Fuck," I said softly. The lounge was downstairs from the ground-floor reception area. It had no windows. Without the electric lights, it was nearly dark. I saw pretty well in the dark, but the fact that the backup generators hadn't kicked into life wasn't making me happy about what the hell was going on. Nor was the fact that none of the other patrons were reacting. When the lights went out, humans usually panicked. Or at least start talking and then moving to fix the problem. But all the humans at the surrounding tables continued to act as though nothing had happened. In fact, one by one, they fell silent, what I could see of their faces in the darkness going weirdly still. If Lancaster was controlling the whole room, I was in some serious shit.

"It's probably just an electrical glitch," Smith said, as though he didn't think it was unusual.

Electrical glitches didn't come with eerie silences.

I ignored him and reached for my phone.

"I wouldn't do that," Smith said. "He won't like it."

"He—"

And suddenly Lancaster was beside our table. He had a gun. I could see well enough to make out the shape of it against the pale skin of his hand.

More bad news. Cleary he had more than joining our conversation on his mind. But it wasn't pointed at me yet. So maybe he thought he had me under control, too? I didn't know if all vampires could tell when a werewolf was shielding, so I needed to give Lancaster no reason to check. I kept still, trying to mirror Smith's uncaring pose. Lancaster would find out if he tried to force me to do something and I resisted. Then the game would really be up. I had to try to keep up the illusion that I was another fly trapped in his web.

"Hello, Baxter," Lancaster said.

Smith looked up, smiled. "Mitchell. What are you doing here?"

Okay, he was definitely under some form of vamp whammy. He'd just been telling me that he feared for his life, that he thought Lancaster was going to kill him, but now he was all smiles.

"I came to meet you. Remember? It was what we agreed."

What the hell? I forced myself not to react. Was Smith under some sort of vamp whammy, or was he in on it, and this was how he intended to get out of the bar and vanish again?

If he was working with Lancaster, then he was a damned good actor. And I was an idiot. But no, Smith had smelled scared earlier, not nervous. I could understand nervous, if he was trying to pull off a scam, but fear had a different scent altogether. I didn't think he was scared of me, particularly. I didn't think he was even scared of the FBI taking him in. But Lancaster was a different matter.

I concentrated, focusing on Smith's heartbeat. Yes, it was faster than it had been before. The body remembered, even if the mind didn't. The body knew when it was in danger.

"Aren't you going to introduce us, Baxter?" Lancaster said.

"Mitchell Lancaster, Ashley Keenan."

"Ashley, it's nice to meet you."

I schooled my face to a smile. I was trying to sort through my memories of the vampires I'd met with Cilla. I couldn't remember if this guy was one of them. But maybe I wasn't supposed to remember if I had. If he'd had these powers then, maybe I wouldn't have remembered anyway.

"Nice to meet you, too," I said and then lapsed back into silence. It seemed safer.

"You and Baxter and I are going to go for a little drive. Did he tell you?"

"Maybe." I tried to sound vague, as though the memory of the last half hour was a fog. "Where are we going?"

"Don't you remember? You were going to show us the Taskforce offices."

The Taskforce? Did he really think we could just waltz in and take…? "Oh, yes," I said. realizing I needed to respond. "I think he mentioned it. What did you want to see again?"

"You were going to show Doctor Smith what your father left for you. He was friends with your father."

Lancaster's voice was soothing. Calm. There was an edge to it that tempted me to listen, to pay attention, but my shields didn't let it go any further than that. But clearly he didn't need to talk to control people. He hadn't said anything when he'd walked into the bar.

But he seemed to be controlling a lot of people. The Geiger wasn't a huge building though. The Taskforce offices were much larger. Too big to control everyone in it, surely? If he could control that many people at once, he could have done this at any time. Walked in there and made us hand over the research. Therefore, I had to assume his powers had limits. So even if he got past Taskforce security with his powers, he wouldn't be able to keep everyone compliant. And then he'd be in trouble. He needed me. I had clearance. I could sign in guests. Get past the scans.

Then what? Did he really want the research?

Smith said they'd argued, so why would Lancaster want to help him?

"I remember," I said.

"Good. That's good. Why don't you finish your drink, and then we can go."

Smith picked up his glass and drained what was left of the wine. My martini was mostly empty, but I gulped it down. Make Lancaster think he was boss and wait for a chance.

Smith rose from the table, and we walked out of the bar, climbing the stairs back up to the lobby. Lancaster walked beside Smith, the gun still in his hand. I couldn't let him shoot Smith. We needed him. Needed to know what he'd done to the virus so the plague vamps could be cured.

So as much as my instinct screamed at me to change, to try for Lancaster, I couldn't risk it. Smith wasn't Jase. He was human. A gunshot could kill him.

Emergency lights flickered over the exits, but otherwise, the daylight coming through the glass doors at the front of the building was the only other light source. The Geiger didn't have a vast glass-fronted lobby like one of the larger hotels.

I was regretting past Ashley's choice of meeting place.

Out in the lobby, no one reacted to us either. The staff behind the front desk were as still and quiet as everyone down in the bar. And there was still no sign of anyone from the Taskforce. That was the worst part, the part that had dread chilling my spine. What if Lancaster had hurt them? Killed them?

But no. I'd know if Dan were dead. Our bond might not be perfect, but I'd feel that. I knew that much.

I shoved the fear away. Dan was fine. And as soon as Lancaster got beyond whatever the limits of his influence were, Dan would come to save me. I just had to keep Smith alive until then.

The elevator was right at the top of the stairs, off to one side. Beyond the edge of the sunlight that came through the doors. Clever. But how had Lancaster known where we were meeting?

Damn it. Had Smith told him? Or had he followed Smith?

Or was it as simple as him using his power? If he could control people, how hard would it be for him to talk to an agent or someone who worked at the Taskforce and find out what was happening? Not all the Taskforce staff were supernaturals. And clearly he thought his powers worked fine on werewolves as long as he had the element of surprise.

What I needed was a vampire or two.

In the middle of the day. Bad timing.

Once, I'd managed to connect with Jase telepathically in a situation like this. Or sent him a scream for help, rather. But that hadn't been the middle of the day. Though, Smith and I had been talking for a while. It must have been closer to three. Jase didn't sleep through until sunset.

Lancaster pushed the button for the elevator, and we went down to the small parking lot beneath the hotel. A nondescript white van—the kind with no windows in the back—was parked among the more expensive cars I assumed belonged to the guests. A man sat in the driver seat, his head lolling back, eyes shut as though he'd fallen asleep.

I hoped he had. Hoped he wasn't dead.

Lancaster walked to the window and tapped on it. "Wake up, Elliot," he said, and the guy jolted awake, his eyes flaring wide with shock or fear for a moment before his expression faded into a familiar calm expression. The one Smith had. The one I was trying to maintain, too.

Elliot lowered the window. "Hi," he said to Lancaster. "Are you ready to go?"

"Yes." Lancaster tugged the side door open. "After you, Ashley."

I gritted my teeth and climbed in. At least I was conscious. Which was more than I could say about most of the other times I'd entered a vehicle with Smith or one of his vampire cronies.

The van had no windows, not even an opening into the front, but it did have seats. Or benches really, lining either side. Which made me wonder what the hell it was normally used for. But it was a simple solution. You didn't need luxury cars with UV screens like Marco had to avoid the sun if you could just choose a van with no windows.

I took a seat and pulled on the seat belt, as I would have done if this was a normal situation.

Lancaster waited until Smith had done the same before he climbed in, too, and slid the door shut. That seemed to be the signal for Elliott to go. The van's engine came to life as Lancaster seated himself next to me and pressed the gun into my ribs.

"My apologies," he said. "But, just so you know, there are silver bullets in this. In case any part of you is awake in there." He rubbed his head a moment with his free hand and then snapped his fingers. "Wake up, Baxter."

Across from us, Smith's expression sharpened, then focused on the two of us.

To my surprise, he smiled. "That went well, then."

Chapter 20

FUCK.

I'd been played.

Or had I?

Double fuck. What the hell was going on?

"We're on our way to the Taskforce," Lancaster agreed. "There's still a way to go yet."

There was tension in his words. Damn it. I needed to know what was going on.

Smith had been genuinely scared at the Geiger. I hadn't sensed he'd been lying when he'd talked about what had happened. Humans got twitchy when they lied. Not in big ways that were always clear to other humans, but for a shifter, it was obvious.

But I couldn't do anything. Not without letting Lancaster know I wasn't under his control.

"You were chatty back there," Lancaster said to Smith.

"You said you needed time to get everyone under control," Smith countered. "And I wanted her to trust me. I told her what she wanted to hear. It doesn't matter that she knows. What matters is that we get the research."

Lancaster made a grunting noise as though he wasn't so

sure. Based on what Felipe had said, he might be right. There wasn't necessarily anything in my dad's research that was going to help Smith.

The van came to a stop, and I heard a beep followed by a mechanical whine. The parking lot gate going up. Okay, so we were headed onto the street. To the Taskforce. There were several routes to take from the Geiger, but they all took about the same time, so I didn't bother trying to figure out which way we were going to go.

Lancaster had a gun. But I had daylight. He could probably shoot me if I tried for the doors, but I might survive it. But if I bailed, we'd lose Smith. Maybe for good. I couldn't imagine him giving me another chance like this.

"Are you sure she's good?" Smith said, nodding to Lancaster.

"She's fine. Her heartbeat's a little fast, but that's normal. You're okay, aren't you, Ashley?"

I kept smiling. "I'm fine."

"Good girl. Now, do you have a gun?"

Fuck. I'd been hoping he wouldn't ask me that question. But I couldn't refuse to answer. Not and maintain the illusion. If he searched me, he'd find the weapon.

"Yes."

"May I see it?"

I reached around to my holster. My fingers closed around the gun. Curled around the grip. Could I shoot him before he shot me? Maybe. But we'd both be wounded. In a fight, it was difficult to say who'd win.

He said he had silver bullets. That could kill me.

I had to give it to him.

I pulled it out and passed it to him, ignoring the howl of fury in my head. I wasn't sure if it was me, or an imaginary version of Dan, or even Tommy, who'd taught me to shoot, who was most disgusted at me giving up my weapon.

"Thank you," Lancaster said.

I nodded, the fake smile making my cheeks hurt. I would be fine. We were going to the Taskforce. There were other agents at the Taskforce.

The sounds of traffic rose around us as the van picked up speed. It was going to take twenty minutes or more to get back to the Taskforce. I'd chosen the Geiger because it was a reasonable distance away, hoping Smith would feel more comfortable knowing the FBI wasn't close.

I had to try to figure something out fast. Lancaster might be good, but he couldn't put vamp whammy on traffic lights.

Esteban had said the glitch in his system had been odd, but now that I knew what Lancaster could do, it was likely Lancaster had used his powers to get into the security team. Or used someone in Esteban's security team to do it for him.

The thought made my stomach twist. Plague vamps were bad enough, but a vampire strong enough to make entire rooms of people forget he was standing in front of them or make them forget entire interactions with him was terrifying. Smith had been underselling it. Lancaster wasn't dangerous, he was deadly.

Marco had said this sort of power was rare. Having seen it on display, I was wondering if the other vampires deliberately kept it that way. Fear crept up my spine, but I stopped the shiver from emerging. They had to think I was happy and compliant.

My fingers itched for my phone or even to hit the panic button. But I didn't want to draw attention to the movement.

"It will be interesting to see Robert's research," Smith said. He was using the same sort of false cheerful-but-calm voice as Lancaster. Talking to me like I was a child to be reassured. His tone didn't have the same weight of power to it as Lancaster's though. It just made me want to punch him in the face.

"It was nice of him to leave it for you. To let you help the vampires," Smith continued.

Was he testing me? "He always liked helping people," I said blandly. "He was one of the good guys."

Smith frowned. "Are you sure she's under?"

Lancaster nodded. "Why?"

"Cilla told me she had a pretty strong shield."

"Well, we can find out," Lancaster said.

Smith frowned. "You can't hurt her. They'll get suspicious on the other end if she turns up with a bruised face. We need her in one piece."

Clearly Lancaster had a history of testing his control in unpleasant ways. Inside me, the wolf prowled, all too aware she was trapped with two enemies. If Lancaster hit me, I wasn't sure I'd be able to stop her taking charge.

"And she's still young for a werewolf. You don't want to test her control. She might get lucky before you can shoot her. She's killed vampires before."

Great minds think alike. Or was that fools seldom differ?

I glanced across at Smith, keeping my face impassive.

Lancaster grunted again, and the gun pressed harder into my side. Interesting that he thought he needed the gun. If I was supposed to be compliant, the way I would be if I was fully thralled, why would he need the gun? How did his powers work exactly? Did they expect me to act like whatever Lancaster thought he was projecting was happening? Or just vague altogether? The people in the bar hadn't reacted at all, but that clearly wasn't what he thought he was doing to me or they wouldn't be talking to me.

"What will you do with the research?" I asked.

"What your father wanted," Smith said. "Help people."

"Cilla said you wanted to help vampires," I said, keeping my voice vague.

The gun pressed harder as Lancaster's hand twitched. Right. Cilla was a sore point with him. Smith had said he thought Lancaster loved her, too.

"We just want what's fair," Lancaster said.

What exactly did he think was fair? Vampires who could breed as well as sire? Vampires who could overrun the humans?

It wasn't logical.

They'd starve without us. Even the artificial blood required cells from real blood to produce it, and the starter colonies didn't last forever.

Maybe Lancaster wasn't so logical either.

"How long?" Smith asked.

Lancaster shrugged. "Ten more minutes, probably. I got the traffic pattern optimized, but you can't just turn off all the signals without someone noticing."

Turn off the signals?

Right. Smith had mentioned that Lancaster had been a computer analyst. Hacking into the traffic system seemed to indicate a level of skill above just your regular computer geek.

I only just stopped myself from frowning. It made sense. Smith had to have someone on his team with stellar tech skills to have stayed as off-grid as he had. Not to mention pulling off a fraud on someone as paranoid as Esteban. Even if you were able to wipe the memory of whoever helped you gain access, you'd need the skills to know what to do once you had it.

Maybe that was why my father had been so paranoid about his data. Did he suspect Smith had someone like Lancaster on his side?

After all, it was kind of what they were doing now. Using me—or the version of me they thought they had under control—to get into the Taskforce, highjack the data they wanted, and get out again.

Though, even with me and my access, it wasn't so clear how they thought they'd just get out again if we got all the way in.

What else did they have planned?

There were more plague vamps out there. Where were they right now?

If they were part of whatever was going down, they had to already be in the Taskforce building somehow. The whole building was vampire-safe once you were inside. The windows had UV screens.

"And the others will be ready?"

"They're in position," Lancaster agreed.

My eyes flicked to Smith. He gazed back with no reaction. But I couldn't help feeling that maybe he was asking these questions deliberately. Feeding me information, maybe. But for that to be true, he had to suspect I wasn't under Lancaster's control.

It made my head hurt. Whose side was he on? What was he trying to achieve?

He'd said Lancaster was dangerous. That he wanted him stopped.

Had that been a lie?

I was sure Smith wanted the data, but it also seemed likely that he knew exactly how dangerous Lancaster's powers were. Maybe he'd decided he was tired of being controlled by unstable vampires. With Cilla gone, he had no emotional ties to Lancaster, and so far, Lancaster didn't seem to be a killer like Tate. Sure, the vampires who'd attacked us yesterday had seemed intent on hurting me, but maybe that was desperation that we were closing in on them rather than any desire to kill.

Or was it desperation to get me right where I was now? To get me to want to meet with Smith?

Had we played straight into their hands? And if we had, how did I flip the game between now and the Taskforce?

Smith's heartbeat was still a little fast, as it had been since we'd gotten into the van. He was nervous. But not more nervous than he'd been back in the bar when all this started.

So, he thought things were going to plan.

But whose plan?

I hoped my poker face was as good as I thought it was. My mind raced, but they had to think I was calm.

Under control.

And I had to wait for the right moment to show them they were wrong about that.

The traffic outside the van sounded normal still. No sirens. No indication anyone might be following us. No one riding to my rescue. Or maybe they were. But right now, I had to plan to rescue myself.

Lancaster pulled out his phone, glanced down at the screen. I didn't look, but in my peripheral vision, I could see a notification bubble.

"Oh, look," Lancaster said. "Our friend on Mercer Island is saying hello."

That made me turn my head, but I stifled the immediate twinge of fear and kept my voice even. "That's where I live. Do you know someone who lives there?"

"I know," Lancaster said. "My friend is familiar with your house."

Bug.

Did he have someone ready to take her? To hurt her?

Inside, the wolf snarled, and I had to fight her back. I couldn't react. Not yet. Not until I had more space and a chance of avoiding a bullet while not letting either Smith or Lancaster get away. We'd put extra agents with Bug. Lancaster didn't have that many vampires to spare. He couldn't send enough to take Bug and have enough to help him at the Taskforce.

At least, I hoped not.

"It's a nice place to live," I said. Somehow, I managed to keep my voice steady.

Lancaster didn't answer me. He was looking down at his phone. I let my eyes glaze over as though I wasn't focused on anything. Kept up the pretense I was under.

Time seemed to crawl. But eventually the van slowed, and

I heard another parking lot gate lift before we drove down a slope. The Taskforce's parking lot was beneath the building. You needed a pass to swipe in, but couriers and deliveries got temporary permission as well. The sort of thing it would be easy for someone with Lancaster's powers to get hold of.

The van parked, and I ignored the prickling down my spine.

This was it.

Either I pulled this off and stopped Lancaster or people were going to get hurt. If Smith and Lancaster got away, then who knew what future havoc they could wreak? Maybe people would get hurt anyway, but we had to stop them.

Even without my dad's research, Smith had caused enough damage for one lifetime. I needed to keep him alive so he could help maybe undo some of it, but no way was I letting him walk out of here. And that went double for Lancaster.

Of the two of them, he was the bigger threat.

Lancaster nodded at Smith, and Smith opened the van door.

"After you, Ashley," Lancaster said.

I undid my seat belt and followed Smith, trying to shake off the rush of adrenaline so I could still seem calm despite the fact that I was all too aware that Lancaster had a gun behind me.

But he wouldn't always be behind me.

The Taskforce lot was laid out like most parking lots. Lots of gray concrete and white painted lines and lighting that was more than adequate for a supernatural but somewhat dingy for a human.

I knew there were plenty of cameras around, but I looked for the nearest one under the guise of shouldering my purse across my body, wondering if we would catch someone's attention. I could probably take down Lancaster without help. But I had to wait for the right moment.

Lancaster climbed out of the van and closed the doors

behind him. The driver didn't emerge, so I assumed he wasn't going to be part of this little adventure.

Good. One less person to worry about.

"The elevator is this way," I said brightly. Like I was just a normal girl, keen to show some friends around her office. "It's the quickest way up to the lobby."

"Okay," Lancaster said, not seeming fazed by the idea of going through the regular checkpoints. Maybe he already knew there was no way around that. And there wasn't. The elevator from the parking lot only went to the lobby. There were fire stairs down from the higher floors, but those spat you out at street level. And they were guarded and alarmed.

Lancaster might have tried for them, but the daylight was still working in our favor, I guessed.

I started to walk for the elevator. Smith and Lancaster kept pace either side of me.

We were halfway there, and I was still trying to decide if it was better to try to do something in the lobby or when we got up to the floor that Dan and I worked on when a voice from behind me said, "Mitchell Lancaster."

Chapter 21

IT ECHOED through the parking lot, ringing with a kind of command I'd rarely experienced. But I knew the voice. Marco.

My knees went wobbly with relief for a fraction of a second. I wasn't alone.

I swung around to face Marco.

Lancaster had already turned.

Smith's hand closed around my arm, yanking me back slightly. Closer to him.

I ignored the grip. I could break it easily enough. Besides, I needed to make sure Smith stayed alive in whatever was about to happen.

Lord Marco stood with Esteban and Niko and…hell, Jase. What was Jase doing here?

"Mitchell Lancaster," Marco said again. "Put down your gun."

Lancaster didn't move. Well, not to lower his gun. He raised a hand as he had in the bar.

Hell, did he think he could use his powers on Marco and Esteban? Vamp powers didn't work that way. A sire could control his offspring, and an Old One could control those of his lineage to a certain degree, but I didn't think the reverse was true. No matter how powerful he was.

"That won't work," Marco said. "Not on us."

Lancaster seemed to hesitate.

"I suggest you listen to Marco," I said, letting enough of the wolf through that the words rumbled.

Lancaster stiffened as he realized I wasn't under his control.

Beside me, Smith laughed softly. "I knew you were faking."

I didn't bother looking at him. "And I know you're a treacherous asshole, Smith, but we can talk about that later. Try to stay alive."

Lancaster spun, gun aimed squarely at me. I stayed still. The gun should have freaked me out, but it didn't.

"Touch me and Ms. Keenan will regret it. So will her aunt," he said.

The snarl turned real. I doubted he could have gotten to Bug, but there was enough uncertainty to terrify me. "If you hurt my aunt, you're dead, Lancaster."

"Well, then, I'll say hello to her in hell," he said to me. "Behave, wolf."

Marco blinked. "Ah. You think you have the upper hand. But in fact, I know Ms. Keenan's aunt is unharmed. She is safe, Ashley. I guarantee it."

Once again, my knees wobbled. I only just stayed upright as relief surged through me.

Marco nodded at me and then focused back on Lancaster. "What do you want?"

"I want a life," he said, turning his head slightly to Marco. The gun didn't waver. "Baxter owes me the life he took from me."

"Cilla gave you life when you were dying," Smith said mildly. "And you volunteered for what came next. I took nothing from you."

"You took everything," Lancaster snarled.

I didn't think he was talking about his life. He meant Cilla.

"Tell us where the other vampires like you are," Marco said. "Then we can talk. We have the one you sent to Ashley's house. I know there are others. If a cure is what you want, then it must be a cure for all of you."

"And you want to lock us up until you find it?" Lancaster's tone was bitter.

"Is there an alternative?" Marco said. "You killed people. You turned others. You have spread this curse without a thought for what it might mean for the rest of your kind. There is a price to pay. At least for those of you who are not mere bystanders." His green gaze turned to Smith.

"You said there were fourteen," I said to Smith. "Is that the truth?"

"Fourteen that I know of. Less the three who died. And then the two new ones Mitchell decided to add to the tally. There could be more. He and I haven't been together for the last few weeks."

Lancaster glared at him. "There aren't any more. We agreed on that."

That seemed difficult to prove, and it was a problem that there was no immediate solution to. Regardless of whether or not he'd created more plague vamps, Lancaster could have recruited other vamps or shifters to his cause. There are scumbags who will do bad things for money in all species. Tate had had underlings. Marco could thrall Lancaster once we had control of him. See if he was lying. Smith, I thought, was telling the truth, but clearly, he was a world-class liar, so I wasn't ready to trust my gut on that any longer.

"Eleven, then," I said. "Or ten if it was a plague vamp you sent to my house."

"Where are they, Mitchell?" Marco asked again.

"Two of my people are probably enjoying themselves back at the Geiger," Lancaster said. "They had orders to keep Agent Gibson and his team busy after I left."

Two of his people? Did he mean plague vamps? That would leave him with only one other, if he'd started with seven. That seemed…low. Or was he lying? I didn't have time to figure it out.

"If you have people back at the hotel, they're probably dead," I said. "Dan doesn't mess around."

"Neither do I," he said.

He lifted his hand again. In it, he held what looked to be a key fob, the kind you used to start a car. But that made no sense. The driver would have the keys to the van…so why?

Lancaster's fingers flexed, and suddenly the parking lot turned to hell as about ten cars exploded. I flung myself toward Smith, tackling him to the ground as debris flew through the air. Something caught my leg, the pain of it sharp and hot, but I focused on Smith. He was human. Fragile. I was not.

He was panting beneath me, breathing hard, stinking of fear.

Hadn't he known what Lancaster had planned?

Honestly, when it came to double-crossing, these two were taking the art form to a whole new fucked-up level.

My retinas flared with wheels of light from the afterburn, and I scrubbed at my eyes, trying to clear my vision. Around me came the sounds of gunshots and fighting. More than would be needed if it was just Marco and the others trying to get Lancaster.

Which meant, I assumed, that the other vamps had joined the fight. I wasn't exactly clear where they might have come from, but at that point I didn't care. It didn't matter.

I wanted to go and help, fighting the urge to change, to defend my friends. But I knew I had to keep Smith alive. If any of the plague vamps survived this—and if there were others—we needed him.

As my vision cleared, my nose registered smoke and the smell of hot metal and gasoline.

Fuck.

Cars on fire next to other cars. The whole place could go up. Not to mention that the ceiling seemed to have caught fire, too.

The safest place to get Smith to was outside.

It was still daylight. The vamps couldn't follow us there.

I stood, hauling him up with me. My leg nearly buckled as pain seared through it again, and I realized I could smell blood. My blood.

But maybe not just mine.

Smith was clutching his side, his fingers stained red. Humans could bleed out fast. No time to waste.

I half dragged him back toward the entrance to the lot, ignoring the fighting behind us and the fact that I was abandoning the friends who were fighting for me.

We made it about three-quarters of the way when a vampire sprang into my path. Not Lancaster. No one I recognized, but it was plain he intended to stop me. That made him one of the bad guys in my book.

"Move," I said. "This isn't your fight."

Any hope that maybe rational argument might work died as the vampire snarled and lunged. Not for me—for Smith.

Fuck and fuck.

I threw myself between them, fighting to stay human. I couldn't drag Smith out of here in wolf form, and I sure as hell wasn't going to do him the favor of biting him by trying to carry him out with my teeth.

The vampire tried to get around me, and I grabbed his arm, twisting it in a move that Dan taught me. Vamps and weres are pretty evenly matched strength-wise. I was hurt, which was a point in his favor.

But he hadn't been trained by an overly protective, paranoid, pain-in-the ass, alpha werewolf boyfriend on top of all the self-defense classes I'd taken over the years. I knew how to fight and fight dirty.

I dislocated his shoulder and followed that up by slamming my elbow into his face. Pain shot up my arm and I hissed, but the vampire wobbled backward, giving me the opening I needed for a more direct attack. I didn't want to kill him if I didn't have to, but I wanted him unconscious. He fought back, snarling, but he was still disoriented, and I wasn't sure he even saw the punch that knocked him out coming.

I turned back to Smith. He was staring back the way we'd come, peering into the red flickering smoky light, trying to see what was happening. I grabbed him and hauled him up toward the exit ramp.

No time for spectating. I couldn't stop and think about who was alive or dead back there. Not until I had him safely outside. I ran for the exit, practically carrying Smith. I got about two paces into daylight when I almost ran into Esme and Dan. I shoved Smith at Esme, relief that they were both alive warring with panic that Smith might die and that Jase and the others were still down in the fire.

"He's hurt. Handle it. Don't let him get away."

Esme nodded and took Smith from me. She cast a look back over her shoulder as she hustled him away, mouthing, "Don't do anything stupid."

Like I had a choice.

I gazed at Dan. So many things I wanted to tell him. But there was no time. Smoke was rolling out of the parking lot entrance, and the flames crackled loudly to my werewolf ears.

"I love you," I said, "but there's no time to explain." That covered a lot of ground. And some of it I couldn't have explained yet if I'd tried. Like what happened back at the hotel. Like Smith and Lancaster and whatever the hell happened between them. Like Marco riding to my rescue. "I have to go back in."

"The fire department is nearly here," he said, shaking his head, silver blazing in his eyes.

I knew I must have looked a mess, stained with blood and smoke and God knew what else.

"Jase is down there," I said. "And Marco. And Niko. And Esteban. They're outnumbered."

"I'll go," Dan said, his voice raspy.

"Not without me." We locked gazes. In wolf form, this might have been easier. "I know it's dangerous, but I have to do this. Come with me."

His mouth quirked and his shoulder relaxed as though he'd finally accepted something. "Okay. Together." He looked me up and down. "Do you have a gun?"

I shook my head.

"Are you going to change?"

I considered. The wolf wouldn't like the heat and the smoke, but neither would I. And the wolf was faster and stronger and saw better in the dark. Besides that, changing would help heal my leg.

I wasn't human anymore. I'd left that behind. Time to use all the weapons I had at my disposal.

I nodded. "Let's do this."

I changed before he could answer, then turned and ran back down into the parking lot. The smoke was worse. The ceiling was definitely alight, and more cars had caught fire. Why hadn't the damned sprinkler system turned on?

Well, sparks might burn my fur, but I'd heal. Fire was more dangerous to a vampire than a wolf.

No time to worry about that. Dan's footsteps came from behind me. He'd changed, too.

"I'm going after Lancaster," I thought at him. *"Don't forget to shield. He's strong."*

"Yeah, we found that out at the hotel. I've got your back." He nosed my neck briefly, then turned to face the fire.

The smoke and flames and shrieking alarms turned the scene into a nightmare. With smoke choking my nose and turning the vamps into blurs, it was hard to tell friend from foe. Or know who the crumpled forms on the ground were.

No time to worry about that. Count the dead later. Save the living now.

I sprang back into motion, trying to find Lancaster. Vampires fought around us, violent and vicious. I caught a glimpse of red hair—or what I thought was red in the weird light—and then Jase's face. I ducked around him and took out the hamstring of the vamp attacking him. The guy fell, clutching his leg. Jase stepped back, frowning, then spotted me.

He lifted a hand, pointing. "He was over there," he said. "He shot Marco. They're still fighting though."

It took more than a single bullet to kill an Old One unless it was a very lucky shot. I ran in the direction Jase had pointed, toward the elevator, I thought. Though the exit light that usually shone above it was invisible, either broken or shrouded by the smoke.

"I'm behind you," Dan said in my head. *"Keep going."*

I followed the sounds of fighting. It didn't take long to find Marco and Lancaster. Marco was only using one arm, and the two of them were slugging it out like prizefighters. If prizefighters moved with vamp speed.

With the sound and the smoke, I guessed Marco hadn't been able to take control of Lancaster. He was an impressive sight in full fight mode, moving faster than any human could hope to.

And for a geek, Lancaster apparently fought better than most of his vampire pals.

I couldn't see a gun in his hands. Where was it? I scanned the ground around us. Red light glinted off metal a few yards behind Marco. The rest of the vampires seemed to be behind us. The gun was safe enough for now. If I changed to grab it, I'd be naked and so would Dan. Not appealing in the hot air, surrounded by flames.

I bounded into the fray, landing on Lancaster's back and forcing him down to the ground. He bucked wildly beneath me, and I snarled in his ear, letting every savage thought the wolf had leak into the sound. I had him now, and I wanted to howl in triumph.

Then the ceiling behind Marco caved in.

Fuck.

I leaped backward on pure instinct, snarling as a cloud of dust rose to add to the chaos.

The place was falling down around our ears.

Marco had bolted forward at the first creaking groan that had preceded the collapse, and now he had Lancaster by the throat.

"We need to get out of here," I thought to Dan. *"Or we need the damn fire department."*

"It's still daylight. The vamps can't go outside."

"Fire stairs."

"Climbing the floors in a building whose basement is on fire isn't a good idea."

"They're concrete. They're tough."

He made a frustrated huff but then dipped his nose in agreement.

I glanced up at Marco, then darted forward, tugged at his coat with my teeth.

He looked down at me. "If you can get us out of here, cara, then our debts will be cleared," he said, coughing at the end of the sentence. "This would be a bad way to die."

I agreed with him there, so I tugged again and then turned, hoping he'd follow me.

He was smart enough to do so and strong enough to bring a struggling Lancaster with him.

It probably only took a few seconds to reach the stairs, though it felt like longer with the fire and the smoke turning the lot to a hellhole. Marco groaned as he pushed open the door with his injured arm, the one not holding Lancaster. He looked back at me. "I can control him, but I can't do that and help you with the others," he said. "I can call Jason, and I can perhaps convince Lancaster to call his children, too. But you'll need to find Esteban."

Great. I got to find the pissed-off Old One.

I turned and plunged back into the smoke and flame. Something seared my right front paw, and I yelped.

"Ash?"

"I'm okay. Just an ember." I coughed, an unpleasant sensation in wolf form. A burned foot was the least of my problems, though it hurt like hell.

As I ran back in the direction of the entrance, Jase loomed out of the darkness, half carrying Niko, who looked dazed, half his face covered in blood. And behind them came the other plague vamps—only four—and then Esteban bringing up the rear. Apparently the ceiling caving in had caught everyone's attention.

I thought I saw Dan in the smoke behind Esteban, but my eyes were stinging, and the smoke was thicker with every second. But he would still hear me if he was nearby. *"Is this everyone?"*

"Everyone I can find."

Above us, there was another alarming creak.

"Head for the stairs." I wasn't sure if it was Dan or I who thought that. It didn't matter. We bolted after the vampires and made it through the door, ducking around Esteban's legs to get inside. He pulled the door closed as he followed us, and there was another crashing rumble that suggested more ceiling had come down.

"Up to the first floor?" I asked Dan.

"The vamps can't go out the door up there."

"No, but it's farther away from the fire." The parking lot didn't run the full length of the building. I was no architect, but I hoped that meant maybe the entire structure wouldn't collapse if it did.

"We can cross over to the other side via the second floor. Everyone in the building should be evacuated, right? Lancaster can't whammy anyone else."

"Whammy?" Dan sounded amused.

"Let's not quibble over terminology for his creepy-ass powers. Just move."

Marco was watching us. "Which way, cara?"

In answer, I brushed past him and headed up the stairs. The others followed, everyone too focused on survival just then to keep fighting. We reached the level where the inner door would open into the lobby. I hoped like hell that the building was empty. Any weres or humans would be fair game for Lancaster's tricks.

Esteban opened the door for me, stepping through ahead of me and beckoning the others. Covered in soot like the rest of us, his suit jacket torn in several places, he didn't look so perfect. He stared down at me as Niko and Jason passed through into the building. "This is not what I expected when I hired you."

I gave him a wolfy grin, then turned to watch the other plague vamps pass us by. Dan had stayed behind Marco and Lancaster, growling softly as he followed them up the stairs.

Marco stepped toward the door, and Lancaster twisted suddenly, shoving him toward Esteban.

He moved fast, too fast, and reached the other door. The one that led outside.

Into safety, but also into daylight. Though maybe, I realized as he started to pull the door open, there might be enough shadow from the buildings this late in the day to protect him. And if he got hold of a human, or managed to disappear into another building, he could get away.

I leaped after him, Dan hot on my heels.

I snapped my teeth but missed the hem of Lancaster's jacket by an inch or two. My momentum carried me forward, and I skidded out onto the concrete. It wasn't so easy to come to a fast stop in this form, and it took me a moment to land safely and get my bearings to spot Lancaster. He was standing at the edge of the road, still safe in the shadow cast by the building. There were firefighters and paramedics a few feet away from him. People he could take control of. Who might help him escape. Werewolves were strong, but I didn't think I'd be able to do much if one of the firefighters aimed their hose at me.

I gathered myself to leap again, to stop him. But before I could move, Dan barreled out the door, twisted midleap, and knocked Lancaster to the concrete. For a moment, there was a blur of snarling wolf and vampire that I couldn't separate. I heard a yelp from Dan, and Lancaster sprang up, trying to get to his feet. But he misjudged, or he'd forgotten where he was, because his leap took him past the edge of shadow and across into the sunlight.

I jumped for him. If I was fast enough, maybe I could pull him back.

But I'd forgotten how fast the sun could take a vampire. Before I could reach him, Lancaster dissolved into flames and ash, the blast of it knocking me back, sending me sliding across the pavement until I hit solid warmth and turned to bury my face in Dan's fur.

Chapter 22

I STILL DIDN'T LIKE hospitals. I doubted I ever would. The weird smell of them would forever be associated with pain and fear. But it helped that, for once, it wasn't me in the hospital bed. I'd been checked out by paramedics at the scene and treated for the burn on my hand, but that was already healed.

Like the rest of me. At least, I hoped so. It still didn't feel quite real.

That it was over.

We had Smith; we had the plague vamps. Smith had told Esme where the others who'd stayed with him were in the back of the ambulance that brought him here.

Maybe he'd thought he was dying, and some semblance of a conscience kicked in.

Whatever the reason, he'd told the truth, and the Task-force had been able to pick up all the other vamps. They hadn't resisted.

The surviving plague vamps were all now at Fort Lyman. So far, they were cooperating.

What happened next to them depended on what I was here to do now.

I stared through the glass of the prison ward at the man lying asleep on the bed inside.

Smith.

He'd made it through surgery, though he was now minus a spleen, and it had apparently been touch and go. The doctors hadn't let us interview him until now, nearly twenty-four hours after his surgery. It was night again, the sun not long set.

But I was used to the night now. My life would never be fully lived in the sunshine like most people. But that was okay. I liked the people who shared the moon and starlight with me just fine. Especially now that I knew there was no longer anything hiding in those shadows that wanted to kill me.

And that the man beside me would always be with me.

I might always carry some of the scars I'd accumulated. Wounds slow to heal. But he would always do his best to ease them.

"Ready to go in?" Dan asked me.

"I'm not sure," I said. I reached for the door, then pulled my hand back.

"This can be the last time you ever have to talk to him, if that's what you want," Dan said. "You don't even have to do this now, you know." He was dressed in his Taskforce agent clothes. Dark suit. White shirt. But he looked more relaxed than I'd seen him in months. Maybe since he'd first reappeared in my office to tell me Tate was back.

I shook my head. "Yes I do." I had to take this all the way to the finish line. So much of my life had been changed by what Smith had done. By his choices. I wanted to see if he would make a better choice now.

I squeezed Dan's hand, his right wrapping around my left. I didn't really want to let him go, and we'd spent most of the last twenty-four hours together. First sleeping, then...well, some other activities involving his bed. We'd spent most of the day with Bug, who had suddenly looked about ten years younger when we told her we had Smith. With the Taskforce building a no-go zone, Esme and Andy handling the retrieval of the vamps, and Smith in surgery, Dan had spent a lot of time on the phone or email, but he'd done it from home, and I'd stayed with him, not wanting to be apart from him.

We'd won, but it could have gone very differently. The fact that we'd both made it through, that we were safe together was something I wouldn't be taking for granted any time soon.

"Let's do this," I said, and Dan nodded at the agent guarding the door to let us in.

Smith didn't immediately open his eyes when we approached the bed, but one of his hands was handcuffed to the bed frame, and I saw the fingers flex, then straighten.

He seemed smaller somehow, lying on the bed. With his gray hair messy and salt-and-pepper stubble shading his jaw, he looked…old. Frail almost, though the doctors had said there was no reason he wouldn't make a full recovery so long as he didn't try something stupid.

Dan pulled the two visitors' chairs closer to the bed, and we sat.

Eventually Smith opened his eyes, turning his head to look at us. He made no move to sit up. I didn't blame him. He had to be in pain after his surgery.

"Hello, Ashley," he said.

"Baxter," I said. "How are you feeling?"

"I've had better days," he said.

"You're alive. That's a good start."

"I guess." He looked at Dan. "Agent Gibson, here to take my confession, are you?"

Dan shook his head. "Not formally. We'll leave that part until you're off the medication. I don't want any questions about the legalities." He stared at Baxter, no pity in his silver eyes. "You understand that you don't have to tell us anything?"

Baxter nodded. "I understand."

"The doctors said you're stable and competent to talk to us. Consider this a preliminary discussion," Dan said.

"Before you drag me off to be thralled by vampires if I won't confess?"

There were legalities around using vampires in interrogation. But I didn't imagine Dan would have any problems getting the permissions he needed in Smith's case.

"I doubt we need an actual confession," Dan said. "We have your other vampires, and plenty of them seem willing to talk to us. So do the thugs Lancaster hired. And we have witnesses." He meant Bug and me.

"So why are you here?" Baxter asked. He turned his pale gaze back to me. "What do you want, Ashley?"

I stared at him. That was a leading question. And he was lucky, perhaps, that I'd had a day for some semblance of distance to begin to set in.

Because there was a big part of me that still wanted a more primal sort of justice than he was going to get through the legal system. But if I gave in to that part, it would make me as bad as the things that had haunted the shadows. I was a werewolf now. A creature of night. But I didn't have to be one of darkness.

I sighed. "I came to ask if you would do the right thing."

His gaze sharpened a little. "What exactly does that mean?"

"A deal of a kind," I said. "It won't win you your freedom, but maybe it can bring a little redemption."

"You think I deserve redemption?"

"I think those vampires you made do," I said. I was under no illusions that most of them had also done bad things. Especially the ones who'd gone with Lancaster. But regardless of that, they deserved a cure, if only to keep humanity safe. If one could be found. "I'm willing to give you what you want. My father's research. And the FBI will provide you with access to a laboratory and other researchers in time. If you're willing to continue your work to find the cure."

"And if I'm not?"

"Well, I'm guessing it's many long boring years in jail until you die," I said bluntly. "No redemption there. You'll only ever be a monster in the history books. A doctor who broke all his oaths and caused misery and destruction, Or you can be all those things, but also be a man who tried to repair some of the damage he did. Who didn't waste so many people's lives for nothing."

I stopped talking. I didn't have anything more to say. I had to hope there was something still decent in him. Or, failing that, that the scientist in him had enough pride to want to finish what he'd started. So, I waited. Until Smith finally nodded.

"All right, Ashley. You have a deal."

Epilogue

I NEVER EXPECTED to marry by moonlight.

But as I stood in my room at the Retreat, sneakily watching last-minute guests arriving through a gap in the curtains, I knew it was right.

Werewolves married under the light of the moon. And even if I hadn't been a wolf, well, there were other people I wanted at the wedding who couldn't have been there by day. Jase. Marco. Some of the Taskforce vamps Dan counted as friends and who I'd gotten to know better in the six months that had passed since we caught Smith.

"Stop scoping out the guests and come back over here," Jase said from behind me. "We need to put your veil on."

I let the curtain fall and turned. Esme shook her head at me while Jase just smiled and pointed at the middle of the room. I moved carefully, not wanting to crumple my gown. It was sleek, deceptively simple cut, the way I'd always imagined, but the fall of white satin was beaded in tiny crystals and iridescent beads, the lines following the curves of my body. When the moon—nearly but not quite full, as was traditional for wolf weddings—caught the fabric, I should shimmer.

In contrast, Jase wore a traditional black tux. He'd insisted that if he was going to be my male of honor, then he was going to do it properly. Esme's dress was slinky and a shade of deep green that was nearly black. I was definitely going to be the center of attention.

Though my own attention would be on Dan.

"How much longer?" I asked as Jase began to drape the delicate lace veil—also strategically beaded—over my head.

"Ceremony starts in fifteen minutes," Esme said. "So let's get this done, and then you can have a few minutes alone with Bug before we have to get downstairs."

I nodded, stomach tightening with nerves. But the good kind. Happy, fluttering butterflies of delight at the thought that tonight was finally the night.

Jase finished pinning the veil in place, folding it back carefully. "There. Perfect."

I didn't know about perfect, but the reflection in the mirror was close enough. The dress and the veil were beautiful —Bug and I had spent long enough looking for them and sending Jase pictures for his input. My hair and makeup artist had done a great job. And I looked happy. I *was* happy. That was the most important thing.

"You look gorgeous," Esme said. She handed me the bouquet of champagne and pink roses, with one lone coral one nestled among them to echo the flowers my mother had carried on her wedding day. I'd even sewn a small strawberry pin my dad had given her into the hem of my dress. I had on Bug's favorite pearl earrings and the engagement ring Dan gave me. My garter was aqua. I was covered.

"Thanks," I said.

Jase kissed my cheek, his lips cool as always.

"Ten minutes," he said as he and Esme opened the door to let Bug in. She'd been up here earlier, helping me with my dress, but had gone downstairs to keep an eagle eye on the preparations.

She stopped when she saw me, a smile that was a little wobbly at the edges lighting her face.

"No crying," I said. "If you cry, I'll cry, and then Jase will kill me."

She nodded, pressing her lips together. "Oh, sweetheart, you look beautiful."

"Thanks," I said. Then took a breath because I wasn't entirely sure that I wasn't going to be the one to break the "no crying" rule.

Bug walked over and kissed my cheek, too, taking the hand that wasn't holding the flowers.

"No point asking if you're sure about this," she said.

I shook my head.

No.

There were no doubts. I'd been ready to marry Dan as soon as we left Smith back in the hospital room. He was the one. The man who'd literally run into fire with me to keep me safe.

We still argued now and then, like any couple did, but I trusted our bond. There was a sense of him, deep and sure, within me. But we'd decided to wait. Wrap up the investigation, prepare for the court case, and just give ourselves some time to breathe. Smith was cooperating so far. He and Felipe and some others were working on a cure for the plague vamps. Adria had unlocked the last of my father's files, and apparently there'd been some theories in his notes that were helpful.

It was as much as I could ask for. Science didn't move at the speed of light. But Felipe was hopeful. Which meant Dan and I could take our time. Revert to normal life—whatever that was.

Bug's house was almost finished. She'd rented an apartment near my house for a few months while her house was rebuilt, though she hadn't yet decided if she was moving back to Caldwell. Stanley had visited often. Everything was good.

Dan and I were even going to go lie on a beach for a few weeks for our honeymoon.

But first, the wedding. And the party. I was looking forward to that part. But not quite as much as making sure everybody knew Dan was all mine.

"Good," Bug said. "It took you two long enough." She grinned at me. "Well, then, let's get you downstairs and married.

* * *

I followed Jase and Esme along a path lit by hundreds of tiny lanterns shaped like stars, Bug by my side and the moonlight falling around me. Every time I walked the woods in the Retreat now, it reminded me of my dad. Tonight, I was sure that, if there was any way they could be, he and Mom would be walking with us. I allowed myself a single thought of *I miss you*, then turned my attention back to where I was headed.

All I had to do was follow the light. The path wound through the trees for a short distance to one of the groves in the woods. Jase and Esme reached the edge of the clearing and stopped to look back at me. I nodded and they walked forward, the music of the string quartet rising around them. Bug's hand tightened around mine as we reached the edge. I squeezed back, but I was focused on the man now standing only about twenty feet away from me, dark hair gleaming in the moonlight, silver eyes as bright as the stars that lit the edge of the aisle. There were no other lights, and the faces of all our friends—our families—were silvery pale. But the joy was clear on all of them.

And the love.

Just like the love drawing me like an arrow down to Dan's side, the fierce happiness on his face telling me he felt the same way I did. That there was no one else just then but the two of us.

I practically floated down the aisle, barely registering Bug as she lifted my veil back when we reached the end, or Esme as she took my bouquet. There was just Dan and his hands on mine and his happiness sweeping through me.

I wanted to kiss him, but there was the pesky matter of the ceremony first. I glanced at the celebrant, "Let's do this," I said.

Dan's laugh echoed through the trees. But he didn't let go of my hands. Not until we'd made our vows under moonlight and he was sliding a ring onto my finger.

"Mine," I said as I slid one onto his as well.

"Yours," he agreed.

And then he kissed me.

THE END

If you'd like to see and exclusive bonus scene with Dan's POV
of the the wedding
sign up to my newsletter!

About the Author

M.J. Scott is an unrepentant bookworm who grew up in a family that fed her a properly varied diet of books. This cemented her story addiction and love of fantasy and romance. So it's not surprising she grew up to write books with both. When not wrestling with the magical worlds in her head, she can generally be found reading, doing something crafty, binge watching, and avoiding housework. She lives in Melbourne, Australia in a small house packed with books, cats, and craft supplies. She also writes romance as Melanie Scott. Her website is www.mjscott.net.

Also by M.J. Scott

Urban fantasy

The TechWitch series

Wicked Games

Wicked Words

Wicked Nights

Wicked Dreams

Wicked Ways

Wicked Deeds

Wicked Lies

The Wild Side series

The Wolf Within

The Dark Side

Bring On The Night

Romantic fantasy

The Four Arts series

The Shattered Court

The Forbidden Heir

The Unbound Queen

Courting The Witch (Prequel novella)

The Daughter of Ravens series

The Exile's Curse

The Traitor's Game

The Rebel's Prize

The Half-Light City series

Shadow Kin

Blood Kin

Iron Kin

Fire Kin

Romance (writing as Melanie Scott)

The Cloud Bay series

Don't Blame Me

Right Where You Left Me

You Belong With Me

The New York Saints series

The Devil in Denim

Angel in Armani

Lawless in Leather

Playing Hard

Playing Fast

Acknowledgments

This series wouldn't exist without a bunch of people who cheered me on from the very early days of my writing career. Agent M, the always awesome Lulus, Sarah, Anne, Kelly and many many more. And also the readers who kept asking me what happened next for Ash and Dan. We got there in the end. Smooches to all!

Excerpt from Wicked Games

Chapter One

My mother was a wicked witch.

An ill-wisher, a doer of dark deeds.

Trading in false hopes, broken hearts, and the not-so-pretty side of human emotion and gullibility.

She liked me to be seen and not heard. She liked magic that served her best interests. And she liked her men tall, pretty, and well acquainted with sinning.

She would've liked the guy standing next to me.

Even if he was a simulation.

He looked like he knew all about being bad. In all the good senses of the word. Tall, dark-haired, and sculpted by a perfectionist. But avatars—skins—can look like anything you want. In real life, he—or she—was just as likely to be a toad as a prince.

I turned back to the game menu, raising my avatar's hand to flick through options. Pretty or not, I hadn't expected company in *Nightruns*. The game was old. Several gens old. Uncool.

I'd retreated here for that precise reason, hiding out from

Nat's coaxing to join her and her team in the latest Phobos offering.

I'd wanted peace and quiet. Time to think.

Which, yes, meant more fool me for coming out in the first place. But Nat was never easy to resist. Though she did know better than to ask me to play any game with magic. I'd known the real thing and seen what it could do; I had no desire to relive it virtually.

But tonight I had no desire to stumble after her and her friends in an unknown game. Nat was a pro. I wasn't. There'd be hundreds of thousands tuned in to the game stream. I didn't want to hold Nat back, nor did I want to sit around and watch her on the screens. So I'd headed for the more obscure parts of the club's catalog.

"You like classics?"

The question startled me. I twisted toward my companion. He studied me with improbably blue eyes, making me wonder again about the real face of whoever was running this skin. "Sorry?"

"Classics?" He gestured at the menu shimmering in the air. "Everyone here tonight seems to be trying to get a slot in the Phobos launch, yet here you are, back in the dark ages."

His voice, like the eyes and the body, was too good to be true, deep and slightly roughened.

Definitely overcompensating. Still, that didn't mean I couldn't enjoy the scenery, given it was so nicely packaged in tight black clothes that hugged every pixel. "Newer isn't every-thing. Anyway, I'm not much of a gamer."

The avatar raised one dark eyebrow. "What brings a non-gamer to Decker's?"

"I'm with friends. They're pros." And could get me comped on the entry fee and game price, which was how my currently slender credit balance could withstand playing in a club like this.

He nodded. "Ranked?"

I shrugged. "Some." I didn't want to get into a boring conversation about the leagues and rankings and upcoming competitions. If he was a game-head, then I'd find somewhere else to hide out. I reached toward the menu in case I needed the exit fast.

"Made a decision?"

I pulled back. "No."

"How about Kingmaker? The palace run? If you feel like company, that is?" One brow quirked a challenge onto that perfect face.

I hesitated. The palace run was my favorite level of Kingmaker, full of the sorts of traps and logic puzzles I enjoyed. Zero magic. I'd been planning on tackling it alone, but a bit of competition could spice things up. Besides, it might be fun to beat pretty boy. "Pairs or head-to-head?"

He smiled, and I had to give points to whoever had designed his skin—the avatar was an advanced lesson in sheer male beauty. I smiled back before I could stop myself.

"Competition is always more fun." He ushered me toward the menu. "Ladies first."

"First to the crown jewels?" I asked, dialing the time to night. Moonlight made playing sneak thief more fun.

He nodded. "I'll be waiting for you."

"We'll see about that," I muttered, then pressed Go.

The walls of the palace shimmered into view and I flung myself into a run, heading for the first challenge point. Pretty boy dropped out of sight behind me. I smiled and then sped up, sinking into the moment, losing myself in the game, enjoying the familiarity, even if the simulation didn't feel entirely real at times and the ageing graphics had a tendency to flicker at disconcerting moments.

My breath sang in my ears as I traversed the darkened corridors, climbing balconies, solving the puzzles guarding each new stage, and dodging guards. Occasionally I caught glimpses of my opponent, muscles rippling under the sleek black shirt and pants as he vaulted over an obstacle or stretched for a handhold.

He was doing pretty well—okay, *really* well—but I thought I had him. If I was reading his route right, he was taking the long way around. He was toast.

Or so I thought, until I dropped onto the balcony above the throne room, creeping carefully through the line of booby-trapped gilt chairs, to find him leaning against the railing looking down at the sumptuous room below with the well-satisfied expression of a king surveying his domain. His avatar didn't even look rumpled. Maybe he didn't like the realism of sweat and heavy breathing, but Nat had built the skin I wore and she was a purist. I knew it showed every inch of effort I'd put into my route. I stopped myself from reaching up to smooth my hair back.

"I wondered where you'd got to," he said with another damnably perfect smile.

I bit back an annoyed retort and looked down at the throne. The crown and scepter we were supposedly here to steal still glittered against the black velvet seat. "Too scared to make the drop?"

"Actually, I wanted to talk to you, Ms. Lachlan."

"How do you know my name?" Alarm prickled my spine, and I backed up a step.

"Easy." He lifted his hands from the railing, holding them out palms forward. "I don't mean any harm."

"How do you know my name?" I repeated, flexing my hand. One quick slap of the release button—the virtual reality equivalent of a safe word—and I'd be out of there.

"Your reputation precedes you," he said. "I've been hearing the names Maggie Lachlan and TechWitch a lot lately."

My mouth dropped open. "You want to talk business?"

"Does that surprise you?"

"Most people just make an appointment," I pointed out.

"I like to know who I'm dealing with. Besides, this is more fun." He hit me with the smile again.

I found it a little less perfect on the face of a mysterious stalker. "I like to know who I'm dealing with too," I said, letting my tone frost a little. "So you've got about five seconds to tell me your name or I'm out."

"Sorry. Where are my manners?" He held out a hand. "I'm Damon Riley."

I sat down on one of the spindly gilt chairs with a thump. It squealed a protest, but I didn't care.

"Game halt." Damon snapped his fingers and the balcony disappeared. The lobby reformed around us, my chair morphing into a plain black cube.

"*The* Damon Riley?" I asked, more to myself than to him.

Those wickedly blue eyes twinkled. Their effect was even more annoying when I realized—having, like everyone else on the planet, seen his picture many times in almost every form of media—that the shade was close to the real thing. His avatar was nudged a little from reality, just enough to hide his identity, I guessed, but not too far.

"Yes. You know who I am," he replied.

It was more a statement than a question. I wondered briefly what he would do if I said no. Probably leave. Unless you were a hermit or otherwise out of touch with the world, you knew who Damon Riley was. "Sure. You own Righteous."

Somehow I managed to sound casual, as if I regularly had people who made world's richest insert-noun-of-choice-here lists come looking for me in game clubs.

His mouth curved again. "I thought you said you weren't much of a gamer?" He sounded amused.

I realized why. Most people would've said Riley Arts. Only the hard-core fans called his company Righteous. "Like I said, I know some pros."

Pros whose heads would explode if they knew who I was talking to. I pictured Nat's expression when I told her I'd played against Damon Riley. Exploding heads would just be the start.

The gamers called the company Righteous because it was. Riley's games were the best. No argument. He was the man who'd developed *Sorcerer's Apprentice*, the must-have game of all time. Almost a cult. It had made him his first million or fifty.

Since then, he hadn't looked back. Riley Arts did both games and game-tech now. Their latest home virtual reality console had sold out worldwide approximately two hours after its release. The games usually took less than that.

"Right." He rested against the railing, stretching out his long legs. "That would be Ms. Marcos and her crew?"

I nodded, my brain trying to catch up with what was happening.

Damon Riley. I didn't have the foggiest idea why someone like him would be coming to me for help. I didn't usually work with his sort of company. My somewhat specialized skills were generally more in demand by boring industries that lacked their own tech gods. Riley Arts had to have more computer geeks per square foot than almost any other company in the world. Why on earth would he want me?

"Yes, Nat's my roommate. Call me Maggie," I added. Ms. Lachlan always made me nervous. Every time the police had knocked on our door in my childhood, they were looking for 'Ms. Lachlan.' Back then, it had been my mother who wore the name, not me, but the sound of it still made me twitch somewhere deep in my gut.

"Of course."

The muscles along the back of my jaw clamped down. I recognized that cool, self-assured tone. Every rich kid who'd ever made my life hell in any of the twenty or thirty schools I'd passed through sounded like that. Like they could snap their fingers and life would provide whatever they needed.

My experience was more like snap your fingers all day

long but life would still hand you whatever the hell it wanted and laugh as it knocked you on your ass.

I forced myself to relax. Working for Riley Arts would be great for my career, no matter how aggravating Damon Riley himself turned out to be. "I guess that's enough of tiresome small talk. Which brings me back to why you're here."

"Your name was brought to my attention."

He waved a hand and a cube like the one under my virtual butt rose out of the featureless white floor. He took a seat, pushing back the sleeves of the shirt. I caught a glimpse of gold on the underside of his right wrist.

An interface chip.

Nice. Better than nice. Covetable, cutting-edge technology. Still almost exclusively the domain of the power players of the virtual entertainment industry. Of which Damon was indisputably king. No wonder he had one, even on his avatar.

Nat had a chip, courtesy of a tournament win a few months back. Me, I couldn't begin to afford one. Even if I could—and I'd had my moments of tech lust drooling over the specs—I wasn't sure I wanted one. The thought of something plugging straight into my central nervous system made me, well, nervous.

Luckily my clients didn't yet expect me to have one. By the time they did, I figured the tech would be tested enough to overcome my instinctive caution and I might be able to afford it.

Of course, if Damon Riley hired me, I'd be able to afford several of the damn things and still have enough left over for my other, more pressing expenses.

"Who gave you my name?" I gave him my best "hey, give me a job" smile. He smiled back, and my pulse hitched.

Just an avatar. Yes, in real life he was plenty pretty too. Not quite as sleekly perfect as the skin, but it wasn't too much of an exaggeration. The real man was tall and dark and built too. But in real life, if I played this right, he'd be a client. Maggie's rules of life included a strict no-lusting-after-the-paycheck clause.

Especially no lusting after the way-too-sure-of-himself paycheck.

He leaned forward, and I mirrored his action automatically. *Damn.*

"Like I said, I've been hearing your name a lot lately."

"And you also heard I was friends with Nat?"

His eyes twinkled. "No, I'm afraid that was something my team dug up."

"You had me investigated?" My jaw twinged again, and several muscles in my back joined in the protest. Twinkles and sinner's smiles be damned, I didn't like people poking around in my business.

"I believe in thorough preparation," he added, not sounding even the slightest bit apologetic.

Paycheck, I reminded myself as my teeth ground a little tighter. "Mr. Riley, you can be as prepared as you like, but unless you tell me what the problem is, I can't help you."

His eyes narrowed. "Who says I have a problem?"

"Maybe the fact that you've hunted me down in a club on a night off and took the trouble to meet me anonymously?"

"Maybe I was just curious to meet the woman who calls herself a TechWitch."

"TechWitch is a business name, not a description. Marketing. Something you understand very well, if the evidence is to be believed."

I didn't like the name. It was something one of my earliest clients had said in recommending me, and it had stuck. It was, like I said, good marketing, nothing more, which was why I'd kept it. And I was sure Riley's investigators had told him as much. He was beating around the bush. Or lying. Or maybe both. Growing up with Sara—my mother—had left me with a well-honed bullshit meter, and the needle was starting to waver.

"So you don't claim supernatural abilities?"

I frowned. Was he serious? Or still trying to avoid getting to the point? "Not at all. I'm very, very good at my job, but that doesn't require magic. As I'm sure you know."

Sara's laughter echoed in my head. How could anyone think I had power? My mother's disappointment—or disgust, rather—had been perfectly clear when I failed to show any signs of power after I turned thirteen. Overnight I became strictly an annoyance and a burden to her, not that she would've won any mother of the year awards before then. I was spared knowing just what she might've eventually done about that burden when she died a few months later.

"Why? Did you want a witch?"

His face went still. "No. No. Just the opposite, in fact."

Some of the tension riding my gut eased even as my curiosity piqued. Damon Riley wasn't a fan of magic either? One point in his favor. Though he was happy enough to include it in his games, so obviously it wasn't completely a no-go. "So what do you want? You do know what I do, right?" I threw his words back at him.

"Yes. The term 'computer whisperer' was mentioned."

I didn't let myself groan. I'd been dumb enough to give the interview to the tech reporter who'd coined that little term. I lived with it, but I didn't have to like it. "That's not the term I'd use."

"What would you use?"

"Troubleshooter, usually. Do you have some trouble that needs shooting?" I cocked my head, waiting for the inevitable questions.

Troubleshooter was a simplification. I was more a cross between cyber engineer and cyber therapist.

I found the problems that technically shouldn't exist. The systems that just didn't seem to like each other. Pieces of code that, in isolation, should've worked perfectly but caused unforeseen complications and glitches when put together with other pieces in adjacent systems.

Despite the cold hard facts that computers were machines and had no feelings, I knew from experience that they did get moody. True, by any test yet devised, no one had yet created a true artificial intelligence. But as each generation of cyber tech became more complicated, more powerful, more autonomous, and we humans generated more and more data to feed them, the systems became . . . touchier. And I, God knew why, had the knack of soothing them. Untangling the knots no one else thought were there.

I assumed I got my cyber skills from my unknown father; Sara had been useless with any sort of machine.

Damon studied me for a long moment. "I might have a systems integration issue in our accounting department."

The needle shot into the red zone. Financial packages— other than the ones used by massive international banks— were not usually particularly temperamental. I could count the number of times I'd been called in to consult on one with less than five fingers. And a bookkeeping problem wasn't impor- tant enough to send Damon Riley looking for me in a game at Decker's, where there'd be no record of us meeting.

I didn't like being lied to.

"Riley Arts must employ more geeks, nerds, and tech heads per square foot than NASA, Wall Street, and the CIA put together. If your people can't solve an issue with your financial package, you should fire them. How about you tell me the real problem?"

"No—"

"I don't appreciate having my time wasted," I interrupted before he could spin another lie.

He held up his hand, giving me an even better view of the chip glittering against tanned flesh. Interesting that his skin reflected that particular bit of what I had to assume was real- life detail when it blurred others. "Let me finish. Not here was what I was about to say. I don't discuss confidential matters in unsecured venues."

I folded my arms. "You're the one who came to me. And at the prices this place charges, I'd think their security would be top of the line."

"Not secure enough."

There was that master-of-the-universe tone again. "Then why did you come?"

"I believe in knowing who I'm dealing with. And being discreet."

"Well, it was nice being stalked by you and all, but I have to get back to my friends." I stood. My chances of landing this gig seemed pretty remote.

He rose too. Apparently he had nice manners when he wasn't being irritating. "Can you come to my office on Wednesday?"

Do this all over again? Why?

I shifted a little in the game chair, aware of my back sticking to the slightly sweaty fabric of my shirt in the real world, but held my avatar still as I tried to figure out if he was playing an angle. "Why Wednesday?" It was still Monday, unless our game had taken more time than I thought. If he did have the sort of problem I might be able to help with, surely it would be a priority.

"I have business in New Zealand tomorrow." He tugged his shirtsleeves down with two sharp movements. "Unfortunately. I will, of course, pay for your time."

Ah. Payment. He'd found my Achilles' heel. The problem with being very specialized was you had to wait for the very specialized problems to come along. And while I did well enough, there had been a distinct lack of computers throwing temper tantrums lately, and there were other demands on my finances.

Which was part of the reason why I was out on a school night. I was sick of cooling my heels at home, worrying about my lack of billable hours and what that meant for my debts. The prospect of cold hard cash flow was even harder to ignore than my curiosity about what might be going on at Righteous. It couldn't hurt to at least find out what the mysterious issue was, even if the boss had pushy and demanding and driven written all over him.

"I'll have to check my schedule," I said finally.

"Is that a yes?"

Check on pushy. "It's 'I'll have to check my schedule.'"

Wicked Games is out now!